OUT OF TIME

BEN ARMSTRONG

To Todd

Ben Armstrong

ARMSTROB

{arms{rob}

Copyright © 2019 by Ben Armstrong

First edition

ISBN 978-1-7342597-0-4

To my beautiful wife, Catrina.
Without whom this novel wouldn't exist.
I love you

CONTENTS

PREFACE

Dear reader,

I've put a great deal of work into what you're about to read, and I have to admit, I am proud of what I have written. That being said, this is my first attempt at a novel, so please go easy on a novice such as myself. I imagine there are some things I missed throughout, but I hope they don't distract you from enjoying the story. Thank you for supporting my efforts as an author.

-Ben

PROLOGUE
DECEMBER 10TH, 1968

DR. ROBERT WILKES SAT UPRIGHT, HIS ARMS CROSSED AND eyes glaring fiercely across the table at his boss. They were joined by a panel of doctors, nurses, and other leading scientists from around the world to discuss their upcoming project.

"I don't think you quite understand," said Dr. Wilkes. "There could be severe repercussions from this if even one small factor is not planned out correctly. What you're proposing is not only unethical, but a majority of it is experimental at best. There are more than just a few lives at stake here, and with all due respect sir, the plan for this project sucks."

His boss slammed his hands onto the table. "No, Dr. Wilkes, what you don't understand is when to keep your ungrateful mouth shut! Do you not realize what I'm offering you? We're going to make history!"

Dr. Wilkes, who was a stern man himself, retreated momentarily but didn't back down. "My lead developer and I have gone over most of the specifications for this project. We both agree that some of the things you're asking for are simply not possible. Also, the timeline is far too compressed. It will take years to write and test all of the code required for this to work."

Dr. Wilkes's boss stood up and paced back and forth, his hands held behind his back. He was dressed in a black 3-piece suit which had been freshly cleaned and pressed. "Not possible? I thought you and your team were the best, Dr. Wilkes. Besides, this isn't up for debate. You'll find a way to get it done. This project will move forward. All you and your team have to do is follow orders and keep your mouths shut. Understood?"

Neither Dr. Wilkes nor his developer liked it, but they nodded in agreement.

"Good. Now, the rest of you, listen carefully. Time is of the essence and we absolutely cannot afford to mess this up. You all have your instructions. Are they clear?"

From around the room, heads nodded in agreement.

"Then we're done here," he said, standing up to leave. Just before he opened the door, he turned to face the panel again. "We will make history, no matter the cost."

PART ONE

THE EARLY YEARS

CHAPTER I

1

IT WAS A COLD, SNOWY MORNING ON DECEMBER 6TH, 1999 IN Redfield, South Dakota. The typical Midwest winter was in full swing by this time. Daniel Williams was enjoying a snow day at his home on the corner of 5th Avenue and 1st Street. Dan loved snow days as much as the next kid, but even more so on this particular day. This snow day gave him more time to play his new video game, Tony Hawk's *Pro Skater*, on the Nintendo 64. It had been an early birthday present from his mom and he couldn't be happier.

"Dan, sweetie, I have to go into work now," his mother said from the other room.

No response. She walked through the living room and stood in the doorway of Dan's room. She smiled as she saw Dan completely immersed in the new video game she had gotten him. Dan was what most would call a loner. He had a few friends that he would hang out with but, more often than not, Dan preferred to be on his own.

He was an average build for his age. According to his last checkup at the clinic, he was 4'7" and weighed 76 lbs. He had striking blue eyes, and dirty blonde hair that always seemed to have the bedhead look to it.

"Psst, Dan," she whispered. Dan gave a quick glance up and then back to the game.

"One second mom, I've almost got the high score!"

She gave a little laugh and nodded. After a couple more moments Dan raised his arms with excitement and tossed the controller on his bed. "Woo! New high score!" Dan said as he ran over to his mom and hugged her. "Thanks again for the game, Mom! You're the best!" Her smile grew as she hugged him back.

"You're very welcome, sweetie. I have to go now. Do you need anything else before I go?"

"Nope! I'm just going to play my game. Bye, Mom!"

She laughed again, watching as Dan grabbed his controller and returned to the world of Tony Hawk.

"Bye, sweetie," she said and walked out towards the front door.

Dan was a good kid. He always received good grades in school, did his chores without too much resistance—all 10-year-olds had some—and was respectful towards everyone. Dan never really asked for much, even for his birthday. So, when Dan had asked for Tony Hawk's *Pro Skater* for his birthday, she knew it must have been something he really wanted.

2

Patricia Williams, 27, was a beautiful young woman with a pale, lightly freckled complexion. She typically wore glasses, and her wavy red hair fell just past her shoulders. Patricia worked as a full-time nurse at the local hospital. She had given birth to Dan when she was only 17. Dan's father had never really been in his life and had left Patricia when Dan was only two. This had left Patricia with a 2-year-old kid and a full plate of nursing school. Luckily, Dan's grandma had been around to help watch him while she was in class. Patricia felt rather guilty about Dan not having a father figure in his life but knew that he was not the man she wanted to marry, nor the man she wanted Dan to call his father. Even though she worked forty-plus hours a week, she felt that she had given Dan the best life she could.

About a year ago, Patricia had met the man Dan would come to call his stepdad, Henry. Henry was a truck driver who mostly hauled cattle to and from auctions. He was an honest man, one who believed in hard work and treating your family right. Henry was an intimidating guy, standing at 6'4", but he was always very soft-spoken and would give you the shirt off his back if you needed it. He was ex-military and had always kept his hair cut in a military style, high and tight.

It wasn't long after they met that Patricia had asked Henry to move in and he had accepted. Dan liked Henry well enough, although he never really felt like he needed a father figure. After all, it had only been his mother and him for the past 10 years. Because of his profession, Henry wasn't home too often, so it was still mostly just Dan and his mom. On occasion his grandma would also come to visit. After Henry and Patricia married, Dan and Henry grew a little closer, but it was still a very shallow relationship.

3

It was 8:45 AM when Patricia pulled into the parking lot

of the Community Memorial Hospital. Her shift today started at 9:00 AM. She had worked there for six years, first in the trauma center, and for the past two years as head nurse. As she sat in her car, she suddenly remembered she had forgotten to order a cake for Dan's upcoming birthday—he was turning 11. She grabbed her phone and quickly called up Siegling's, the local grocery store, hoping it wasn't too late. Along with the video game, Dan had asked for a Dragon Ball Z cake for his birthday, so when the man asked Patricia what kind of cake she wanted, she made sure he had it just right. "My son loves Dragon Ball Z. You know, the cartoon show where they have the crazy hair." In all honesty, she had never quite understood the fascination Dan had with the show, but she wasn't one to pass judgement. If he liked it, that was good enough for her.

"Yes ma'am, I'm actually quite a big fan of the show myself," the man replied. "Do you know what he would like on the cake?" Luckily for Patricia, Dan had been quite specific with this request.

"Yes, he would like Gohan, specifically from the Cell Saga," she said. The guy on the phone laughed as he wrote down the specific details of the order.

"Your son sure knows what he likes. I'll get this order put in right away and it will be ready on December 10th."

"Thank you so much! Have a great day," she said and ended the call. She looked at the time and saw it was 8:58, two minutes before her shift. *Dan is going to love his birthday cake. I hope it's a birthday he never forgets,* she thought to herself as she walked into the hospital entrance. How right she was.

4

Tuesday, December 7th started just like all school days did for Dan. He was startled awake from a deep sleep by his alarm clock and dreaded the thought of having to get up. He had a habit of staying up way too late on school nights—the new Tony Hawk game certainly didn't help.

"Good morning, Dan! Only three more days until your birthday!" his mom said, passing his room as she collected her things for work.

"Hi Mom," he managed to mumble as he rubbed his eyes. She always was a very cheerful person in the morning. Dan never really understood this, but never let it bother him either. Dan's bedroom was a modest one, barely able to fit his twin-size bed, tv, and dresser. But to Dan, this was all he needed. He liked his small room; it made him feel safe and at home. It took another twenty minutes before Dan had managed to make it to the shower (mornings really were not his thing). As Dan was getting out of his shower, he thought he could smell pancakes. "Hey Mom, are you making pancakes?"

Patricia smiled, and replied from the kitchen: "Yes, dear. Quite the nose you have...how many would you like?" Dan finished drying off and came out to the kitchen in his towel.

"I'll take three, please," he said and went to his room to get dressed for school.

"Ready in ten," she replied.

Dan made quick work of his pancakes and then it was off to school. "Have a good day at school, sweetie," his mom said as she left for work.

"Bye Mom!" he replied.

5

Dan's school schedule was pretty easy. He was in 4th grade

and had the same teacher for almost all of his classes, Mrs. Nielson. She was an older lady, in her mid-sixties, Dan thought, but was a nice enough teacher. She always insisted that students pay attention and be respectful. Dan could remember many times when Mrs. Nielson had sent kids to detention for talking out of turn or being disruptive. Luckily for Dan, Mrs. Nielson liked him, primarily because he was a straight A student and never caused any trouble.

During his lunch break, Dan asked one of his friends, Jake, if he wanted to come over on Friday for his birthday. "My mom got me Tony Hawk's *Pro Skater!* I was thinking we could hang out and play it," Dan said. Jake McMiller was one of Dan's closest friends. They'd only met about a year ago but in that year they had established quite the bond. This was primarily due to the fact that they were both quiet, loved video games, and lived only a few houses apart.

"Oh man, that sounds awesome! I've been wanting to play that one," Jake responded. "I'll ask my parents tonight and let you know later."

Dan was excited. Jake's parents were really cool, so he was certain they'd let Jake stay over. The rest of the day was pretty standard for Dan, and after school he walked right home to play Tony Hawk.

6

Later that evening, Dan heard the phone. He immediately jumped up from his bed and ran out to the living room, "I got it, I got it!" he yelled, "it's probably Jake." He picked up the phone, almost out of breath, "Hello, Jake?" he asked.

"Hey, man," Jake said, "parents said Friday is cool with them. Want me to bring anything?"

Dan did a little dance in the living room—it was going to be a great birthday. "Nope, I don't think so. Mom said we can order pizza too! I'll see you in school tomorrow, Jake," he said, and hung up. "Jake's parents said he could stay the night on Friday, Mom," Dan said.

"That's great, sweetie," she replied, "I know you two are going to have a great time." Dan hugged her and went back to his room. After a few more hours of gaming, Dan fell asleep.

December 8th, 1999—a Wednesday. This was the day that would be forever ingrained in young Danny's mind. It was the day the dreams started.

CHAPTER II

1

Dan opened his eyes and found himself right in the middle of Main Street, Redfield. It was Main Street—yes, that was certain, but something wasn't quite right. As Dan walked south, he realized the buildings didn't look the same. They were different than he remembered. The brick that covered most of the buildings was much more vibrant than they had been the last time Dan saw them. They looked—newer. I don't recognize hardly any of these, *he thought as he continued walking down Main Street.*

He began to notice other things, too. The cars parked along the street looked odd to Dan. They were rather long and had a generous amount of chrome on the body. The tires had a strange white ring on the front of them, which went all the way around them. Dan also noticed the traffic light; or rather, the lack thereof. Dan knew that wasn't right. It had been there for as long as he could remember, but now it was gone.

"Danny, wake up, Danny." Dan heard this voice, but it seemed far away. The world around him began to shake, his vision became blurry, and then went black—

Danny awoke suddenly, his heart rate slightly elevated. He had a confused look on his face—unsure of what just happened. He noticed his mom, who was standing next to his bed.

"Danny, are you okay?" she asked. "You must have been having quite the dream! You were mumbling to yourself about buildings, and cars, and traffic lights."

Dan rubbed his eyes, more confused than ever. "Yeah, I was. It was weird, Mom. I was on Main Street, but it was...different. It was like in the old times or something," he said.

"That sounds very interesting, sweetie," she said. "You'd better hurry and get ready for school or you'll be late!"

As Dan went to get out of bed, the pain hit him like a truck—his head felt like it was going to explode. "Ouch!" he cried, putting both hands on his head. His mom came running back into the room.

"What's wrong, sweetie?"

"Ugh, my head, Mom...it's killing me."

"Oh no, I'm sorry, Danny. Let me go grab you some medicine," she said, leaving his room and heading to the kitchen. A moment later she returned with two Advil and a glass of water. "Here, take these, they should help," she said. "I have to get going to work. Please call me if your headache gets worse." Dan took the pills and drank the water.

"Okay, will do. Thanks, Mom!" he said. Dan leaned over to grab his book bag for school, and as he did another wave of pain shot through his head. *Ugh, I sure hope that medicine helps my headache.*

2

As his second class finished, Dan noticed (with great clarity) that his headache wasn't going away. He raised his hand and asked Mrs. Nielson if he could go see the nurse.

"Not feeling well, Dan?" she asked.

"No, Mrs. Nielson. I've had a headache all morning and it doesn't seem to be getting any better."

Mrs. Nielson wrote him a pass and Dan was on his way to see Mrs. Kline, the school nurse. Mrs. Kline took Dan's temperature and did the routine check-up.

"Well, Dan," she said, "I don't see anything out of the ordinary, but I do know that you rarely ever ask to come see me, so this shouldn't be taken lightly. I'd better send you home so you can rest." She wrote on his pass that he was to be excused from class for the remainder of the day. "I'll call your mom and have her come pick you up, Dan," she said. Dan gave a brief smile.

"Thank you, Mrs. Kline, but I can walk. It's just across the street," he said.

Once he was home, Dan took off his clothes and put on some shorts and fell into bed—he was exhausted. Unfortunately, his head wouldn't allow him much sleep— none, in fact. After an hour or so, he decided it was useless and got up. The remainder of Dan's day was spent playing Nintendo, with the sound turned way down and the lights off. His head was still throbbing, albeit less than it had been at school. *I hope my headache is gone by Friday*, he thought. *I don't want to deal with this on my birthday*. The day turned to night, and Dan managed to drift into a dreamless sleep.

3

Two days passed and it was now December 10th, Dan's

birthday. Dan had still been complaining about his head and his mom feared it could be something more severe.

"Do you think we should take him in?" she asked Henry, her face revealing the overwhelming concern for her son. "Nothing seems to be helping his head," she continued.

Henry considered this for a moment, and replied, "Yes, I suppose we better. Might be nothing but on the off chance it is, we don't want to take that risk. Some birthday, huh?"

Patricia froze— "His birthday!" she said. "Oh, Henry, I forgot his cake! Could you go get it while I call the clinic?"

Henry smiled, "Of course, dear! I'll head there now." He got up, kissed her on the forehead, and left to get the cake. Patricia picked up the phone and dialed the Redfield Clinic. When the receptionist answered, Patricia asked for the soonest available appointment with Dr. Hodgin.

"I'm sorry, Mrs. Williams, but Dr. Hodgin's schedule is booked for the next week or so," the receptionist said. "Would you like me to look at his schedule past then?"

"Oh, gosh, no," Patricia replied, "That's much too long to wait! My son has had a headache for the past couple of days and we're very worried. Is there someone else that could see him?" The line was quiet for a few moments, followed by some keystrokes and mouse clicks. After what seemed like an eternity, the receptionist spoke again.

"Oh, actually, Dr. Hodgin just had a cancellation, and now has an opening this morning at 10. Would that be okay?" Patricia looked down at her watch, saw it was only 9.

"Yes, that should work fine," she said.

"Okay, great!" the receptionist replied. "So, I have you down for 10 A.M with Dr. Hodgin. Is there anything else I can do for you?"

Patricia checked her watch again, just to be sure, and then

replied, "No, I don't think so. Thank you!" As she hung up the phone, she saw Dan enter the living room.

"Hey, Mom, who was on the phone?" asked Dan.

"Oh, good morning, honey. Happy birthday! That was the clinic. I scheduled you an appointment for this morning to see what's up with your head," Patricia replied. She ran her hand gently through Dan's hair. He winced and let out a small cry that told her his headache wasn't improving.

"I guess that would be good," he said. "I'm going to go take a shower." She smiled at Dan as he walked out of the room.

"Okay, sweetie. We'll want to leave in about forty minutes or so," she said. Dan muttered something, which she took to be acknowledgement.

A few moments later, Henry arrived home from picking up Dan's birthday cake.

"Honey, I'm home," he announced just as Patricia was coming into the kitchen.

"Oh, hi, babe! Did you have any trouble getting the cake?" she asked.

"Nope," he said, "no problem at all. It looks good!" The cake really did look good. It was a standard sheet birthday cake, chocolate flavored of course, and covered with white buttercream frosting. They had done a wonderful job of decorating the cake. Gohan looked just like he did from the show, and Patricia knew Dan would love it.

"I sure hope the doctor can figure out what's wrong," she said. "It's such a shame he has to be this miserable on his birthday."

CHAPTER III

1

DAN AND HIS PARENTS ARRIVED AT THE REDFIELD CLINIC JUST before 10 A.M. It was a small, one story building that was built in 1950. The building was brick, brown and tan colored, and had black trim all around the sides. Henry parked the vehicle in front of the building. The three of them got out and walked towards the entrance, which was a set of plain cement stairs with a tan handrail placed in the center. Dan felt something that wasn't quite right about the building, but it was a brief feeling that passed almost as quickly as it had appeared. Once inside, they were greeted immediately by the receptionist, whose name according to her badge, was Amy.

"Good morning, how can I help you?" she asked in an almost alarmingly cheerful voice.

"Hello, my son Dan has an appointment at ten with Dr. Hodgin," Patricia said. Amy smiled and proceeded to check her computer for Dr. Hodgin's morning schedule.

"Ah, here we go, Daniel Williams. It says here Danny is

complaining of a headache. Is that the only symptom he's experiencing?" she asked and looked over at Dan. Dan looked briefly up at his mother, who smiled and gave him a look that said, *it's okay, go ahead and tell her.* Patricia found it odd that the receptionist was asking about his symptoms but chalked it up to being a small clinic.

Dan looked back at Amy and nodded. "Yes, just my head. It hurts so bad."

Amy took down a couple more notes and told them that they could have a seat and that the doctor would be with them shortly. No more than ten minutes later, they were accompanied by a nurse back to one of the patient rooms. Dan sat on the table, which was lined with the usual paper—the stuff that made sure the slightest movement was announced at a resounding noise level. The nurse placed a light touch onto Dan's shoulder after closing the door.

"How are you feeling, Danny?" she asked. "Does your head still hurt?" Dan nodded, just as he had done earlier at the receptionist's desk.

"Ye-yes," he said with a noted hint of nervousness. Understandable, of course. Nobody really liked going to the doctor, especially kids. Dan just hoped he didn't have to get a shot. He hated shots.

"No need to be scared, Dan, Dr. Hodgin is a great doctor. He'll make sure you get to feeling better in no time!" she reassured Dan. His expression remained unchanged at the attempt of reassurance. The nurse did the routine checks: pulse, temperature, blood pressure, etc. "Everything looks good with your vitals, Dan," she said, "I'll tell the doctor you're ready for him. Hang tight." She left. Dan was more nervous now than he had been. *What's wrong with me?* He thought. *I hope Dr. Hodgin can fix my head. I just want to feel better for my birthday.*

As if she sensed Dan's concern, his mom put a hand on his knee and said, "Don't worry sweetie, Dr. Hodgin will make you feel much better." Dan took in a deep breath and released it out. He tried to relax.

A knock on the door came, and Dr. Hodgin entered the room. He was a tall man—towering at 6'7" and had arms that seemed to stretch out forever. At sixty-five, his hair (what was left of it, anyway) had gone completely grey. His eyes seemed not so much to look at Dan, but rather through him. Dark blue, almost stormy eyes that made his blood run cold.

"Good morning, everyone," he said in a raspy voice. He shook hands with Dan's parents and then focused on him. "What seems to be the trouble, Danny?" he asked. Dan had tried to relax before, but now he was downright terrified.

"He's had a headache for the past couple of days, doctor," Patricia replied. Dr. Hodgin turned and looked at her, "Aww, that's too bad. A headache can be the worst," he said.

"We're probably overreacting, but we wanted to be sure," Henry added.

"It's also my birthday," Dan said—he sounded no less nervous, though.

"Your birthday? Well, this sure isn't a great way to spend it," he said. "Let me do a few checks on you and then we'll see if we can get you on your way." Dr. Hodgin asked Dan to open his mouth and say *ahhh*, and then looked at Dan's eyes through his retinoscope. He felt around Dan's neck, both in the sides and towards the back. "Okay, Dan, I'm going to ask you a few questions. Is that alright?"

"Sure," said Dan. He felt he could handle a few questions.

Dr. Hodgin proceeded to ask Dan if he had hit his head recently, experienced any light-headedness, dizziness, or concerns with his hearing. Dan answered no to all of these questions.

Dr. Hodgin jotted a few notes down, he turned to face Patricia and Henry. "I'm afraid I can't tell what's going on just yet," he said. "I would like to run a few tests on Dan. Would that be okay?" Dan's eyes grew wider, and his complexion had almost immediately one ghostly pale. He gave his mom a sudden terrified look that said, *please don't let him operate on me, Mom.* Dan's parents looked at each other and then Patricia spoke.

"What kind of tests, Dr. Hodgin?" He smiled, which revealed a set of teeth that belonged in some horror novel by Stephen King.

"Nothing invasive, I assure you," he replied. "I would like to do a CT scan on Dan. It's the quickest and easiest way to determine what might be going on. It could just be something as simple as excessive stress...albeit unlikely at his age but still possible. Likewise, it could be much more serious that we would need to rule out quickly." Before a word was said, Dr. Hodgin turned to Dan as if he had read his mind, "No need to worry, young Danny, it's completely painless."

A sudden chill came over the room, and Dan gave a slight shiver at Dr. Hodgin's remark. Patricia gave another look at her husband and then to Dan. She was the typical concerned mother, but she knew (being a nurse) that ruling out any serious concerns was imperative. With that thought at the forefront of her mind, she gave Dr. Hodgin the go ahead for the CT scan. He smiled again and walked towards the door, stopped at the door and turned to face them and spoke. "I'll get the order put in right way. A nurse will be by to get you, Dan and I'll meet you in the CT room."

After the door closed, Dan turned to his parents with a look of apprehension. "What's a CT scan?" he asked. Patricia took this one as she replied.

"It's pretty neat, Danny. It's like a really powerful camera that allows the doctor to take really high-quality pictures of your head that will tell the doctor what's causing it to hurt." Dan relaxed a little at this response. He thought he could handle that. It actually sounded pretty cool. He relaxed a bit, but his head was still throbbing.

After what seemed like an eternity to Dan—it had really only been 15 minutes—the same nurse from earlier opened the door and asked him to come with her. Dan slipped off the bed, which created an obnoxiously loud crackling sound, and walked towards the door. Just as Dan's parents stood up to join, the nurse raised her hand, "Oh, no, I'm sorry, no one but the patient is allowed in the CT room," she said. "You can wait here, and I will come get you once we're done." Patricia reeled back at this as if physically hit with the words.

"Surely we as the parents can be with him to watch. He's just a boy. He might be scared." The nurse's expression changed to a slight smile, one that wouldn't pass for much more than modest concern.

"I'm sorry, but it's doctor's orders. Due to the radiation involved, as well as the necessity for Dan to be perfectly still, we ask that the parents stay outside," she said. "Please, trust me, the doctor knows what he's doing. I'll be back soon." Patricia started to speak again, but the door closed before any words could come out.

2

The nurse walked with Dan down a long, brightly lit hallway. At the end of the hallway, the nurse directed Dan into a room marked *CT Scan*. When Dan walked in, he noticed a large rectangular table in the center of the room. Attached to the table was a giant circle. The table was on a track that seemed like it would go straight through the circle. On the wall to the left of the machine was a one-way window. Other than the CT machine, the room was void of anything else. Like the rest of the hospital rooms, the walls were plain white with no decor of any kind.

"Please have a seat, Dan. Get comfortable and relax. I'll be right back," the nurse said as she closed the door behind her.

Dan sat down, but he was the furthest thing from comfortable or relaxed. Something didn't sit right with Dan, but he wasn't sure what it was. His gut had told him Dr. Hodgin was a bad man—a very bad man. The room door opened, and for a moment the thoughts went to the back of his mind. The nurse came in with something behind her back—the bad feeling returned to the front of his mind with full force.

"Wha-wha-what do you have in your hand?" Dan stuttered.

The nurse smiled as she put out her hand, revealing a cupcake. It had a candle in the shape of an 11.

"I hear it's your birthday," she said.

Dan showed the first sign of a slight smile since he had been at the clinic—the bad feeling was still there, though. Dan hesitated, and then took the cupcake. The nurse smiled at Dan, who had already started to eat the cupcake. "I need to go into the next room to prep the machine Dan, but I'll be back in a moment. Enjoy your cupcake."

Dan barely heard the nurse as he was thoroughly enjoying the cupcake, which was pistachio flavored. He finished the cupcake, and a few moments later started to feel dizzy. *Something isn't right,* he thought. *I think something was wrong with that cupcake.* The room grew colder—his vision had started to become foggy.

The nurse came back in the room. "I'm sorry, Danny, but it's for the best. The doctor won't be able to see anything on the scan if you move too much," the nurse said. The world went black for Dan and he fell backwards onto the table.

CHAPTER IV

1

"Danny, hey, Danny. Wake up, the scan is all done," said the nurse. Danny made a groaning noise as he tried to open his eyes. He quickly noticed they felt...heavy.

"Wha—what happened?" he asked. "I feel...sleepy."

The nurse smiled. "I'm sorry, Danny, I had to give you something to relax during your CT scan," she said as Dan sat up from the bed. "If you're feeling okay, Dan, I'll take you back to your parents now," the nurse said.

"Yeah, actually I..," Dan stopped, "I actually feel really good! My headache is gone!" It was true—he felt great. Dan's headache was gone. Dr. Hodgin came in the room and stood next to Dan.

"How are you feeling, Danny?" he asked, doing his best to sound genuinely concerned. Dan told the doctor that his headache was gone and wondered if he could see his parents now. Dr. Hodgin smiled and motioned towards the door, "Of course! I need to fill them in on what was going on with your head anyway," he said. Dan had been so relieved about his head not hurting, he had forgotten to ask why it had stopped. Before he could ask, the nurse took his hand and directed him out the door and into the hallway.

2

They reached the exam room and the nurse knocked and opened the door to let Dan inside. "Danny!" his mom shrilled, "Are you okay? I've been worried sick!" She ran towards Dan and gave him a big hug. The nurse smiled as she moved out of the way to allow Dr. Hodgin inside as well.

"I'm great, Mom!" Dan replied. "I don't know what the doctor did, but I feel great!" Patricia smiled and turned to Dr. Hodgin with a relieved look.

"What took so long?" she asked. "It's been nearly two hours."

Dr. Hodgin hesitated for a moment but replied with confidence. "I do apologize for the wait, Mrs. Williams. The scan took much longer than I had anticipated due to some technical difficulties. Plus, I wanted to be thorough to make sure I didn't miss anything."

Patricia seemed satisfied with this answer. "Oh, I see," she said. "So, what did you find out?"

"Well, I have good news and bad news," he began, "the good news is the scan didn't show any signs of a tumor or swelling. I gave him a strong dose of pain medication, which appears to have subsided the pain in his head for now." Henry, who had remained seated at Patricia's side, let out a sigh of relief.

"Well, go on. What's the bad news?" Patricia cried, hardly hearing the good news.

"The bad news, which could have been much worse, mind you, is that Dan appears to have a rather severe case of *Toxoplasmosis*," he replied. Henry had a rather blank expression on his face, but Patricia knew very well what Toxoplasmosis was. "Now, Danny, do you recall eating any food recently that didn't taste quite right?" Dr. Hodgin asked. "I ask because the leading cause of *Toxoplasmosis* is exposure to contaminated food."

Dan thought for a moment. "Umm, no...I'm sorry, doctor, I can't think of anything," he said. Dr. Hodgin smiled.

"Oh, that's okay, Danny, I myself can rarely remember what I ate for lunch." Dan was hesitant to ask his next question, but knew it was necessary.

"So, am I going to be okay, doctor?" he asked.

"Oh, don't worry, Danny, you're going to be fine, I promise," he said. "If it's okay with you, Danny, I'd like to have a quick talk with your parents outside. It'll only take a moment." Patricia didn't like the sound of this, but she agreed.

"We'll be right back, sweetie. Don't worry," his mom said, gently placing her hand on his shoulder.

The three of them stepped outside the exam room, leaving Danny by himself. Danny was a little nervous but remained strong. He moved closer to the door and put his ear up to it, hoping to hear something—there was nothing. Disheartened, Dan sat back down on the table and waited. *At least my head doesn't hurt*, he thought. A few minutes later, the exam door opened, and his parents came back in.

"Mom! Dad!" Dan said. "What's going on? Am I going to be okay?" Patricia smiled and gave Dan a big hug.

"You're going to be fine, honey," she said. "The doctor just didn't want to potentially scare you with any medical terminology, especially since some of it can sound way scarier than it is." Dan thought he sensed something off in his mom's voice, but couldn't place it, nor did he pursue it. "Dr. Hodgin gave us a prescription for you to take. Just a pill once a day. Easy as that!" she said.

"How long do I have to take them?" Dan asked.

"Well...the doctor isn't sure, unfortunately. It depends on how well your body takes to the medication," she said, knowing all too well how wrong this sounded.

"Oh...alright," Dan said. Nothing felt right to Dan, but he trusted his parents, and they knew best. They filled Danny's prescriptions and headed to the car. Once inside, Dan got that feeling again—something wasn't quite right. But as before, it faded away.

3

For the rest of the afternoon, Dan sat around the house, never feeling quite right. He didn't have a headache anymore, but he just felt weird. After school had got out, Jake showed up at Dan's house, which made him feel much better. Dan had almost forgotten about his plans for tonight.

"Hey, Jake!" Dan said, closing the door behind him.

"Hey!" Jake replied, "How's it going? You weren't in school today." Dan put his hand up to his head.

"Yeah, I'm alright...I'd been having a pretty bad headache the past couple days, so I went to the clinic. Got some medicine, so I'm good now. Let's play!" Jake smiled, kicked off his shoes and followed Dan to his room. Several hours went by as they played Tony Hawk. Later on, Patricia ordered pizza for dinner.

After dinner, Patricia had asked Dan and Jake to come out to the kitchen for some dessert.

"Dessert?" asked Dan. "I didn't know we were having dessert."

As the two of them entered the kitchen they noticed a large, decorated cake sitting on the table. Dan's mouth fell open once he saw what was on the cake, it was Gohan from *Dragon Ball Z*.

"Oh man, that's awesome! How'd you know, Mom?"

Patricia smiled. "You told me, silly. Plus, you're always talking about how Gohan is your favorite character. Which piece do you want?"

Dan was still distracted by the incredible level of detail that had been put into the cake. "Um, it doesn't matter. I almost don't want to cut it," he said.

"I want a corner piece!" said Jake. "I like the extra frosting. Is that okay, Dan?"

"Yeah, of course man, any piece you want. I'll just have the piece next to the corner, Mom."

The three of them finished their pieces in no time at all— it was as tasty as it was detailed.

"Thanks again, Mom. The cake was delicious! Come on, Jake, let's go play some more."

"You're welcome, sweetie. I'm glad you're finally having a great birthday."

Dan and Jake continued playing Tony Hawk, trying to beat each other's high scores.

"Thanks for having me over," said Jake, "it's been great so far."

"Of course," said Dan. "That cake sure was good, wasn't it? Oh, by the way, who's your favorite DBZ character? I think I know, but I'm not sure."

Jake contemplated this for a moment, and then replied.

"Hmm, I'd have to say Trunks. I like his purple hair when he's not a super saiyan. And yeah, that cake was delicious!"

Dan laughed at the purple hair comment. "Yeah, Trunks is cool too. He's in my top five for sure."

It was well after midnight when they began to get sleepy. Dan shut off the TV and lay down to sleep. "Goodnight, Jake," he said, "Thanks for hanging out with me on my birthday."

Jake, who was already almost falling asleep on the floor, replied: "No problem, man, that game is awesome!" The time was 12:43 AM.

TICK TOCK

Dan's bed began to shake violently, tossing him around like a boat on rough tides. He tried to open his eyes but was unable to. A moment later he was thrown from his bed and landed onto Main Street, again. Dan looked around, feeling more disoriented and confused than he had been in the previous dream. Things were the same as before, except not quite.

Dan noticed there were other people this time, walking up and down the sidewalks on either side of the road. Like the cars and buildings, they looked strange to Dan. Not the people themselves, per se, but what they were wearing. Everyone seemed so formally dressed to Dan. He himself was wearing a pair of gym shorts and a t-shirt—standard sleeping attire. All the men Dan saw were in suits and the women were either wearing dresses or skirts. It was bizarre to Dan. He had obviously seen adults wear this sort of thing before but only on special occasions, not simply walking down the sidewalk on a Saturday. Was it Saturday? he thought. To be honest—he didn't know what year it was.

Dan approached a well-dressed man in a three-piece suit. The suit was comprised of fitted charcoal grey trousers and sport coat, complete with a thin black tie. "Ex..excuse me, sir?" asked Dan, sounding as nervous as he felt, "could you tell me what the date is?" The man stopped and looked down at Dan with a puzzled look.

"It's Saturday, son, first of January. Are you lost or something?"

"What year?" asked Dan, astounded by how real this dream was. The man's face had changed from puzzled to utterly bewildered.

"What year is it? Did you hit your head or something?" he asked, "It's 1965, of course...brand new year!"

Suddenly the street began to shake, Dan's vision blurred again, and he had to struggle to maintain his balance. The man didn't seem to notice and was waiting for Dan to say something. Before he could reply, everything went black.

4

The time was 12:43 AM. Dan woke up, again with a slightly elevated heart rate, as well as more confusion. To his disappointment, his headache was back—worse than before, in fact. *1965? Did I hear that right? Why am I dreaming of 1965?* Dan looked over at his clock and saw it was exactly the same time as he had fallen asleep. A chill fell over him, causing gooseflesh to form up and down his body. *What the...*he thought. *I was in that dream for at least thirty minutes—maybe longer.* Dan knew that the time spent in dreams was not the same as in reality, but even so, he felt something wasn't quite right. Dan considered going to tell his mom, but decided against it —he would mention it in the morning if he remembered. Dan lay back down and fell asleep. He didn't dream for the rest of the night.

5

The next morning, Dan woke up to his head still hurting

from the previous night. He had a vivid memory of the dream last night, which he planned to mention to his mom.

"Hey, Mom," he called, walking out into the kitchen. She was at the stove making breakfast—eggs and hash browns, by the smell of it—and turned to face him.

"Good morning, dear, how are you feeling?" she asked, her face turning to a smile.

"Ugh, my head hurts again, Mom. I also had another dream..." he trailed off. Her smile fell slightly but was still there.

"Aw, sorry about your head, sweetie. Here, take your medication, that should help," she said, handing him one of his pills. "What was this dream about?" she asked.

"It was the same dream," he said as he took his pill. "I was on Main Street, and things were all old-timey looking. This time there were people. I even talked to a man that was walking by me. He told me it was 1965! He had on a grey suit and a black tie." Her eyes widened at the amount of detail Dan recalled from the dream.

"That's very interesting, honey. What else happened?" she asked. Dan frowned and looked down at his feet.

"That's all. I woke up after that. But when I woke up, I noticed it was still 12:43, the same time I went to bed," he said.

"Now Dan, you know that's not possible. I'm sure you were just sleepy and didn't read the clock right," she replied. "Go wake up Jake and hang out in the living room. I'll bring the food in shortly." Dan started to raise his hand in protest but reconsidered and did as his mom said.

6

As Patricia finished up making breakfast, she couldn't help but think of what Dan had told her. *Dreaming of Redfield, 1965? I sure hope this doesn't get any worse. What if he never gets better? And this thing about the time being the same as when he went to bed? What is going on?* She didn't like it—not one bit. She told herself she would mention it to Henry, and if it kept happening, she would consider taking Dan to see someone—perhaps a therapist.

Once Henry and Jake entered the kitchen, the four of them sat down and ate breakfast together. "How's your head, Dan?" Patricia asked.

"Better, actually," he said, "that medicine sure works fast." She smiled. Dan didn't mention the dreams at the table. Patricia was thankful for this but also not surprised. While Dan had no problems with Henry, he rarely talked to him about anything personal in nature. Their conversations were typically very brief and superficial—small talk, mostly.

After breakfast, Dan said goodbye to Jake, who had to go home and do chores, but said he would probably be able to come back later. Dan went back into his room to play Nintendo—a typical Saturday for an 11-year-old. Once Dan was engrossed in his game, and the dishes were cleaned up, Patricia asked Henry if they could talk.

"Uh, sure, babe," he replied, "everything okay?" Henry sat back down at the table next to her, placing his hand on her leg.

"I don't know, exactly," she said. "I think something might be going on with Dan. The last two nights he's been having this dream, a very detailed dream of Redfield in 1965." At first Henry didn't say anything and before he could, she spoke again. "This morning he told me about a man he spoke to in the dream...he described the guy's suit and tie. He mentioned the buildings and the cars too. I don't know, maybe I'm just overreacting or something." Henry moved closer and embraced his wife, doing what he could to comfort her.

"It'll be okay, babe," he said. "I don't think there's anything to worry about, but if it makes you feel better, we can keep an eye on him, and if things get worse, we can discuss the possibility of seeing a therapist." She let out a short sigh of relief and hugged her husband tighter.

"Thank you. I just worry about him, Henry. What if we were wrong to put him on the medication? I don't know if I could handle that. Maybe we should have gotten a second opinion." Henry was never very good at heart-to-heart conversations—or much of any conversation at all, really. But at the end of the day, he was a hard-working guy who cared deeply for his family and would do anything for them.

"We aren't wrong, dear. I feel like Dr. Hodgin knows what he's doing. It's good that we took him in, trust me. It just might take a little more time," Henry said.

"I love you," she said. "Thank you for being so under-standing. Let's go see how Dan is doing." She started to get up, but Henry grabbed her arm.

"I'm sure he's fine, dear," he said. "What do you say we go out and do some shopping? Dan will be busy with his games for hours anyway."

Patricia smiled and put her hand on top of his. "Sure, babe. I'll get my things," she said. She got up and went to their bedroom to change her clothes while Henry went out to start the car.

7

The time was 10:46 AM. Dan had been playing Nintendo

but started to get unusually tired and decided to lie down. The moment his eyes closed the bed began to, once again, shake violently. He was scared, but he was paralyzed—unable to open his eyes or move. He felt a cold wave rush over his body and then he felt himself forcibly tossed out of his bed and landed on Main Street, 1965.

TICK TOCK

He opened his eyes, slowly getting up from the rough landing he had just experienced. Wha—what was that? he wondered. This dream would be number three, if this were actually a dream, anyway. Dan was seriously beginning to wonder what was going on. As he looked around, he noticed everything was the same as the previous two trips here, with one notable exception—the people. They all seemed to be paying more atten-tion to him—staring at him—as if he didn't belong. It was a bit unnerv-ing, to say the least, but he tried to ignore them. This couldn't be real, after all. He decided to do a little exploring while he was here, maybe figure out why he kept dreaming of 1965.

As with the past two dreams, Dan had landed at the intersection of Main Street and E 5th Avenue, facing south. To his left he saw the library. This didn't surprise Dan, as he knew the Carnegie Library was very old. It honestly didn't look too different from how it did in 1999. It still had the wide, cement steps with a round, metal handlebar splitting them down the middle. The steps led up to the glass door, which was surrounded by red brick. At the top of the stairs loomed four large pillars, which were in noticeably better condition than he remembered seeing them. Other than the apparent condition of the building, the only difference was the familiar trees surrounding the library, which were significantly smaller.

As he continued walking south on Main Street, he came to another familiarity—Siegling's grocery store. It was a bigger building that looked freshly painted. Dan was surprised by how new it looked. He wasn't sure when the grocery store had been built, but he figured it must have been sometime this year (1965).

Dan came to a crossroad, 6th Avenue, and as he looked to the west, he froze. Dan caught a glimpse of something peering from behind the building on the corner of Main Street and 6th Avenue, which at this time was apparently a bank.

He rubbed his eyes and looked again—nothing. He strained his eyes, trying to see what had been there—it was something, he was sure of that. But whatever it was, it was gone. I'm going crazy, he thought. Dan considered investigating further but decided to chalk it up to everything else in the surroundings being weird. He turned to continue down the sidewalk when something bumped into him and knocked him off balance. The world went dark, and he woke—

CHAPTER V

1

THE REST OF 1999 CAME AND WENT WITH NO DREAMS OR headaches, but Dan couldn't help but wonder what the previous dreams had meant. Had there actually been something peering at him from behind the bank? Were they really just dreams? Dan would come to have many more questions before he had answers. Many, many more.

January 3rd, 2000 was a bitter Monday. Dan was back in school after Christmas break. He was feeling as if he hadn't slept at all, even though he had gone to bed unusually early Sunday night. Dan was in his math class when he felt his headache return. *Oh no, not this again*, he thought, *I thought this was over.* He didn't want to go to the nurse again—that was too much attention on himself. He gritted his teeth and decided to try to fight through it.

Mrs. Deaver was writing fractions on the whiteboard and Dan was finding it harder and harder to focus on them. As he was copying the equations in his notebook, a terrifying thing began to happen. The lines of his fractions started to wobble back and forth. It reminded Dan a little bit of a teeter totter. He felt a chill pass over him, which caused goosebumps to form on his skin. As the wobbling intensified, he noticed the entire whiteboard began to turn fuzzy, like it was out of focus. He closed his eyes and shook his head. *No, nope...this isn't happening*, he thought, trying to convince himself.

Dan felt a tap on his shoulder. He opened his eyes and turned to see Jake, looking at him with a look of concern. "You okay, Dan?" he asked, keeping his voice to a whisper so he didn't draw Mrs. Deaver's attention.

Dan nodded. "Yeah, I think so. My head just really hurts. I might ask if I can go see the nurse."

He turned back towards the whiteboard and saw the lines were still, just as they're supposed to be. An excruciating wave of pain shot through his head, giving Dan a painful reminder of its existence—a reminder that was certainly not needed. He reluctantly raised his hand to ask if he could be excused. "Yes, Dan?" Mrs. Deaver asked.

"Mrs. Deaver, my head is killing me. May I be excused to go see the nurse?" he asked, feeling bad for interrupting.

"Of course, by all means," she replied, giving Dan a genuine look of concern. "No need for a pass, I'll take you myself." Dan felt his guilt and embarrassment rise—both of which were intensified by the gawking of his classmates.

"Oh, that's okay Mrs. Deaver, I don't want to be a bother," he said.

"Nonsense! We're almost done here anyway," she said. "Class, please finish up copying these equations and then you may have free time." She motioned for Dan to come with her.

Dan had always liked Mrs. Deaver. She was a beautiful lady who was in her late twenties. She had dark blonde hair, which always looked perfect. He admitted to himself that he may have had a slight crush on her but would never say it aloud. As they walked down the hall towards the nurse's office, she asked Dan if he had been having issues with his head for long—she always was concerned about him. "They started about a month ago. My parents took me to the doctor, and he gave me some medicine to take. Today is the first time I've had a headache since then," he said. "The dreams...gosh I hope those don't come back too..." he said, somewhat under his breath.

"What was that?" she asked. Dan felt his face flush and turn hot. He trusted Mrs. Deaver, more than anyone else, aside from his parents, of course. Even so, he still wasn't sure if he should mention the dreams to her. This last dream was the most concerning, as it had appeared to be even more realistic, as well as terrifying. Dan knew he had seen something behind that building, he was sure of it. *Why am I still remember all of this so vividly? Don't people usually forget dreams almost immediately? And those stares—those disconcerting stares—*

Mrs. Deavers noticed that Dan seemed distracted, almost in a trance. "Uh, Danny?" she asked, "Are you okay? Did you say something about dreams?" The question startled Dan from his thoughts.

"Sorry Mrs. Deavers, I've been having a tough time focusing," he said, the feeling of embarrassment returned. *Maybe I should just tell her. After all, she has always tried to look out for me.*

Dan proceeded to explain to Mrs. Deavers that the past three dreams he had were of Redfield, but in 1965. He said that the first two were more or less the same. During these, he had walked around a bit, just trying to figure out what was going on. He had mentioned that, in the second dream he asked a man what year it was, and he had said 1965. Dan paused for a moment, and then continued.

"The third dream, though, it was awful, Mrs. Deaver. Everywhere I looked, people were staring at me, studying me. They all had a look that was of confusion, or maybe concern?" Dan said, trying to keep himself composed. "It wouldn't be so bad if they were just dreams. Having multiple dreams wouldn't be that uncommon, but they're so real, and I have control over what's going on in them, too.

"And then there was the thing at the bank. I had looked down 6th Avenue, and I swear I saw someone peeking around the corner of the bank. But when I looked again, there was nothing. Maybe it was nothing, but afterwards I felt so cold...it was scary."

At that point they had reached the nurse's office. They stopped just before her door and Mrs. Deaver kneeled down so she was at eye level with Dan.

"I'm worried about you, Dan. It seems like you have a lot on your mind, and it might be helpful to see some-one...someone more specialized in this area," she said.

Dan wasn't sure, but he thought he knew what she was talking about. "Like, a therapist?" he asked. Mrs. Deavers nodded and then the nurse opened her door and smiled at them.

"Hello, Mrs. Deavers. Hello, Danny. Please, come in," she said, motioning towards her office. Mrs. Kline closed the door as they stepped inside, promptly taking a seat in her laughably large chair. Mrs. Kline had been the nurse at Redfield for the last twenty-five years and that chair had been there since day one. Dan sat on the couch, which was primarily for students complaining of headaches or upset stomachs to rest on. It was a light brown color with three oversized cushions to lay on.

Mrs. Deavers sat on the opposite end of the couch, still looking concerned at what Dan had told her. "So, what's going on, Danny?" Mrs. Kline asked. Dan hesitated and then Mrs. Deavers spoke.

"Go ahead, Dan, tell her what you told me. She just wants to help."

He was nervous, and almost felt like he was in some kind of interrogation, like the ones he had seen on *Cops*, a show his dad always watched. Regardless, he proceeded to go over everything he had told Mrs. Deavers on the way there. When Dan finished, Mrs. Kline had an almost identical look on her face as Mrs. Deavers had in the hallway.

"My, Danny, that's quite a story," she said. "I'm afraid this is a little out of my realm of expertise. However, I do know someone that might be able to help." Mrs. Kline got up and walked over to her desk. She grabbed a card and wrote something on the back of it, and then returned to her chair. Mrs. Kline handed Dan the card which read:

Dr. Andrew Priam
Registered Psychologist

Below that, it had two contact numbers, as well as his website and email. Dan took the card, giving her an uncertain look. He didn't like the idea of having to tell someone else the story of his dreams. He had been hesitant to even say anything to Mrs. Kline, and now he wished he hadn't. His first thought was to just throw the card away once he was outside but had a feeling Mrs. Kline would also call his parents—he was right. "I'll also be giving your parents a call, Dan," she said, making a note on her calendar to do so. "I'm worried that this could be a symptom of something more severe, and I just want to make sure you're okay." Dan winced as another wave of pain shot up through his neck and into his head.

"Thanks, Mrs. Kline," he said, not at all sounding (or feeling) genuine. Mrs. Deaver left with Dan and back down the hall.

"You can be excused for the rest of the day, Dan," she said. "I'd better get back to class. I hope you feel better soon."

"Thank you, Mrs. Deaver. I hope so too."

Dan looked down at the psychologist's card again. The letters on the card began to wobble, just like the fractions had earlier. He dropped the card in his panic and took a few steps back. *What's happening to me?* After a moment, he bent down and picked up the card—it was fine now. He stuck it in his back pocket and walked home.

CHAPTER VI

1

DR. ANDREW PRIAM, THIRTY-EIGHT YEARS OLD, WAS A lifelong resident of Redfield. His office was on the corner of 7th Avenue and 1st Street. He was happily married, almost thirteen years now, to his college sweetheart. No kids, but a few pets to keep them company. Dr Priam was a very soft-spoken individual. He had short, black hair that was always neatly styled, never a hair out of place. His suits were cleaned and pressed, custom tailored, and always in good taste.

During his nearly fifteen years of being in business, he had helped hundreds of clients, both young and old, get through their troubled times. Dr. Priam had a way of getting to the root of what was going on in the minds of his clients which he did with unparalleled ease. Dr. Priam was, for all intents and purposes, a great psychologist. The day he met Daniel Williams triggered a chain of events that forever changed him —not for the better.

2

As Dan and his parents walked into Dr. Priam's office, Dan felt a similar cold wave from his dreams pass over his body. He also had a sense of not feeling welcome, but it wasn't from Dr. Priam—if he had been older, maybe he could explain it, but at his current age, he was stumped. Luckily, the feeling left when the doctor spoke.

"Hello, Daniel," Dr. Priam said, presenting Dan with what looked like a genuine smile.

"Hi," he said. That was more than he wanted to say. Dan's parents had urged him to see Dr. Priam, and after quite a bit of pressure from them, he finally gave in.

"I understand if you're nervous, maybe even a little apprehensive," Dr. Priam said. "That's a completely normal feeling, especially the first time you visit. It's my job to make sure you feel safe and relaxed."

The doctor asked if Dan would rather have his parents in the room or not. Dan looked over at his parents, who gave him a look that said, *it's up you, sweetie.*

"They can go somewhere else if they want," Dan said. Dan's mom came up to him and kissed his head.

"We'll go get a few groceries for tonight and come back," she said. Dan nodded, and waved at them as they left. Dan turned back towards the doctor, who had sat down on a stool in front of his couch.

"Please, have a seat, Dan—may I call you Dan? What would you prefer?"

"Dan or Danny is fine," he said as he walked towards the couch and sat down. It was an overstuffed couch, much larger than a standard sized one. When Dan sat down, it nearly swallowed his small frame. He felt...somehow comforted by it. As he looked around the room, Dan noticed several bookcases lined the back of the wall. They were filled with all sorts of books, games, and toys. Along with being overstuffed, the couch had several large decorative pillows thrown onto it.

"So, I hear you've been having some dreams about, uh...1965?" he asked. Dan nodded, still not sure if he was comfortable enough to speak. "Can you tell me a little about these dreams? It's very important that I get as much information as possible so I can help." Dan shook his head,

"I... I just don't know if I can yet," Dan managed to say. "This last one was...it was bad, doctor." Dr. Priam jotted something on his notepad, and then looked back at Dan.

"I completely understand, Dan," he said. "Dreams can be scary, especially ones that seem real, which I am to understand is what's going on with yours. Why don't we talk about something else...anything at all. Just to sort of break the ice if you will." Dan smiled, thinking of his Tony Hawk Nintendo game.

"My mom got me a new Nintendo game for my birthday! Tony Hawk's *Pro Skater*," Dan blurted out. "Oops, sorry, I didn't mean to say that so loudly," he said, sounding a bit embarrassed.

Dr. Priam chuckled. "Gosh, no, Dan, no need to apologize. I do believe that is an excellent ice-breaking topic," he said.

With this, Dan went on for a good twenty minutes about his new game. "For my birthday, my best friend Jake came over and we played it for hours and hours...it was great! We had pizza for dinner and then played some more. And then..." He had come to the dream.

"Okay, Dan... I think we've talked enough for this session. We do need to discuss these dreams, but I don't want to rush you," he said. "Let's pick this up in a couple days. How does that sound?" he asked. Dan, who was in somewhat of a trance, looked up at Dr. Priam.

"What? Oh, yeah...that sounds good, doctor. Thanks for listening to me. I get excited about games," he said. Dr. Priam smiled—his expression showed that he was worried about Dan though.

"You can call me Andrew if you'd like, Dan."

"Okay, sure," said Dan, a little unsure of his response.

About ten minutes later, Dan's parents arrived back at the office and took him home.

3

Dr. Priam sat at his desk, leaning back in his chair, looking over the few notes he took on Dan. *Very peculiar,* he thought. *I most certainly need to hear about these dreams of young Dan's...otherwise I'm afraid of what might happen to him. I'm not sure what it is, but something tells me there's much more to these—dreams—than any of us can imagine.* He sat up in his chair, closed his notebook, and got up to leave for the evening. The time was 7:03 PM.

4

When Dan and his parents arrived at home, they all sat down in the living room to relax. Dan could tell his parents were anxious to find out how it went but he was hesitant to tell them—mainly because he hadn't told Dr. Priam anything about the dreams.

"So, Danny, how'd it go with Dr. Priam?" his mom finally asked.

"Okay," Dan replied. He could tell she wasn't happy with his response—he had expected this reaction. He sighed and continued, "He's nice, actually. When I first met him, I got a really bad feeling from him but after sitting and talking with him for twenty minutes or so, I realized the feeling was wrong. He seems genuinely concerned and that made me feel comfortable. I'll talk to him about the dreams...I just needed this first session to—break the ice—as he put it."

Both Patricia and Henry were taken aback a little by his detailed answer—but at the same time—they were relieved.

"That's great to hear, Dan," his mom said. "Don't worry about not opening up during the first session, sweetie. We totally understand and honestly didn't expect much from it at all. It's not easy to talk about things like this, especially at your age. It can be scary and we're proud of you for doing this." Dan got up and hugged his mom and dad—he was content.

"I'm going to head to bed," Dan said. "I'm pretty tired." A few minutes later, Dan was in bed, and his eyes began to close. It was 10:06 PM.

TICK TOCK

Dan's bed began to violently shake, even more so than the last time. He heard parts of his bed frame cracking from the force. He tried getting up, tried opening his eyes—no use. Oh no... not again. I... I can't. Please make it stop! *And then everything dropped out from under him —the bed, the frame, the floor—everything. Dan fell out of his bedroom and landed squarely on his back. To his surprise, there was a complete absence of pain given the velocity of the fall.* Maybe this is all a dream, *he thought.*

Dan slowly got to his feet and was startled when he looked around. It was different—much different. "Whoa...this definitely isn't Main Street," *he said.* "I don't even think this is Redfield." *He also wasn't sure what year it was. Dan was inside some sort of building—pretty new by the looks of it. He was standing in a long corridor—seeming to lead on forever in both directions. The walls of the corridor were a ghastly grey color and appeared to be made of some kind of metal.* What is this place?

Dan walked down the hallway, coming to a large, blood red door with a standard lever handle. Dan carefully put his ear against the door to see if he could hear anything from inside. At first there was nothing, but then he heard it—a faint ticking. Is that a clock? *Above the handle Dan saw an electronic pad, which had an image of a thumbprint on it.* A fingerprint scanner, *he thought. He remembered seeing one in the movie* Back to the Future II. *Dan put his thumb onto the pad which had a smooth, cold surface. He heard the pad begin to scan his print. A moment later it turned red and it emitted two short chimes which echoed throughout the hall. Dan jumped back, startled by the echo. His world went black. Dan felt himself hurled away from the corridor and away from the building. A moment later he landed again, softly this time. He awoke in his bedroom —the time was 10:06 PM.*

As Dan looked around his bedroom, he felt the usual elevated heart rate, complete with the unpleasant headache. "Wha—what was that?" Dan asked. Dan looked over at his clock, and not surprisingly it still read 10:06 PM. He stared at it for a moment, and then watched as it changed to 10:07— not good. *So, the clock works...what's going on with me? Should I talk to Mom and Dad again? What good would that do...they'll just tell me they're dreams and that I looked at the clock wrong. I guess I should talk to Dr. Priam.*

Dan rolled over and tried to sleep. *What was behind that door?* The question lingered in his mind as he drifted off to sleep.

CHAPTER VII

1

THE NEXT MORNING, DAN WOKE UP AROUND 9 AND WAS feeling surprisingly well-rested, all things considered. He slowly strolled out of his room and found his parents in the kitchen having coffee. They were both seated at the table in the center of the room. It was a medium-sized, rectangular table with dark brown wood. Dan had always liked how it looked. It had three extra leaves to make it larger which were never used, at least that Dan could remember.

"Good morning," Dan said, grabbing a bowl to get some cereal.

"Hi sweetie," his mom replied with her usual morning smile. "How are you this morning?" Dan picked out his favorite cereal, *Cinnamon Toast Crunch*, and filled his bowl to the brim, leaving little room for milk.

"I'm good, Mom," he said. "I had another dream last night...but afterwards I slept great!" The first part reduced the smile Patricia donned by at least half, but she quickly pulled it back together.

"Well, I'm glad to hear you got some sleep," she said. "I think we should go see Dr. Priam again."

Dan had just stuck a huge spoonful of cereal in his mouth and then replied, in a mumbled tone, "Mhm, me too. Can he see me today?"

She got up and grabbed the phone. "I'll give him a call. I believe his schedule is pretty flexible during this time of the year."

The phone rang only twice before Dr. Priam picked up. "Hello, Dr. Priam's office," he said.

"Hi Dr. Priam, this is Patricia Williams. Would you be available to have another session with Danny today?" she asked. Dr. Priam pulled up his schedule on his computer and saw that it was completely empty.

"You're in luck, Mrs. Williams, my schedule looks pretty barren today. What time would you like to come in?" he asked. Patricia looked up at the clock—it was 9:25.

"We're just finishing up breakfast here, would 10:30 work for you? That will give us time to get ready and drive to your office," she said.

"That would be fine, 10:30 it is. I'll see you then," the doctor replied and hung up the phone. Patricia smiled and put the phone back on the receiver.

"Okay, Dan, 10:30 today with Dr. Priam. Finish up your cereal and go get dressed," she said. Dan nodded as he continued to devour his breakfast.

2

"What in the fuck was that?" the man screamed. "Are you trying to sabotage everything?" The other man flinched.

"I—I'm sorry sir. This isn't very easy, you know. The algorithms behind this...they're incredibly complex and I told you at the very beginning tha—"

He was interrupted by a heavy hand slapping him across the face—it stung immediately.

"I don't want to hear your excuses!" the man screamed. "I was told you were the best. Is that not so?" The other man was holding his cheek, still trying to understand what had just happened.

"I—I am, sir. I mean, I think so...but sir, please try and understand. What we're trying to do here has never been done before. We need more time to clean up the code and make sure the bugs are ironed out. We simply can't do a full implementation like this...there's just too much interference," he said, bracing for what he thought would be another harsh punishment. The man raised his hand to do so but stopped and sighed.

"Fine. You're right, we can't afford to mess this up. I'll make sure you get what you need. I need to make a few calls. As you were."

3

It was 10:24 when Dan and his parents pulled up to Dr. Priam's office. For a Saturday in January it was a fairly nice day, around 40 °F—Dan felt good. As they stepped into the doctor's office, they noticed he was on the phone. Henry raised his hand to him in a *sorry, didn't mean to interrupt* motion. Dr. Priam motioned them to have a seat as he continued on with his phone conversation. "No, that's okay...yes, that will be fine," he replied. "Yes sir, I under-stand...if that's what you think is best. Uh huh...Okay, good-bye." He hung up the phone. Dan felt a chill go over his body—he shivered—something wasn't right, but he couldn't place it.

"Sorry about that," Dr. Priam said, walking over to greet them. "I had forgotten I scheduled that call until after you and I got off the phone." He shook hands with Henry and Patricia and then looked towards Dan. "Hello, Dan," he said. "Ready for our next session?" Dan had been fidgeting with his hands but stopped when the doctor addressed him.

"Ye—yes, Dr. Prium...I mean, Andrew. I think so," he said. Again, Dr. Priam asked Dan if he'd prefer to have his parents there or not—he decided they could stay this time. Dr. Priam nodded. He grabbed his notebook and motioned towards the door to his therapy room.

"Come on in, everyone. Make yourselves at home," said Dr. Priam, sitting down in his chair. "Okay, Danny, where would you like to start?" he asked.

"I—uh, guess at the start of the dreams. I think it was a year and a half ago that they started," Dan began.

"The first dream was short...maybe only 5 or 10 minutes. I was in Redfield...on Main Street, but it was...different. I didn't know at the time that it was 1965, I found that out in the second dream. I just knew that it wasn't 1999."

"What made you think that?" Dr. Priam asked, making a few notes while awaiting Dan's response.

"It was everything," he said. "The buildings and the cars mostly. The cars were longer...more rectangular than cars from 1999. The buildings that looked old in 1999 appeared to be almost brand new in my dream. Oh, and the traffic light...there was no traffic light in my dream."

Dr. Priam continued to jot down a couple things, and then looked back at Dan.

"Sounds like this dream was the least concerning. Is that right?" he asked. Dan nodded.

"Yeah, it was short and didn't give me any of the strange feelings the others did. What do you think is wrong with me, doctor?" Dr. Priam paused from taking notes and thought for a moment before responding.

"It's much too soon to make any definite conclusions, Dan. Right now, the only thing I can really see is a boy who has an active imagination...nothing unusual about that. That being said, I do understand that this is bothering you, and rest assured I will help figure out what's going on. Let's continue. What happened in the second dream?" Dan nodded again and took a deep breath before speaking.

"The second dream started exactly the same—I was suddenly standing on Main Street. Same place as the first time but this time there were quite a few more people than last time..."Dan paused for a moment. "Actually, I don't think there were any people in my first dream...at least none that I can remember. The people also didn't seem right. The men were all dressed in suits and the women were in dresses or skirts. It was like they were all dressed for church, or maybe a wedding."

Patricia reached out and grabbed Henry's hand. Hearing all of this again had made her emotional. A tear fell from her eye as Henry put his arm around here.

"It's okay, dear," said Henry, "this is a good thing."

Dr. Priam nodded. "Go on, Dan, this is good to get out."

"Towards the end of this dream, I approached a man and asked him what year it was. Of course, he was rather confused as to why I didn't know, but that's when I found out it was

1965. After that, I don't really remember anything...things sort of went dark and then I was back in my room. The third dream is where it got really bizarre. It was much longer than the first two...well, it seemed like it anyway."

"What do you mean by that? Like, it felt like a long time, but when you woke up it had only been a few minutes? Time passes differently in dreams, Dan."

"I know that, doctor, but this wasn't like that. Time hadn't passed at all. I came out of the dream at the exact same time I went to bed. It was the same with all four dreams."

This caught Patricia off guard. "Four dreams? You didn't tell me anything about a fourth dream, Dan." Dan figured this would come up, but hadn't given it much thought yet. He began again.

"Sorry, Mom. It only happened last night. I'll get to it. Because the third dream lasted longer, I was able to walk around a bit and explore. I couldn't believe how real it seemed. The people seemed to notice me more this time, too —much more. It was if they knew I didn't belong.

"Then there was Sixth Avenue...it was such an awful feeling. I looked to the west, and for just a second I thought I saw someone, or something, looking at me from behind the corner of the old bank building. After I rubbed my eyes and looked again there was nothing, of course. But in that moment, I experienced such a cold chill...I'll never forget that feeling. I felt it in my bones..."

From behind Dr. Priam, Dan saw a couple of books on the doctor's shelf start to wobble. The wobbling intensified and then Dan noticed the books began to take on a blurry, pixelated appearance—almost like they weren't really there. Dan would later come to realize this was a glaring red flag. "Oh no... not again. Not now...please, please make it stop!" Dan covered his eyes, curled up into a ball, and cried. Patricia tried to comfort him, but he pushed her away. Dr. Priam was quite taken aback by what was going on, even after his phone call earlier. He hadn't known what to expect—but this wasn't it.

Dr. Priam knew he still had to fulfill his end of the deal, even as regrettable as it was. As Dan began to calm down, Dr. Priam leaned forward and put a hand on Dan's shoulder.

"Dan, it's okay...these things can be difficult, especially at your age. Do you think you can continue?" he asked. Dan didn't know it, of course, but the more he spoke about his dreams, the tighter he was sealing his fate. Dan sat up slowly, nodded at Dr. Priam while wiping his face with a Kleenex wipe his mom had given him. Dan sniffled, due to the crying, and took a moment to collect himself.

"Almost immediately after seeing...well, after whatever I thought I saw by the bank, I was pulled out of 1965 and back to my bedroom. Do you want to hear about the fourth dream?" Dr. Priam looked up at Dan and for just a fleeting moment, Dan thought he saw something behind the doctor—again. It was a flash of dark red smoke that appeared to be right behind the doctor's shoulder. A moment later, it was gone.

"Hello? Dan? Are you alright?" Dr. Priam asked.

"Uh, yeah, sorry," Dan replied, "I thought I saw that thing again from my dreams." Dan felt he maybe shouldn't have relayed that last bit of information, but it was too late now.

4

"That's very interesting, Dan," Dr. Priam said. He jotted the following in his notebook:

Client appears to suffer from paranoia, hallucinations, difficulty sleeping, and chronic headaches. Initially these seemed to be isolated to dream states but appear to also occur in the conscious state.

These symptoms all point to early-onset schizophrenia. Recommend admission to Clearwater Psychiatric Institute for early treatment.

"If I may, I'd like to have a word with your parents in private." Dan seemed to be surprised by this, but his parents seemed okay with it.

"It's okay, sweetie," his mom said. "I'm sure it's protocol." Dan looked as if he were on the verge of tears, but he remained on the couch as his parents and Dr. Priam stepped outside the office.

Once outside, Dan's parents stood with Dr. Priam, who had taken on a much more serious demeanor.

"So, I don't want to beat around the bush here, Mr. and Mrs. Williams," he began, "your son is ill. He doesn't know it, nor do I think he'd ever believe it, but it's the truth. Young Dan is showing all the symptoms of *early-onset schizophrenia.* Paranoia, hallucinations, difficulty sleeping, and headaches are all tell-tale signs of this awful disorder." As he finished saying this, he himself realized it was all bullshit. *But what choice do I have?* he asked himself. Patricia put her hand over her mouth as tears formed in her eyes. Henry seemed unaware of what the doctor said—he was emotionless.

"Wha—what can we do?" Patricia finally asked. Dr. Priam was silent for a moment, contemplating every other possibility, but there was no way to avoid it—he had his orders.

"There's an institute, it isn't cheap...but it's renowned for its success rate. It's called Clearwater Psychiatric Institute, located in Fargo, ND. I would personally write the order and guarantee that Danny would receive the best care available." Patricia winced at the word *institute,* and immediately broke down at the thought. She fell to her knees, filling the hall with the sound of her sobbing.

"Oh, honey, I'm sorry. I know this is hard, but it'll be okay," said Henry, kneeling down to try and comfort her.

Patricia pushed Henry away. "I don't want to send our son to a mental institute!" she cried. "He's only ten!" She tried to take a breath, but her sinuses had become congested from all the crying.

Dr. Priam had been in similar situations before, but this one was especially difficult—he was starting to regret agreeing to what he did.

"I'm so sorry, Mrs. Williams," said Dr. Priam. "Normally, I wouldn't jump to such drastic measures, but schizophrenia is best addressed immediately. The earlier we can get Dan help, the better his chances are of recovery. Dan will not be so easily persuaded, however, because he's not convinced there's anything wrong with him. I will need your help. Can you do that?"

Patricia had managed to somewhat pull herself together. She made it to her feet and looked to Henry for help. Henry saw that her eyes were bloodshot, and her mascara was smeared down the sides of her cheeks.

"I think we should take the doctor's advice, sweetie," said Henry, doing his best to not upset her. Patricia sniffled and took in a deep breath, then exhaled.

"Okay...okay, let's do it then," she said. "I just hope Dan doesn't take it too hard, but I know he will." Dr. Priam smiled (albeit forced) and led them back into his office.

CHAPTER VIII

1

PROFESSOR JAMES KERN WAS A BRILLIANT SOFTWARE ENGINEER
—the very best. He had graduated Summa Cum Laude from
Oakwood University at just nineteen years old. Not long after
graduating, he had been hired on by his college to teach their
programming courses. Dr. Robert Wilkes had recruited him
for a project that was classified above Top Secret. James was
given the absolute minimum details necessary for him to do
his work. He was told that they would be making history,
although not necessarily for the greater good.

Dr. Wilkes was, to put it mildly, a malicious doctor with no
regard for anyone's well-being but his own and he certainly
had no time for incompetence. The first time James had
"failed" was when a full implementation of the project had
been attempted. James had warned Dr. Wilkes multiple times
that the system wasn't ready and that his team needed more
time—Wilkes wouldn't hear it. He insisted on moving forward

and so James did. As James predicted, the system partially crashed and corrupted multiple drives.

"James, how is the testing going?" Dr. Wilkes asked, walking into the main laboratory of The Elysiam, the secret research facility he operated. Dr. Wilkes was a slender man, weighing 150 lbs soaking wet. He had short grey hair that was almost always slicked back. His eyes were an emerald green, the likes of which didn't quite look at you so much as they looked through you.

James looked up from his large, U shaped desk, which was cluttered with stacks of papers that appeared to have no sense of order. The majority of his desk was taken up by his six monitors, which were used to access the primary servers running the project.

"We're on track, sir," said James, standing up to meet Dr. Wilkes. "What are we doing about the little hiccup from last week?" Dr. Wilkes grinned, placing his hand on James's shoulder,

"Don't worry about that, my dear James," Wilkes said, "it is being taken care of. The situation is being rectified. Once that is complete, you'll have adequate time to complete your testing." James felt a sense of remorse pass over him, and not for the first time. The more that was revealed to him about the project, the more remorseful he felt. "Tell me, James, how long do you think you'll need to reach 100% readiness? And please, be honest...the more honest with me you are, the more I can help you." James hesitated, not wanting to upset the doctor but also not entirely sure of the answer. He knew that Dr. Wilkes was only playing the nice card to get what he wanted, which was results—at any cost.

"Uh...two, maybe three years? James finally replied. "I know that seems like a long time, sir, but what we're dealing with here...it isn't just as simple as checking emails or looking up a recipe online. There are literally millions of lines of code left to sift through." James braced for reprimand, but none came. Dr. Wilkes seemed to be holding back any anger or maybe there wasn't any——but James thought that seemed unlikely. Dr. Wilkes closed his eyes, took a deep breath, and exhaled.

"Okay, James...okay," he said. "Three years it is. I'd prefer much sooner, but you, as well as all of your colleagues, have made it quite clear that this is how it is. You came highly recommended, James, don't let me down. You won't like what happens if you do." He turned and walked out, slamming the door behind him.

2

Dan hadn't heard any of the discussion that had taken place outside of Dr. Priam's office. He was completely distracted with the books he swore had been wobbling earlier. *What's going on with me? Maybe I am crazy. No, I saw these books wobble, I know I did. And there was that fuzziness about them...what was that about?* Dr. Priam and Dan's parents came back in—he startled at the sound of the door. "Mom! Dad! Is everything okay?" he asked, running over to them. He stopped at the sight of their expressions—everything wasn't okay. Patricia and Henry had wanted to try and pretend everything was okay with Dan, but it just wasn't possible.

"Danny, sweetie, listen," his mom began. "Dr. Priam thinks there's something funny going on in your brain. He thinks this is why you're having all these weird dreams and visions, as well as the headaches." She wasn't happy with how that all came out, but it was done.

"Something wrong with my brain?" Dan asked. "What's wrong with it, doctor?" Dan was a little frightened and wished he hadn't said anything about the dreams, or visions. Dr. Priam could see tears forming in Dan's eyes and he felt some remorse building inside him, but he had to push through it.

"Now, Dan, there's nothing to be afraid of. It might sound scary at first, but I promise that I'll do everything I can for you." Dr. Priam proceeded to explain to Dan about *early-onset schizophrenia* and how it was typically treated. He explained that while there are a number of medications available, psychotherapy was far more effective in patients his age. Dr. Priam also assured Dan that while at the institute, his parents would be allowed to visit as often as they liked. After the doctor finished, Dan sat down on the couch (which no longer seemed comforting to him) with his parents and tried to take in everything Dr. Priam had said. To Dan's surprise, he wasn't as scared as he thought he'd be.

"So, am I crazy?" Dan finally asked. Startled, Dr. Priam was speechless at first, then replied.

"No, no Dan, you're not crazy. This is another common mistake people make when talking about schizophrenia. Your brain is just wired differently than others, so it needs some help getting things straightened out, that's all." Dr. Priam felt happy with the response and Dan seemed to take it okay as well. Dan looked at both of his parents, who were both trying to be as supportive as possible.

"What should I do?" Dan asked. "I'm scared, but I want to be better." Henry still seemed like he hadn't fully absorbed the information yet, so Patricia took over.

"Honey, we want you to be better too, but we also know you're scared. I think you should give the institute a chance. Dr. Priam says they do great things there, and remember,"

Patricia paused, placing a hand on Dan's shoulder to comfort him, or perhaps herself, "we can visit you whenever you'd like us to. Right doctor?"

Dr. Priam nodded. "That's right. Also, if it helps make your decision easier, Dan, this will be treated as a voluntary admission. You'll be free to go home at any time." Dr. Priam found it hard to keep his composure while saying what he had. Dan forced a smile, the first time this whole visit, mainly to try and make his parents feel better.

"Okay, let's do it. I want to get better," Dan said. Dr. Priam forced another smile as he got up and went to his desk. He pulled out some paperwork from one of his drawers and returned to his chair.

"I have some paperwork that will need to be completed prior to admission. Most of it is done by myself, so you won't need to worry about it, but I do need a few signatures from you, Mr. and Mrs. Williams," he said. Both Henry and Patricia skimmed over the paperwork and barely read any of the content—not good. At the bottom of page 5, there were two signature lines for *parents or legal guardian of patient*. They hesitated a moment, and then signed and dated the paperwork.

3

As the three of them left the office, Dr. Priam fell back into his chair with a sigh of frustration. *What have I done? I know it's not right. Damn that phone call.* He poured himself a tall glass of bourbon. It was only one this time but the events surrounding Daniel Williams would be the beginning of Dr. Priam's long, painful battle with alcohol. In the end, it would take his life.

The date was January 10, 2000.

CHAPTER IX

1

CLEARWATER PSYCHIATRIC INSTITUTE WAS ESTABLISHED IN 1902 and was one of the oldest psychiatric institutes in the area. It was positioned on the outskirts of Fargo, northeast of I-29. The institute was designed to house up to 500 patients throughout its nearly 100-acre site. It was built using the *Kirkbride Plan*, which had the administrative building front and center with eight housing units (four on either side) sprawling outwards from the admin building. The arrangement gave the structure a "bat wing" appearance.

It was January 14th when Dan and his parents pulled up to its entrance. The time was 8:00 AM.

As Dan stepped out of the car, the administrative building was what first got his attention. The admin building was a colossal, faded red brick structure—covered in a thick layer of moss due to the years of neglect it had withstood. At a height of five stories tall, it was rather daunting to small town Dan and his family.

A tower stood prominently at the building's center. Its immense height commanded the attention of onlookers, large- and small-town folk alike. While the institution itself was five stories, the tower loomed at almost double that. Windows lined both sides of the building. Near the top of the tower Dan noticed a large, circular clock that currently read 8:30 AM. As he stared at the clock, Dan thought he heard a faint ticking sound. The ticking seemed to only be in his mind, but it was terrifying, nonetheless. Gooseflesh formed over his entire body at the sound of it. *Wha—what's going on?* A moment later it stopped.

Dan noticed more buildings, which had an identical appearance, sprawled out from the admin building. *This place is scary,* he thought.

"I... I don't like it, Mom," Dan said, fighting a welt in his throat.

"Oh, it's okay, sweetie. It's just an old building, that's all. I'm sure it looks much nicer inside. Come on!" his mom said, taking a hold of his hand. Just as Dan felt his mom's hand touch his, his vision began to go blurry and darken. *Oh no...no, no. I'm not sleeping...wha—what's going on?* Dan felt himself fall backwards, helpless and unable to say anything. He landed with a *thud.*

When he got up, he was still in front of the admin building—but it was different. The building he saw a moment ago was showing signs of old age, but the one in front of him now looked ancient. A majority of the red bricks were faded to brown and some were crumbling. As he walked towards the door, he looked up and saw that the large clock had shattered, leaving nothing but an empty hole. He turned to look behind him and saw that there was nothing. In fact, the only tangible thing he could see was the building. The rest of Dan's surroundings were covered in what looked like dense fog. Once in front of the admin door, Dan saw a white sign hanging on the wooden entrance door that read:

BUILDING CONDEMNED
NO ENTRANCE ALLOWED
VIOLATORS WILL BE PROSECUTED

Dan wasn't certain he knew what prosecuted meant, but based on the tone of the sign, he assumed it wasn't good. A cold, deathly hand caressed his back, sending shivers all up and down his body. "Ah!" he screamed, "Go away!" Dan turned quickly but saw nothing. He felt his heart race inside his chest and sweat drop down the small of his back.

"Danny? Danny are you okay?" he began to hear his mom's voice—far off in the distance.

"Mom? Mom, where are you?" shouted Dan. He ran towards the door and tried to open it—locked. He felt the cold hand on his back again. His vision went blurry, and then dark.

His vision returned to normal and he was back in 2000—back with his parents as if nothing had happened.

"Wha—what's going on?" Danny asked, realizing he actually had fallen.

"Oh my god, Danny," Patricia gasped. "What happened? Your expression went blank and then you fainted. My gosh you're drenched, Dan. What happened to you? You've been out for almost ten minutes!" *Ten minutes? There's no way that was ten minutes...it only felt like a few seconds.* Dan had started to understand that time was funny while he was *over there.*

"I—I don't know what happened, Mom. I'm okay now, though. Let's get going," Dan replied, not entirely certain he really was okay. Patricia had a terrified look on her face as Dan grabbed her hand.

"Sweetie, are you sure you're okay? Gosh, I'm so worried about you. I sure hope they can help you here," she said. As they approached the admin building, they were met with a short set of six stairs which led to a plain looking, wooden door marked *Admin Entrance*.

Not very welcoming, thought Dan. Both Patricia and Henry shared this thought as well.

"At least it doesn't have a condemned sign on it," sighed Dan quietly under his breath.

Henry noticed a doorbell near the wooden door. A short time after ringing it, a buzzer blared its deafening chime which caused the three of them to jump. The door clicked open and Henry hesitated before opening it. A moment later they were inside Clearwater.

As they walked up towards the large front desk, Dan realized that his mom had been right. The inside, at least the lobby, was gorgeous. The centerpiece of the room was a large, rectangular desk. The top was covered with a large slab of black marble, with the front lined with strips of complementary dark brown wood—quite the first impression. The ceiling was stark white, adorned with recessed lighting that shone down on the desk, offering it a very modern feel.

In the center of the entrance area hung an enormous, circular chandelier. The chandelier looked like it was original to the building but modernized with brighter lights that glistened against the thousands of crystals that adorned the massive thirty-foot structure. It covered a majority of the ceiling.

"Whoa," Dan managed to say. "This is really nice." Dan's previous fear washed away at the beauty of the entrance.

They walked toward the front desk, admiring their surroundings, from the ornate ceiling to the stunning white marble floor.

At the front desk, a friendly face greeted them. "Hello, welcome to Clearwater! My name is Rebecca, how can I help you?" Patricia glanced at her name tag and noticed it read *Rebecca Peters, RN.*

"Hello, my son Dan is here to receive treatment. I believe there should be an order from Dr. Priam." Patricia replied.

"Oh yes," the nurse said. "I was just about to enter Dan's information into our system. Here are a couple of forms that we will need filled out. You may have a seat over there. Just bring them up when you're finished. Please let me know if you have any questions."

The nurse had pointed to the corner on Dan's left, which was lined with stereotypical waiting room chairs. In between the chairs were desks that each had a lamp and a few stacks of magazines.

"Thank you," Patricia said as she took the paperwork from the nurse. She found it strange that an RN would be working as a receptionist, but this was her first time at this type of facility, so she let it go. The three of them wandered over to the waiting area and Patricia began to read over the paperwork while Henry thumbed through a random magazine that caught his eye. Dan continued to admire the beautiful lobby. *Something about this waiting area feels wrong,* he thought. The waiting area of the room was remarkably different than the rest of it. The chairs and desks were new, but very poor quality. The lamps appeared to be nothing more than props, as they weren't plugged in to any power source. It was as if this specific area had been put here recently—just before their arrival.

Dr. Priam had advised Patricia to pay close attention to these forms, as places like Clearwater typically had a fair amount of fine print. Unfortunately for Dan, Rebecca had kept the first three pages of said fine print. Among these pages were such passages as *Clearwater will not be held responsible for any injuries to patients, whether caused by themselves or staff.* Another was, *We at Clearwater reserve the right to medically restrain patients at our discretion.* The final page that Rebecca had kept, which would be the most relevant to Dan, stated that *Clearwater reserves the right to provide experimental/untested treatments to patients at their discretion.* Dan didn't know it yet, but he was not going to enjoy his stay at Clearwater, nor would he remember a good majority of it.

2

"How many protocols do we have written, Joe?" James asked one of his colleagues.

"Um, one moment sir, let me check the latest count," Joe replied. James had nearly thirty of the smartest scientists and software engineers under his leadership and, together with Dr. Wilkes, they intended to make history. "It looks like our current count is fifteen, sir," he replied.

"Okay, thank you, Joe. I think we should run another test on a random protocol...see how well the code is holding up. Agreed?" Joe nodded in agreement and James initiated test protocol 10, chosen at random.

"What's this one do? Can we test it?" Joe asked as he pointed at James's computer screen.

James hesitated but then responded, "We don't discuss that, Joe. It's far above either of our pay grades...and honestly, from what I've seen, it's best to leave it at that." James wasn't sure his answer was good enough, but it was the truth. Joe thought about the response for a moment but then seemed satisfied.

"Duly noted," he said.

3

Dan watched from his room at Clearwater as his parents got in their car and drove off. They had stayed for several hours for a tour and to help Dan settle. It was an enormous facility, so seeing all of it in a single tour was not feasible. During the tour, Dan and his family got to see the more common parts of the facility. The tour had started in the cafeteria, which always had at least two cooks on duty. While in the cafeteria, Dan had noticed a few of the other patients, who appeared to be roughly his age, eating a late breakfast. *I wonder if they're here for the same reason,* he had thought. After the cafeteria, Dan was shown the dormitories, and they had made a stop at his room to drop off his bags. The rest of the tour had been a quick overview of the layout of the facility, as well as a quick look at the gym and game rooms that were available to Dan.

Dan felt a sense of melancholy as he watched his parents' car disappear out of sight along the driveway. After a few moments, Dan turned away from the window, which was fronted by steel bars, and looked around at his room. The room looked like a college dorm, of which Dan had no concept. It was almost identical in size to his room at home. It consisted of a twin bed tucked away in the corner with a small desk for writing situated at its foot. The barred window was immediately to the right of the bed with a closet built into the wall on the other side. The floor of his new room was white tile, reminiscent of a hospital—certainly not the elegant marble they were greeted with in the lobby. There was a single fluorescent light on the drywall ceiling that illuminated the room. For all intents and purposes, it was a dorm.

It was just after noon, Dan's parents had left an hour ago, and he already wanted to go home. He had been left in his room and was unsure whether or not he could leave to wander. Dan was about to open his door when he heard a knock. "Hello...Daniel? Can I come in?" the unfamiliar voice asked.

Dan was a bit shaken but managed a faint reply. "Ye—yes."

The door opened and a tall man in a white medical coat walked in with a clipboard. He was accompanied by a small kind-looking woman. Dan assumed the couple to be his new caretakers, his doctor and nurse, respectively.

"How are you doing today, Dan?" the doctor asked. The doctor was a short man, Dan had guessed he was in his 60s, and his hair had gone grey.

"I feel pretty good right now, doctor. My head is starting to hurt again but that's okay," he replied.

The doctor looked over at the nurse, who quickly jotted something down on a notepad, and then back to Dan. "Those darn headaches. From your chart here I see you've been dealing with them for a while now. I'll make sure to get you some pain medication that will help alleviate them. In the meantime, do you have any questions about the facility?" he asked.

Dan thought for a moment and then asked the first thing that came to his mind. "Can I wander around or do I have to stay in my room?"

The doctor gave a hearty chuckle at this and smiled. "Oh

heavens no, Dan... you're not a prisoner! You're free to wander as you please. Just keep in mind, this place is rather large so it's easy to get lost. Also, there are places that are strictly off-limits. The outermost ward, where we keep our most dangerous patients, is restricted to staff only. Aside from that, feel free to wander as you please."

Dan smiled, "Cool," he said. *Maybe this won't be such a bad time after all,* he thought. The doctor wrote something on his prescription pad, and then handed it to the nurse.

"Please have this filled and brought to Dan. I want his stay to be as comfortable as possible," the doctor said, showing what Dan thought to be a genuine smile.

"Right away, Doctor," the nurse replied, "I'll be right back." She turned and walked out of the room. The doctor turned to leave as well but just before he walked out the door, he turned back to face Dan. "Once she fills the prescription, just let someone on staff know when you need a dose for a headache. And remember, aside from the off-limits areas, you're free to roam, Dan. We'll start your therapy in a day or two. We like to give new patients time to adjust." He left the room.

As the door closed, Dan lay down on his bed. He figured he would wait for the nurse to return with his medicine before wandering—his headache was quite persistent. A few moments later, the nurse returned with his updated prescription. Shortly after taking it, he fell asleep. Dan slept through the night—no dreams.

CHAPTER X

1

JACK AND HELEN STEVENSON HAD WHAT YOU'D CALL THE perfect marriage. They had met in high school—Jack in his senior year and Helen in her junior year. Both graduated with honors from Redfield High School. After graduating, Jack went to the Stonewall Institute in Westwend, South Dakota, where he received a doctorate degree in both pharmacy and psychology in 1960. Just like the noted professor, James Kern, Jack graduated Summa Cum Laude. Westwend was a modest-sized town of about 65,000 people. It was only twenty miles southwest of Redfield, so Jack and Helen still got to see plenty of each other. Helen had planned on attending college, but during her senior year, she became pregnant.

Mary Stevenson was born on Thursday, April 7th, 1955. While Jack and Helen had not been planning to have Mary, it was unequivocally the happiest day of their lives. She weighed 6lbs 4oz and had a generous amount of red hair. The resemblance to her mother was uncanny. Jack and Helen had agreed that Helen would stay home with Mary. Not long after his graduation, Jack was hired on as the lead pharmacist at the hospital in Redfield. Things were going great for the small family.

About three months after getting the pharmacist position, Jack bought his family a house. He felt it was about time they leave the apartment life, as Mary was now five and growing like a weed. She was in perfect health and even a little above average in height. Both Jack and Helen had agreed that they needed a room and yard of their own for Mary to grow into.

The house was a beautiful single-story home with a two-stall attached garage. While Jack could have afforded much more, he was a fairly modest man and felt this was all they needed. The house was bright yellow with white trim. It was located on a corner lot with a big oak tree in the front yard. Jack thought it would be the perfect place for a tree swing. Life was good at 398 W. 3rd Ave, Redfield, South Dakota. Unfortunately, life for Mary Stevenson would not stay this way for long—it would get worse, in fact. Much worse.

2

Dan awoke the next day and found he felt much better. "Man, that new medicine is great!" he exclaimed. He got dressed and left his room to explore the facility. He walked past a map of the facility, which told him his room was in Ward A, the closest to the admin building. The wards were split into eight sections lettered A-D, with men and women also being separated. Ward A was the least dangerous, and Ward D held the most dangerous patients—these were the farthest from the admin building. Dan walked up to the front desk and as he did, he noticed Rebecca was working again.

"Good morning, Dan," she said. "How was your first night?" Dan had quickly become distracted by the marble floor—it really was quite an impressive floor.

"What? Oh...it was good. I slept great!" Dan finally replied. "I was wondering if you could tell me what there is for kids to do here? The doctor said my therapy wouldn't start for a few days." Rebecca smiled and Dan heard her type a few things on her computer and then looked back at him.

"Well, that depends on what you like to do. We have a pretty great video game room. Do you like video games?" she asked. It was as if she had read his mind.

"Yes! I love video games," Dan said, quite literally jumping up and down. Rebecca laughed heartily.

"Sounds like we have a winner then," she said. "Come on, I'll show you myself." Rebecca took Dan's hand and led him through a door that was to the right of the desk. The door led to a long, brightly lit hallway with five or six doors on either side. She stopped at the fourth one on the left, which was labeled "Game Room." She opened the door and waved her hand inside. Dan took a step inside and was met with several massive televisions, all of which were hooked up to a dozen different video game consoles. His eyes were the size of silver dollars and his mouth was nearly on the floor. Dan turned around and on the opposite wall were hundreds and hundreds of video games.

"Holy crap..." he said. "This is... incredible!" Rebecca stepped into the room, slowly shutting the door.

"Yeah, we like to keep this room stocked for our younger patients. If it was ever released, we probably have it," she said. "You're welcome to play them for as long as you like. I'll leave you to it. Let me know if there's anything else I can do." She left the room.

Dan walked around, his eyes and mouth both gaping at just how many games were in the room. "There has to be at least 500 games here... probably more," he said. They were sorted by console, and then alphabetical. Dan had gotten to the N64 section when he noticed a few of the game cases start to wobble on the shelf. "No... please, no," he said. The wall began to turn fuzzy, and Dan thought he knew what came next. He took a step back, but the wobbling intensified, and then his vision went black—he fell.

TICK TOCK

The floor dropped out from underneath him and he fell. He landed back in Redfield, 1965. Dan got up, rubbing his head, which hurt from the fall. I didn't think you could get hurt in dreams, *he thought.* Wait, am I dreaming? I don't recall falling asleep at all, or even feeling tired.

The idea quickly left as Dan noticed he wasn't on Main Street this time but rather some kind of neighborhood. It wasn't an area he recognized, but it seemed familiar at the same time. He walked south, shivering as he trudged through a fresh layer of snow and found the first intersection, the signs read 4th St W and 3rd Ave W. Oh, now I know...I think the pool is near here..at least, it is in the year 2000 anyway. That's why this looks familiar, *he thought.*

Dan wandered farther down 4th Street until he came to a bright yellow house on the corner. For some reason, this house stuck out to him, although he had no memory of seeing it before—even in the present. Dan thought it was odd, but he got a really good feeling from this house. It was a small, single-story house with an attached garage. The front yard had several pine trees and a giant oak tree, complete with a tire swing, all covered in snow. I don't understand what's so special about this house, *thought Dan.*

Dan stood there staring at the house and after a moment he saw someone—a girl. She was bundled up in black snow pants and a puffy, pink coat. Her shoulder-length hair was a vibrant red, covered mostly by one of those winter hats adorned with what looked like a snowball on top. She dashed out the front door at a sprint and jumped into the first snowbank she found—she giggled.

It was a few moments before Dan caught himself staring—the same moment she looked over at him. A wave of fear washed over him and he turned to run but slipped and fell on a patch of ice. As he fell, he clenched and braced for the familiar crack of landing face first on the ice, like so many winters of his youth. However, instead of the unforgiving pain, he felt—nothing. When he pried his eyes open, he realized that the road had fallen with him as he continued to fall down a dark and cold hole. Nothing but darkness welcomed him.

After falling for what felt like an eternity, Dan landed with a loud thud. "Ugh, there's the landing I was bracing for," groaned Dan. What on earth was that? He thought.

As he got up, he noticed he was in front of the same yellow house—except it wasn't the same, at least not exactly. Before the dark fall, this house had made Dan feel good, safe. Now, however, when he looked at the house it felt cold and—wrong. The tire swing had been cut down from the tree and the paint on the house was peeling off in multiple places. The yard looked as if it hadn't been tended to in years, and a broken strand of yellow caution tape was waving hauntingly in the wind.

Dan took a few steps towards the house to see if anything else had changed. He had nearly reached the front yard when his vision became blurry. Oh n—no... now what? thought Dan.

His vision became increasingly blurry and just when the world was going dark once more, he saw a black shadow wisp by out of the corner of his eye. Dan felt gooseflesh form over his body; whether it was from the cold or from immense fear, he didn't know. A tremendous force pulled him *backwards, knocking the wind out of him. Everything went black. The last thing he could make out was the number on the yellow house—398.*

3

Dan awoke with a brutal headache and found himself shivering while also being drenched in sweat. *Why am I shivering? Wasn't it just a dream?* He noticed he was back in his room. *How did I get here?* He thought. Dan also realized it looked darker outside than it should. *How long was I out?* He looked over at the clock on his bedside table, and saw it read 10:30 P.M. *No... no that's not possible! It was morning when I went to the game room, and I was only in the dream... or whatever it was, for a few minutes.*

Dan started to feel his pulse elevate, and somehow his headache, which was already unbearable, was getting worse. He sat up in his bed and realized just how badly he felt overall —not just his head. He tried to stand up but fell back down. *My legs...they feel so weak. What's going on?* He glanced over at the bedside table and as he did, something caught his eye. There were several empty containers, the ones used to hold medication, sitting on the table. Dan felt tears coming to his eyes. *I don't like this...I want to go home.* The door to his room opened and the same nurse from yesterday walked in.

"Well, hey there, sleepy head. How are you doing? You gave us quite a scare." Dan wasn't sure how to respond but did the best he could.

"Uh, I'm not sure, honestly. Wha—what happened to me?" The nurse gave him a concerned look—it seemed genuine enough.

"You fell, sweetie. Must have gotten too excited about the games and tripped on the carpet. We've seen it happen before.

Hit your head pretty good too." Dan rubbed the back of his head and noticed it was pretty sore. He pointed at the clock.

"Have I really been asleep since this morning?" he asked. The nurse looked at him with a perplexed expression.

"Dan, what day do you think it is?" He felt a giant lump form in his throat—he couldn't speak. *What day do I think it is? What's going on here?* He thought. Finally, Dan managed to respond.

"It—it's Saturday," said Dan, sounding more like a question than an answer. She smiled, but Dan thought it was more sinister than sincere.

"No, it's Wednesday, Dan. Wednesday the 19th." The room began to spin around Dan. The nurse seemed to fade away in the distance and his surroundings became wobbly and blurry.

Wha—what's going on? "Nurse!" Dan shouted. "Nurse, please make it stop!" He closed his eyes and started to cry. The room stopped spinning and when he opened his eyes—his vision was normal, and the nurse had left. *Was she ever here at all?* Dan wondered.

What's happening to me? Dan asked himself. He wanted to get up, but he was somehow still tired. He was, to put it lightly, emotionally, physically, and especially mentally exhausted. While he wanted nothing more than to be back in his room at his parents' house, the only thing he could do was sleep. So, sleep he did.

4

For the next few weeks, Dan drifted in and out of consciousness. He would dream for what seemed like only a few minutes, and then wake up to find that entire days had passed. The nurse continued to assure him everything was fine. She always made sure Dan took his medicine, a common occurrence that Dan could only vaguely remember, and then he would fall back asleep. He began to wonder why his parents hadn't been to visit, and the thought of this made him sad. *I hope they come visit soon. I miss them. How long has it been? I've been here for...wait, I can't remember. Two weeks? Has it been two weeks already?* Time was funny sometimes—wrong, even.

"Danny, wake up, Danny," Patricia said. Dan groaned a little and opened his eyes—it was his parents.

"Mom! Dad!" he cried as he jumped up and hugged them. "Oh, Mom, where have you guys been? I've missed you so much. Why haven't you visited sooner?" Patricia and Henry looked at one another with great concern, and then turned back towards Dan.

"I'm sorry, sweetie, the last couple of days have been crazy at work," she said.

"Yeah, and I had a last-minute haul to make down south. Sorry about that, bud. We figured you'd be okay for a few days...trying to adjust and all," Henry added. Dan's face immediately went white—all the blood drained from it.

"Wha—what? A few days??" Dan asked. "What are you guys talking about? It's been three weeks!" Patricia now had a worried expression on her face.

"Dan, what are you talking about?" she asked. "It's Wednesday...we dropped you off on Friday. It's only been four days, sweetie." Before Dan could respond, there was a knock on the door and then the nurse came in.

"Ah, hello, Mr. and Mrs. Williams...how are you doing today? So nice of you to visit Danny," she said.

"Dan seems to be confused, nurse. He thinks it's been

weeks since we dropped him off," Patricia said, holding on to Dan's hand, which felt cold and clammy.

"Oh my, yes..." the nurse said. "May I talk to you and your husband outside?" Dan tugged on his mom's hand and protested against her leaving.

"Please stay, Mom," he said. "I don't think this place is safe!" Patricia looked worried but also knew that Dan wasn't well.

"I'm sorry, sweetie," she said. "I know this must be scary, but you want to get better, right? We'll be just outside the door, and only for a moment. I promise." Dan let go of his mom's hand and watched the three of them walk out of the room. He felt a sense of helplessness wash over him. *Why didn't his parents believe him?*

5

The research being done at The Elysiam was classified above top secret, with even the source of funding for the research classified. The massive research facility was operated by Dr. Wilkes. The visible portion of the building was three stories tall, with dozens of barred windows lining the walls. All of the windows were tinted, reinforced, and bulletproof. Leading up to the entrance was a long, winding driveway lined with trees. The entire facility was surrounded by eighteen-foot-tall electrified barbed wire fence. It had been rumored that the underground portions of Elysiam were where the most profound and sometimes questionable research was performed.

Professor James Kern knocked on Dr. Wilkes's office, planning to update him on the latest test performed. "Come," Wilkes said. James stepped into the office and sat down in the nearest chair. Dr. Wilkes had a large, cherry oak desk that took up the back third of his office. Behind it, the wall was lined with his medical achievements as well as recognitions from countless research assignments. The front of his office contained a small, round desk that was surrounded by two chairs, one of which was where James now sat. "So, James, what's the word on testing?" Wilkes asked.

James handed Wilkes an updated progress report from the most recent test.

"Things are looking good, sir," James replied. "Our recent test was performed on protocol 10. We ran the test for approximately fourteen hours, and all the results look promising." Dr. Wilkes nodded with approval as he looked over the report.

"Excellent news, James, thank you. Please continue testing and let me know of your progress."

James stood up and was turning to leave but stopped.

"Um, sir," he began.

"Is there something else?" Dr. Wilkes asked.

"We—well, sir...I was wondering about...you know, the other..." he trailed off.

A miffed expression formed on the face of Dr. Wilkes. His eyes narrowed to a mere sliver as he got up and walked around his desk, stopping in front of James. He grabbed hold of James by his tie and yanked him forward.

"Listen here, James, you know better than to bring that up. We have our orders," Wilkes said. "The people who gave them have a higher pay grade and security clearance than either of us could ever dream of. Hell—I don't even know who *they* are. I've run this facility for twenty-five years, and not once have I thought to question my orders. I suggest you do the same. Are we clear?"

James, who was quite shaken at this point, nodded in

agreement—or maybe out of fear. It was most likely a combination of both. Dr. Wilkes released James and walked back to his desk. "Now, if you'll excuse me, James, I have a call to make and then I am needed over at the other facility."

James nodded again and left the room at once.

6

Once outside of Dan's room, the nurse turned to face Henry and Patricia. "I'm sorry if I scared you," she began, "but Dan's behavior has been rather disturbing. Multiple times he's awakened screaming. When I went into his room, he was confused as well as scared. His heart rate was elevated, and he was covered in sweat." Patricia put her hand over her mouth, and a slight tear formed in her eyes.

"Oh, Danny," she cried. "What's wrong with him, nurse?" The nurse took hold of Patricia's hand.

"He's very sick," she said. "I've called our head doctor and he said he'll be right over to speak with you. When we received the initial report from Dr. Priam, his status didn't look too severe. Not great, of course, but certainly not severe." The nurse was about to continue when Dan's doctor walked up to join them. "Ah, hello doctor," the nurse said. "I was just about to tell Henry and Patricia the status of young Danny. Would you like to take over?"

The doctor smiled and sat down next to the nurse.

"Yes, of course," he said. "I'm sure you're concerned about your son, so I'll get right to it. Dr. Priam's diagnosis of early-onset schizophrenia was spot on, but I believe the severity of his particular case was greatly underestimated. In the short time Dan has been here, I've noticed multiple outbursts from him. During a few of these, Dan has become almost violent in nature. Because of this we've had to keep him medically sedated for both his and my team's safety." Patricia began to cry. Henry put his arm around her, trying to comfort his wife.

"Is there nothing you can do for him?" asked Henry, almost pleading. The doctor put out his hand as if to say, *I didn't mean he's beyond help.*

"Please don't misunderstand, Mr. and Mrs. Williams, of course we will help Danny. We just need to reevaluate our plan now that we have a better idea of his mental state." Patricia managed to control her tears for a moment and looked up at the doctor.

"Please help him," she said. "I can still remember the first time I heard him wake up from...from one of those dreams. He sounded so confused and scared." The doctor nodded in an understanding manner.

"I have seen this kind of thing many times before, Mrs. Williams. It's scary, no doubt, but with the right treatment, it can be overcome. This brings me to my final point, which is Dan's stay here. Unfortunately, he will need a much more extended stay than initially planned. The treatment I'm recommending to him can take upwards of three years to complete, if it is to be successful."

Patricia let out a small cry upon hearing the news. Henry remained silent—he had yet to process what the doctor had said. *Three years? My little Danny would be fourteen—a teenager— by then,* Patricia thought. After a moment Patricia cleared her throat and spoke.

"I—I guess if that's what you think is best, doctor. Danny won't be happy about it. Are we still allowed to come visit him? Please tell me we can visit." The doctor was silent for a moment. He looked over at the nurse, who was having trouble making eye contact with him, and then back to Patricia and Henry.

"Yes, of course," he said. "We would never want to isolate a child from their parents." On any other day, Patricia would have heard the hesitation in his voice, but today she was too concerned about her son's well-being. The doctor sat up and motioned towards Dan's room. "Shall we go in and talk to Dan? You can say goodbye and then it will be time for Dan to take his medicine."

"Um, would it be possible for us to stay a little longer? Dan is so scared, and I think it would help for him to spend more time with us," said Patricia.

The doctor shook his head solemnly. "No, I'm afraid that won't be possible. The best thing for Dan right now is rest, and the medicine we have him on tends to make him drowsy."

Patricia and Henry followed the doctor into Dan's room, their heads hung low in disappointment.

7

It was Mary Stevenson that Dan had seen in his recent trip to 1965. She was so excited to play outside in the snow that she burst through the front door to jump into a giant snowbank. She was having a good time, but something drew her attention across the street. Wha—what's that? she thought. Across the street was a boy, at least it looked like a boy to Mary, about her age who was just standing there—staring. Mary wasn't sure he was real, though, because something wasn't quite right about him. "You could see through him" is what Mary would later tell her parents. If she had been older, transparent is the word she probably would have used. Mary tried to wave, but the boy appeared to look terrified of her, or of something. She saw him turn and try to run, but then he vanished.

"Mom!" cried Mary. "Mom, Dad! Come outside, quick!" Mary's

mom and dad came running outside, almost knocking the screen door off its hinges.

"What is it, sweetie?" asked her mom. Mary pointed to where the boy had been, but of course there was nothing to be seen.

"He was right over there, Mom," said Mary. "It was a boy. He looked... weird. I could see him, but also through him... kind of like looking through fog, or smoke." Her parents looked at one another with concerning expressions.

"Are you sure you saw something, Mary? You do have quite the imagination, little lady," said her dad. Mary stomped her foot on the ground.

"I'm sure I saw him! I tried to wave, but then he looked scared and tried to run...then he vanished." Her mom put an arm around Mary and hugged her.

"It's okay darling, we believe you. Let's go inside and relax for a bit." January 18th, 1965 was a very weird day for young Mary Stevenson— and it would get even weirder.

8

Not long after Dan's parents and the nurse had left his room, Dan had fallen back asleep. When the door opened again, he bolted upright in his bed and screamed. Patricia ran over to Dan and put her arms around him—he was drenched in sweat. "Oh, sweetie...was it another dream?" she asked. Dan nodded as he leaned against her.

"They just keep happening, Mom...even when I feel like I'm wide awake. I'm scared." Patricia kissed his head and felt tears forming again. She looked up at the doctor, who was watching them with a strange, almost inquisitive expression.

"Please...please help my son," she pleaded to him.

"I promise, Mrs. Williams, my team and I will do our

absolute best to help Dan." Patricia turned to Dan and spoke as calmly as she could.

"Listen, sweetie, we've talked with the nurse and doctor, and they feel that your symptoms are worse than Dr. Priam initially thought." Dan opened his mouth to speak, but his mom put her hand up and stopped him. "They can still help you, Danny, but because of these more severe symptoms, they need to approach your treatment differently. The doctor is recommending a more extensive plan. You'll have to stay a little longer, until you're well."

"How long is a little longer?" asked Dan, looking up at his mother with sudden concern.

Patricia sighed. She had known he would ask. "Well, um...it all depends on how you respond to the new treatment." The moment the words had left her mouth, she knew that Dan would hear the hesitation. He did.

"I don't believe you," cried Dan. "Tell me the truth!"

He's never going to forgive me, Patricia thought, *but he deserves the truth.*

"The doctor says the treatment plan could take up to three years." Dan immediately pulled away from Patricia and shook his head.

"Three years? No, no way, Mom. I thought I could leave whenever I wanted. What happened to that?" Dan began to cry. Patricia hated to see Dan upset. She turned to the doctor and gave him a *can't you say something* look. The doctor didn't have to be very observant to catch this look.

"Listen, Danny," the doctor began. "I understand that you're scared, I really do. I've been working here for twenty-five years and in that time, I've seen kids just like you in the exact same position. Because of that, I won't try to convince you that how you feel isn't warranted...it can be a scary experience. I want you to know that your well-being is my utmost priority. I told your parents three years because that's typically how long we like to have to do our treatment. However, there's a very good possibility that we can cut that time in half, or even more if things go well. It all depends on how you respond to treatment."

Dan shook his head and continued to cry. "I don't wanna," he said. "I want to go home and play my games. I want to be normal. I don't want to have these dreams." The doctor knelt down and put his hand on Dan's shoulder.

"I'll make a deal with you, Dan. Give me six months with the aggressive treatment plan. If after six months we are seeing significant improvements in your symptoms, I'll recommend that you be allowed to go home and receive the rest of your treatment there." The doctor paused. "How does that sound?" Dan was able to pull himself together for a moment as he thought about what the doctor said. Dan finally nodded in agreement.

"Okay, six months it is. Please make me better, doctor." Dan took in a deep breath and exhaled.

"I'm proud of you, bud," Henry said, who had been trying to stay out of the way the best he could.

"Yes, sweetie, what you're doing is very brave," Patricia added. Patricia hugged Dan and then got up from the bed to join Henry. The doctor also stood up, but continued to maintain his focus on Dan.

"Unfortunately, Dan, your parents will have to leave now. I know you won't like hearing this, but they won't be able to visit as often during these six months. We don't want to isolate you, of course, but it's very important that we try to limit outside interaction during this treatment." Dan wasn't happy about this but, to the surprise of both Patricia and Henry, he didn't try to protest. The doctor motioned for the nurse to lead them out of the room. Dan got up and ran to give them a hug goodbye. Dan began to cry again, which also caused Patricia to cry.

"It'll be okay, sweetie. We can still visit, just not as often. Please be brave." Dan hugged his mom tighter and after a few moments let go. The nurse led Patricia and Henry out of Dan's room. The doctor smiled at Dan and then left the room as well.

Dan let out a big sigh and sat down on his bed—alone again. It was just after 5 P.M. and Dan watched out his window as the sun began to set. *Six months...* he thought. *I sure hope the doctor can help me. Six months is a long time, but I want to get better. I really want to get better.* He saw his parents get into their car and back up out of the parking spot and then drive away. He waved but knew they wouldn't be able to see him through the dark, barred window. Dan heard a knock on his door and turned toward the sound.

"Dan, it's time for your medicine. May I come in?" the voice from outside the door said—it was the nurse. Dan wondered if he would be able to make it through six months of aggressive treatment. *I don't even know what that means, honestly,* he thought. *But what other choice do I have?*

"Yes, come in," he replied.

CHAPTER XI

1

THE FIRST MONTH AT CLEARWATER WAS A BLUR TO DAN. Most of what he could remember from it was being in and out of sleep—waking only to take more medication. The *aggressive treatment* seemed to be nothing more than sleeping, taking medication, and occasionally talking with the doctor. As the second month passed, Dan noticed the frequency of his medication had decreased. He was also able to remember more things day to day. It was the start of month three when Dan really started to show improvements. He hadn't had a dream or even a strange vision in three weeks. Dan didn't want to get his hopes up, however, as he had experienced temporary breaks from them in the past.

When April changed to May, four months after he had started the aggressive treatment plan and still no dreams or visions occurred, Dan started to believe that he might just be cured.

Dan was sitting in his room reading the second book in

J.K. Rowling's Harry Potter series. He wanted to reread all three of them prior to the fourth coming out in July. A knock came at the door. Then, the doctor entered with his clipboard and sat down on the bed beside Dan. "Good morning, Dan," he said, seeming more cheerful than usual today.

"Hi," Dan said, looking up momentarily from his book. Dan suddenly realized how strange it was that he'd never learned the doctor's name, or even bothered to ask what it was.

"How are you feeling today? I see you're reading Harry Potter. The fourth one comes out soon, doesn't it?" he asked. Dan smiled.

"Yup! In two months, I think. And I'm feeling great, doctor. I'm really looking forward to being able to go home soon. Our deal is still on, right?" The doctor laughed and gave Dan a thumbs up.

"Of course, Dan. I'm not one to go back on my word. A deal's a deal. You have about two more months of therapy left, and if you're doing as good as you are now, you'll be home just in time for the fourth Harry Potter book." The doctor stood up and walked towards the door. "I'm very happy with your progress, Dan. Keep it up and you'll be home in no time." He was about to leave when Dan spoke up.

"Um, doctor?" The doctor paused and turned to face Dan.

"Yes, Dan? Something wrong?" he asked. Dan sat down his book and felt himself become quite nervous.

"N—No... nothing is wrong. I was just...well, I don't know your name." The doctor, who had his hand on the doorknob, appeared to consider the question for a few moments. Dan was about to ask if he had heard him, but the doctor finally replied.

"Oh, sorry, Dan, got a lot going on upstairs, and sometimes the simple things like that slip my mind." The doctor pointed to his head. "My name is Bob, Dr. Bob Walsh. It's a pleasure to meet you, Dan." For reasons Dan couldn't explain, a chill fell over him—gooseflesh covered his body. Something about the doctor's response wasn't right. He shrugged it off, however, and figured it was just him being too cautious.

"Ni—nice to meet you too," Dan managed. The doctor smirked and opened the door, and then left the room. "Have a great day, Dan. I'll see you soon." Once the door closed, Dan picked up his book and continued to read it. Dan would spend a majority of his time reading over the next few weeks—it was calming. He found it helped keep his mind off of missing his parents.

2

James was debugging a large chunk of code when Dr. Wilkes dropped a monstrous folder onto his desk. James took off his headphones and looked at the folder. On the front was stamped:

TOP SECRET
PROJECT DESTINY: PHASE TWO

"It's time," Dr. Wilkes said, tapping on the folder. "You'll find your orders inside. If you have any questions, don't bother. You know the routine...same as before." James nodded and pulled the folder in front of him.

"I'll get to work on this right away, sir," he said. "When is go-live?"

"Phase two is split into three parts," said Dr. Wilkes. "Part one will need to be ready to go in about four months, ideally three. Part two and three are still undetermined. You'll receive further notice at a later date. Get it done ASAP and no mishaps this time!"

Dr. Wilkes turned around and walked out of James's office, making sure to slam the door on his way out.

3

Patricia and Henry were doing their best to adjust while Dan was receiving his treatment. It was tough at first, but after the first month or so it had gotten a bit easier. Henry had picked up a few extra-long hauls and Patricia was working overnight shifts—both just trying to stay busy. They had called Clearwater a few times to ask about Dan, but all they were told was that he was receiving his treatment. Patricia couldn't help but worry. *Did we make the right decision to leave him there?* she thought. *What if the treatment is making his condition worse?* She also had a feeling that the six-month deal the doctor had made with Dan was just a ruse to get him to stay for treatment. It was a very strong feeling indeed.

4

June came and went for Dan without a dream or vision— he couldn't believe it. It had been almost five months since his last dream. July 10th had finally arrived. It was exactly six months since Dr. Walsh had made a deal with him. If the doctor was true to his word, Dan would get to go home today —he was elated. Dan began to pack up his things he had acquired during his stay at Clearwater. He had, believe it or not, started to enjoy his stay at Clearwater. Most likely this was due to no longer having any dreams or visions, but either way, the six months had gone way better than he had imagined. After Dan got all his things packed up, he began to feel a little tired. He wasn't surprised, though, as he hadn't slept much the night before—too much excitement. He checked the time and saw it was only 10:00 A.M. He decided he would lie down for a little bit to rest his eyes.

5

It was a little after 2:00 P.M. when Dan was awakened by a knock on his door. "Come in," Dan managed to say. Dr. Walsh walked in, followed by the nurse.

"Good afternoon, Dan. Today is the day." Dan was happy, but after sitting up, he realized his head was throbbing. He felt like someone had his head in a vice—*but I didn't have any dreams,* he thought.

"Good afternoon, Dr. Walsh," Dan replied. "Are my parents here yet?"

The nurse took this question. "I just got off the phone with them, Dan. They're on their way." Dan couldn't remember a recent time that he'd been so excited.

Dr. Walsh told Dan he could grab his stuff and go wait in the lobby if he wanted. Dan went to pick up his bags and stopped—something wasn't quite right. *These aren't right,* he thought. *My bags are blue and black. These are green and black.* These thoughts quickly left Dan's mind as he remembered his parents would be arriving soon. Dan grabbed the two bags and they all left the room together. As Dan walked out of the room, he felt a strange, cold draft against his back. It caused him to shiver—he knew this feeling. *No, I'm not dreaming.* He thought. *This is real. I get to go home.* Dan grabbed the door handle and closed the door without a second thought. *There, it's done. No more draft.*

Dan walked down the hall and out of the door that led to the lobby. Dan stopped in the middle of the lobby and looked up—something was wrong. *Wasn't there a chandelier here?* He thought. *I know there was...I'm sure of it.*

"Hi, Dan," Rebecca said from the front desk. "Everything okay?" Dan was caught off guard by her overly joyous tone.

"What? Oh, hi, Rebecca," he said. "Wasn't there a chandelier here? I could have sworn there was." Rebecca frowned and looked up at the ceiling where Dan was pointing. She thought about it a moment.

"I've worked here for about six years now, and I sure don't remember ever seeing one." Dan looked around at the rest of the lobby and saw that the rest of it was the same. The stark white ceilings, the breathtaking marble floor, and the large front desk that was lined with dark brown wood and topped with a slab of black marble. *I know there was a chandelier here...I know it.* The thought left when he caught a glimpse of his parents.

"Mom! Dad!" he shouted and ran towards them. His mom wrapped her arms around him and gave him a big hug. Henry hugged both of them.

"Oh, sweetie. I'm so glad you're doing better," his mom said, squeezing him tighter and tighter.

"I'm excited to be going home, Mom. Can Jake come over and play?" he asked. She laughed and released her grip on him.

"Of course, sweetie, but I'd like us to have at least a little family time first. Deal?" Dan nodded.

"Deal!" Henry grabbed Dan's bags and the three of them walked outside to the car. "When did you guys get a new car?"

Dan asked, noticing right away that their old, rundown Camry had been replaced by a much newer one. Henry looked over at Patricia and gave her a confused look. She shrugged and then replied to Dan.

"What do you mean, sweetie? This is the same car we've had for almost a year." At first, Dan wasn't able to reply—his mind was a blur. He simply stood there with a blank expression on his face. After a few moments, Dan snapped out of it.

"Sorry, guess I'm still a little out of it from my nap earlier," he finally replied. "Let's go home!" Henry and Patricia both smiled as the three of them got into the car and left Clearwater. *What's going on?* Dan thought. *It's like I'm in another dream...but I'm not. I'm awake. Then why are certain things noticeably different?* This question was one that Dan couldn't answer, and there would be many more questions to come—many with answers that wouldn't be pleasant.

6

About four hours later, they pulled into their driveway on East 1st Street. Dan had never been happier to see his house. Even more so, nothing seemed out of place, at least from the outside. "Welcome back home, sweetie," his mom said as they got out of the car and walked up to the front door. Dan was beyond excited to get inside and be in his room—he missed his room. The moment the front door was opened, Dan stormed inside and jumped onto his bed. *Good ole bed* he thought. *I've missed this bed...the bed at Clearwater was too hard.* He looked around his little room and couldn't see anything out of place. It all seemed to be as he left it, right down to his Tony Hawk game, which was still in his N64.

"Hey, Mom, can I play my N64?" he asked.

"Of course, sweetie, dinner will be about thirty minutes. We ordered some pizza." *Mmm, pizza,* he thought. Dan turned on his Nintendo and began to panic—his progress was gone. He looked through all the save points on the memory card but found nothing.

"No way!" he cried, pounding the controller down against his legs. His mom had heard this and stepped into Dan's room.

"Everything alright, Dan?" she asked. He looked up at her, a sense of frustration clearly visible on his face.

"No, Mom...my game didn't save! All of my progress is gone!" He was frustrated, but at the same time a bit confused. *I know I saved my game...I always do. Multiple backups, in fact...just in case.* Dan looked through the saves once more but found nothing.

"I'm sorry, Dan, I don't know much about those things. Nobody was in your room while you were gone, though, promise." Dan knew this was the truth. His mom would never touch his games; she didn't want to risk messing anything up. The cold draft he felt at Clearwater returned, and it caused goosebumps to cover his body. *Please, no. Let this just be a coincidence.* Dan was upset, but it didn't take long for him to get over the lost progress. It just meant more time to practice the previous levels—maybe there were some hidden secrets he missed the first time.

Dan had just finished the first level when he heard his mom call him for dinner. The three of them sat at the living room table and enjoyed pizza—stuffed crust meat lovers and cheese sticks. Dan enjoyed being with his parents again, but the pizza was "meh." It wasn't bad, just wasn't the same as he remembered. "Does the pizza taste weird to you guys?" Dan asked, putting the rest of his second slice on the plate and pushing it aside.

Henry, who had just shoveled a fourth slice into his mouth, shook his head and mumbled, "No, tastes great to me." Patricia laughed at Henry and also agreed with him that it tasted really good. Dan shrugged his shoulders and tried the cheese sticks, but they too weren't the same as he remembered. He decided not to mention this to his parents and just pretend to enjoy the rest of his dinner.

After dinner, Dan returned to his room to continue replaying the levels that were lost.

7

In the living room, Henry sat in his *La-Z-Boy* chair while Patricia relaxed on the couch. Their living room had recently been remodeled. It had freshly painted walls, all of them white except one accent wall which was a burnt orange. Dan hadn't understood this concept, but believed his parents knew what they were doing. The floor, previously covered in carpet that was easily twice as old as Dan, was now covered with beautiful dark, espresso tiles that brought new life into the room.

"Did Dan seem...I don't know, different to you at dinner?" asked Patricia. Henry had begun to doze off, more than likely due to all the pizza he just ate but appeared to have heard her question.

"I guess I didn't really notice anything, dear," he grumbled. "I guess there was the thing about him saying the pizza tasted weird, but that's nothing to be concerned about." Patricia sighed.

"Yeah, I suppose you're right. I guess I'm still on edge is all. I want him to be better, Henry, more than anything."

Henry, who was more awake now, looked over at his wife with loving eyes.

"He's doing better, babe. The doctor wouldn't have sent him home otherwise; you'll see." She smiled at him and then turned on the TV.

They didn't realize yet that Dan wasn't doing better.

CHAPTER XII

1

"JUST ONE MORE THING," JAMES SAID, TYPING THE FINAL FEW lines of code of his assignment. "There, that should be it, sir. I just need to do a final build and it'll be ready to launch." Dr. Wilkes stood up from the chair he had sat down in almost thirty minutes ago.

"Good, it's about time, James...what took so long?" Dr. Wilkes asked. James, who had just written nearly 700,000 lines of code in three months, sighed.

"Sir, like I've said before, this isn't like checking your email or reading news articles. What we're trying to do has never been done before, ever. My team and I are doing our best to accomplish this monumental task, sir, I promise." Dr. Wilkes had a rather bored look on his face as he stood by James's desk.

"I don't need to hear about the details, James. Just finish up whatever you need to do and do it now. This phase needs to go live in ten minutes...can you handle that?" James mumbled something under his breath—*asshole* was the something—but replied in a more professional manner.

"Yes, sir, we'll be ready." Dr. Wilkes was about to leave but decided to stay until the task was done. He sat back down in the chair and waited. James made an obscene gesture towards Dr. Wilkes before returning to his code—the doctor didn't see it. *700,000 lines of code...in three months, and this is what I get?* James thought as he ran a build command on the final piece of phase two. *This better work. If it doesn't, and something goes wrong again, I'll be fired...or worse.* A bead of sweat began to form on his forehead as he waited for the final build to complete.

It took about ten minutes for the compiler to return a successful build. James sat back in his chair, exhausted and relieved that the build finished. He knew that didn't mean there weren't bugs, but unfortunately Dr. Wilkes wanted this done now, so this would have to do. "It's ready, sir," James said. Dr. Wilkes stood up once more and grumbled about being tired of waiting or something along those lines.

"Okay, great," he said, "push it out." James had never wanted to object to something as much as he did now but knew that it was useless. Dr. Wilkes had his orders, just like James himself did.

"Yes, sir." James ran the command to execute phase two. Dr. Wilkes smiled (this was not a common event) and slapped his hand down onto James's shoulder.

"Good work, James. Go on, take a little break, you've worked hard the past few months," he said as he walked past James and left the room. James struggled to remain calm as he watched Dr. Wilkes walk away. *Just...relax, James, it's okay. You executed the code on time, and everything is fine.* He took a few deep breaths and then got up and left his office to take a break. James was, without question, one of the most talented developers ever to sit in front of a keyboard. However, he could only watch over his development team so much, especially on a project the size of Destiny. Something was going to go wrong again—very wrong.

2

Several hours passed while Dan played his Nintendo, and it was close to midnight when he decided to call it a night. He walked to the bathroom to brush his teeth. Dan was aware that he didn't do this nearly often enough, but he tried to get it done as often as he could. As he stood in front of the mirror brushing his teeth, the mirror began to go fuzzy and his face went out of focus. "No! No, no, no," cried Dan. He dropped his toothbrush in the sink and closed his eyes, almost falling backwards. He opened them but found that he was still seeing a blurry reflection of himself. The mirror had begun to look almost like it was made of some kind of liquid metal.

Dan reached out with his hand and pressed his finger up to the mirror. To his surprise, or maybe not such a surprise, the mirror gave way to his finger and it was partially immersed inside the mirror. *Whoa...* thought Dan. He pulled his hand back and his finger felt cold. *I think I'm actually going crazy.* Dan looked down at his hand with a confused expression. He reached out again, this time pushing more of his hand inside the mirror, up to his wrist now. Dan closed his eyes again, tighter this time, and then opened them. His hand was still inside the mirror, up to the wrist. Dan felt a slight tug on his hand and horror struck at his heart. "What the hell?" said Dan. Before he could say anything more, he was violently pulled into the mirror.

His vision went black, and a few seconds later he landed flat on his back with a vicious thud. "Ugh, that hurt..." *groaned Dan.* "Where am I?" *he asked. It didn't take long at all for Dan to realize where he was— it was Clearwater, but it was different. He had landed in the lobby, and while it may have been pretty, the marble floor made for a rough landing. The floor appeared to have a generous layer of dust on it as if it hadn't seen foot traffic in years.*

Dan slowly got to his feet and walked over to the impressive front desk. This, too, appeared to have a large amount of dust on it, and also wasn't so impressive anymore. Most of the dark wood was splintered and the large slab of black marble was cracked. What happened here? *wondered Dan.* Something isn't right. This isn't the year 2000— it can't be.

Dan walked around to the other side of the desk. The computer screen that Rebecca had spent many hours in front of was also shattered, and the keyboard was covered in dust. To the right of the keyboard, Dan found one of those calendars with a funny joke or quote for each day of the year. The most recent one was September 19th, 2000. September? *That's only two months after I left.* What on earth could have happened? *Dan didn't know much about dust, but he felt this was quite a lot for only three months.* Yeah, this definitely can't be the year 2000...no way.

The thought left his mind almost immediately. A dark shadow appeared in the corner of his eye and then it was gone. Dan ran out from behind the desk and into the middle of the lobby. He felt a tap on his right shoulder and froze. No, this isn't happening. Don't look...it's all a dream.

Another tap, harder this time, and then—wham—Dan was shoved down with tremendous force. As he fell towards the floor, it transformed into what looked like liquid metal—it was a giant mirror. He felt the frigid cold liquid envelop him, and then he landed hard, again, back in his bathroom.

Dan got to his feet and right away noticed his head was in a vice again. *First the past, and now the future? I'm not even asleep...was that real? No, couldn't have been.* He argued with himself. *I'm just tired, that's it. Too many video games tonight.* Dan picked up his toothbrush and washed it off, then put it away and went to bed. He slept through the night without any more dreams. Although, Dan was starting to wonder if these *happenings* were really dreams at all.

3

The next morning at breakfast, Dan was contemplating whether to tell his parents about this *happening* or not. He decided not to—*it was a one-time thing,* he reassured himself. "Everything alright, sweetie?" asked his mom. "You're very quiet this morning." Dan looked up from his plate of eggs and toast, startled from his thoughts.

"Yeah, I'm okay, Mom, just waking up still." Dan smiled at her and this eased her mind. As Dan went for the first actual bite of his breakfast, he noticed that it, too, tasted funny. *First pizza, and now eggs...what's going on?* "Hey, Mom, is something wrong with these eggs? They taste weird." She glanced over at Henry, who shrugged, and then she looked back at Dan.

"They taste fine to me, Dan. Are you sure you're feeling okay?" Dan was about to play the *yeah, I'm fine* card when a horrid sight came into his vision. The entire living room, including his mom and dad began to appear blurry—not much, but enough to appear just slightly out of focus. Dan closed his eyes and rubbed them, hoping when he opened them again, things would be okay. He opened his eyes, and to his relief he saw that the blurriness had receded. Both of his parents were looking at him with great concern, but at least they were normal.

"I'm okay," said Dan. "If it's okay with you guys, I'm

going to go for a walk. I think some fresh air will help wake me up." Both agreed that that was fine but told him not to be gone too long. Dan cleared his plate into the trash and put it in the sink. "I'll be back in a little bit," said Dan, throwing on some clothes and heading out the front door.

Dan stepped outside and ran down the front steps as he had many, many times before, but this time it was different. He tripped on the bottom step and fell. Dan got to his feet, noticing that he had scraped his elbow on the sidewalk, and looked back at the steps. *That's weird...I don't ever remember there being five steps there...it was always four.* He shrugged it off, like he had with the bags and the car, and started out on his walk. It was a gorgeous Saturday morning in July, not too hot or too cold—it was perfect. Dan walked west towards Main Street. He reached the intersection of 5th Ave E and Main St and noticed something else was wrong—very wrong.

To his right, he looked and saw that the old Mason building was where the library should be. *Okay, this is getting a little scary. I don't really know what the Mason building is, but I know it isn't supposed to be here.* Dan turned to his left and walked on to Main Street, and on the corner was the library. Dan stood in front of the library for a full two minutes, mouth open slightly as he tried to understand what was going on. *This isn't right,* he repeated to himself. He thought about running back home and telling his parents, but then decided against it. *It would be just like the pizza and eggs thing...they thought everything was normal. Maybe I am the one who's crazy.* Dan continued walking south down Main Street and everything else he saw seemed to be in the correct place. He reached the corner of 6th Avenue and saw that Leo's was still there. "Well, at least that's how I remember it," said Dan aloud. *Maybe I'll try some of their food, see if it tastes okay.*

Dan stepped inside and was greeted at the counter, and then told to sit wherever he liked.

Leo's had been in Redfield for many years. Dan had only ever eaten breakfast there, but he knew most of their food was good. Prior to 1984, the building Leo's was in had been a bank, and Leo's had been diagonally across the road from it. Dan sat down in a booth on the far wall and waited for a menu. A moment later a waitress brought Dan a menu and a glass of water. "Anything else to drink besides water?" asked the waitress. She was an older lady, in her late sixties Dan guessed. She had curly white hair and wore thick rimmed glasses.

"No, water is fine. Thank you," said Dan. She walked away to give Dan time with the menu. As he looked over the menu, he noticed a few of the words begin to wobble—not good. He quickly shut the menu and set it aside. *Nope...not happening today. I want a normal morning with good tasting food.* The waitress returned and asked him if he was ready to order. Dan was about to reply, but when he looked up at her, she appeared to be at least thirty years younger. Her hair was now a dark brown, and no sign of the glasses.

"You okay, dear?" asked the waitress, waiting to take his order. Dan, who couldn't believe his eyes, simply stared and said nothing. She snapped her fingers and that brought Dan out of his trance.

"Oh...sor—sorry, I don't know what happened there," said Dan, "I'll just have two scrambled eggs, hash browns, and some toast, please." She wrote down the order and smiled as she walked away. Before she had turned away, Dan noticed her face had gone back to looking 60 again—weird.

Dan got his food about fifteen minutes later, and to his disappointment, it also tasted weird. The taste wasn't necessarily bad, but it tasted—fake. Dan pretended to enjoy his meal and twenty minutes later he was back outside on Main Street. He froze with a horrified look on his face. Across the street, diagonally, was Leo's. "But...that's not possible," said Dan. He turned around and looked at the building he just came out of. Across the front of the building it read *Redfield Bank*.

Dan stumbled backwards and almost fell into the street. *It can't be...* thought Dan. *I'm wide awake, not dreaming, but I think I just walked into 1965.* A moment after this thought crossed his mind, he saw a car drive by that was most certainly not from the year 2000. It was a long, boat-like car that had chrome fenders, hubcaps, and mirrors. The body of the car was a sea green color and it was a convertible. The man driving it had on a black suit with a black hat to match. He raised his hat off his head as he looked at Dan.

His vision started to become blurry and he looked farther down Main Street and saw things were changing in front of his eyes. He tried to start walking back home, but it was no use. He stumbled off the curb and barely managed to stay upright. His vision went black and he felt himself fall backwards and hit his head.

4

"James, what's the status on part two?" asked Dr. Wilkes, storming into James's office and showing little respect for anyone else—his norm. James, who was going on little to no sleep since who knows when, yawned before he was able to respond.

"We're a little behind, sir. The specifications of part two are rather daunting, even for me." Wilkes sat down in one of the chairs beside James's desk and put his head in his hands.

"Listen, James, I have a call to my boss in twenty minutes. He's going to ask me about part two, and I know he's going to want it to happen in the next few days. Can this be done or not?"

"I... uh, I'm not sure, sir," said James, "it's not straight-forward."

"Well, what's the problem? You're the best in your field; you should be able to come up with a solution."

James let out a deep sigh and contemplated how he wanted to handle this situation. "Sir, permission to speak freely?" Dr. Wilkes motioned with his hand. "Granted," said Wilkes. James swallowed and began.

"Sir, the specifications of part two involve theoretical physics that are, A: far beyond my understanding, so I'm having to work closely with one of our physicists, which is fine, but it takes longer. And B: technically impossible, so that's a rather large obstacle as well. This has literally never been done before, and personally...I think it's quite questionable morally."

"Thank you for that, James, I will make a note of your morals. Now, as for the first part...that's why we have such a large team of physicists here. Use them. And impossible as it may seem, the boss wants what he wants...and that's what he'll get, period. Is there anything else?" James took a moment, trying to decide if Wilkes really cared about anything he had just said—he decided not.

"Nothing more, sir," said James. Dr. Wilkes stood up and walked towards the door.

"I want part two ready in three days, James. No less. I

have to make a call." Wilkes opened and closed the door, making no attempt to do so with any measure of subtlety.

Dr. Wilkes was preparing to have a conference call with his boss about the status of Project Destiny, particularly the first part of phase two which had recently been completed. Dr. Wilkes was a stern man, but he was terrified of his boss. He knew little about the man, only that he didn't like things not going his way. His job title, location, and even his name was all classified way above top secret. He had contacted Dr. Wilkes many years ago regarding Project Destiny, and sometimes he wished he hadn't accepted—today was one of those times. They were behind schedule, and Wilkes knew that his boss was going to be furious.

His boss picked up after two rings and Wilkes could already tell he wasn't in a great mood. "Status of phase two, part two?" his boss asked, not wasting any time.

Wilkes hesitated, and then replied. "Uh, well, sir...I spoke with my lead developer and he said they're a little behind schedule. I—"

Wilkes was interrupted by his boss slamming the phone down on his desk. "No, Wilkes...I don't think I heard you correctly. You're behind schedule?" Dr. Wilkes was trembling at this point. He knew all too well what was on the line if things didn't get done on time.

"No, sir...that's what my lead dev said, but I told him that's not an option, and that he was to have part two ready in three days." There was silence on the line for a few seconds, which seemed like hours.

"Very well, Wilkes. If it isn't live in three days, you'll never see the light of another day." Wilkes heard the phone slam down onto a receiver and then silence. He sighed and hung up his phone. *James better get his shit together,* thought Wilkes.

PART TWO

THE FACILITY

CHAPTER I

1

DAN AWOKE TO ANOTHER HEADACHE—ONE OF THE WORST YET.
The pain was almost unbearable, but it was quickly overtaken
by the shock of what he saw. He was back in his room at
Clearwater, and it looked exactly as it had before. The empty
pill boxes on the end table, the Harry Potter book he had been
reading, and the bags he had brought here full of clothes—the
right colors too. *No...it can't be. That couldn't have all been a dream.*
There was a knock on the door, and after a moment Dr. Walsh
walked in. "Good evening, Dan. Are you feeling okay? You
don't look so good." Dan could say nothing, he just sat there
with a blank look on his face.

"Wha—what day is it, doctor?" asked Dan, his voice
breaking.

"Why, it's July 10th, of course." said Dr. Walsh. "Are you
okay, Dan?" *July 10th? No, that can't be...my parents came to get me,
and I had been home at least two days.*

"No, that can't be right, doctor. My parents were here...they came and took me home!" cried Dan. Dr. Walsh walked towards Dan and sat down on the bed.

"I'm sorry, Danny, but that isn't quite the truth. Your parents did visit you, but unfortunately, I couldn't send you home. Your progress has been promising, but I still feel like you need additional treatment. Your dreams have become much more elaborate, and I fear that they could become worse if you were to go home."

Dan looked up at the doctor with a shocked expression.

"I—I don't understand," said Dan, "it was so real...I—"

With that, he fainted.

2

The doctor tucked Danny in and walked out of the room and closed the door. He walked to his office and placed a call. After two rings a voice on the other end picked up.

"Hello?" said the voice.

"We're ready," said the doctor, and then hung up.

3

It was the afternoon of January 18th, 1965, and Mary Stevenson decided to stay inside for the rest of the day. It hadn't warmed up much since the morning and she wanted to get more work done on her novel, or maybe it would be a novella. Mary was home schooled by her parents and they had given her the day off due to recent events. Mary was an intelligent girl, although quite shy. She showed a particular interest in reading and writing. Her overall language skills were off the charts for her age. When asked what she wanted to be when she grew up, Mary had said a writer, without any hesitation. Her mom had told her that she should start smaller, and just write whatever she found enjoyable.

Mary was sitting at her desk, which sat next to the window, looking out at the back yard. Mary was deep in thought when a bright flash caught her eye. At first, she thought it was the sun glaring off the snow, but it was an overcast day—no sight of the sun. She got up from her desk and stood next to the window, and as she looked out towards the fence, she saw something in the corner of the yard. She squinted out the window, but all she could see was what looked like a pile of clothes. She raced out of her room and ran towards the back door. She threw on her coat and boots, and went outside, all before either of her parents could say a word. The back door opened to a large, oakwood deck that stretched almost the full width of their house. She ran to the far railing and looked at the odd pile of clothes in the corner of the yard—it moved.

Mary gasped, and without realizing it, jumped back from the rail. Mary walked down the steps of the deck and began trenching through the snow. There was plenty of fresh snow from the storm last night, which made crossing the yard a strenuous task. She had nearly reached the corner when she heard her dad from the deck. "Mary, sweetie, what are you doing out here? You'll catch a cold." She had been focusing so much on keeping her balance in the snow that her dad's voice had startled her, and she nearly fell.

"Sorry, Dad," replied Mary, "I saw something out here from my window and wanted to come look at it." A low grunting noise came from behind Mary and she lost her balance and fell into the snow. Her dad, who hadn't heard the noise, began to laugh from the deck.

The pile of clothes started to move again, and then began

to stand up—it was a boy. Mary's dad stopped laughing at once and ran off the deck towards Mary.

"Move away from the corner, Mary!" shouted her dad as he also trudged through the heavy snow. The boy opened his eyes as he got to his feet and saw the girl, Mary, and his eyes widened.

"I—I've seen you before..." said the boy, and then he fell over into the snow. Mary screamed as she jumped back from the boy but would later feel bad for yelling in his face.

"What in the world was that about, Mary?" asked her father. Mary shrugged, still not able to speak. Jack leaned down and picked the boy up off the snow-covered ground. "Come on, Mary, we better get this boy inside before he catches pneumonia." Mary followed her father back through the snow and into the house. Mary's mother got up from her chair as soon as she saw Jack come inside with the boy.

"What's going on Jack? Who's that?" Jack shook his head. "I don't know hun. When I went out to see what Mary was doing, he was in the corner of our yard. I heard him say he had seen Mary before, but then he passed out." Helen put a hand over her mouth and let out a small gasp.

"That poor boy," said Helen. "He must be freezing...and scared." Jack nodded.

"I'm going to take him to the guest bedroom to warm up and rest. Hopefully after a few hours he can tell us who he is, or who his parents are."

4

Two days had gone by since Dan had passed out at Clearwater. On the morning of the third day, Dan woke up once again to another headache—this one took the cake, though. Tears were already forming in his eyes due to the immense pain. The pain was so severe, it took him a few moments to notice his surroundings. He was in a bedroom, that much was obvious, but aside from that it was completely unfamiliar to Dan. The comforter on the bed had a pink and purple floral design, not exactly Dan's taste. The floor was covered with an olive-green carpet, and the walls were covered with dark wood paneling.

Against the wall near the foot of the bed was a dresser with a mirror attached to it. Next to the bed was a small end table that had an old looking lamp with a glass shade over it. Also, on the end table was an alarm clock, the old-fashioned kind that had the hour, minute, and second hands on it. *I don't like the look of this*, thought Dan. *Something tells me I'm not in 2000 anymore.* Dan got up from the bed and looked out the window, which faced a large oak tree, and a tire swing. "The tire swing..." whispered Dan. *Is this another dream?* he wondered. *It sure doesn't feel like the other ones. This one feels...solid, I guess. I'm not getting the same wobbly feeling as before. They've all been pretty real, but this one feels like I'm actually here. Is that possible?*

A knock came at the door and Dan turned to face the sound. "Um, young man?" a voice called, "may I come in?" Dan was terrified, not sure he could speak.

"Ye—yes, I guess so," he finally managed. A moment later Jack Stevenson stepped into the room. Mary had wanted to come in with him, but Jack had refused, at least until he had spoken to the boy. Jack, now thirty, was a slim, well-dressed man who was known all over Redfield as being very kind and understanding. Today was an exception, at least in regard to the well-dressed part, as he had run out in knee deep snow to carry Dan inside. Jack was wearing a pair of black sweatpants, a white thermal shirt, and a fuzzy pair of maroon slippers—he looked cozy.

"Hello there," said Jack, "my name is Jack, Jack Stevenson. What's your name?"

Dan had been nervous a moment ago, almost terrified, but as soon as he had heard Jack's voice, his nerves had all but vanished.

"Hi, Jack, my name is Daniel, Daniel Williams, but you can just call me Dan."

Jack took a few steps towards the bed and sat down next to Dan. "Nice to meet you, Dan. How are you feeling? You gave us quite a scare."

"I have a pretty bad headache, but otherwise I'm okay. I hope I didn't startle the girl too much...I didn't mean to."

Jack chuckled a little, which made Dan feel even better. "Oh gosh, no, Dan, she's fine. In fact, she was begging me to let her come in here too, but I wanted to have a little man to man talk first, I guess you'd say." There was a moment of awkward silence before Jack added to his last statement. "Sorry, please don't take that *man to man* thing too seriously. You aren't in any trouble with us or anything, I'd just like to find out what your story is firsthand before my daughter starts to interrogate you, and believe me, she'll ask you questions all day long." He laughed again—Dan did too. Dan liked Jack, he felt he could trust him. Initially, Dan wasn't sure at all what he would tell Jack. *Find out what your story is* had been what Jack had said. *What was his story?*

"It's okay, Jack, I didn't think you meant it in a bad way. You seem nice, and I'd like to tell you the truth about me, it's just...complicated.";

"Take your time," said Jack. "I'm a great listener."

Dan nodded, and sat quietly for a moment to gather his thoughts. *Where do I start?* Wondered Dan. *How can I know my story? I don't even know where I am right now—or when right now is.*

"Say, Jack...um, this is going to sound strange, but what year is it?" Jack seemed only slightly startled by question.

"It's 1965, Dan. Are you feeling okay?"

So I am in 1965...well I guess that's as good of a place to start as any—tell him I'm not from this time.

"Uh, yeah, I'm okay. So, I guess the most important thing to know is...I'm, uh...not from here," said Dan, "and no, I don't mean Redfield. I mean, I'm not from 1965. I came here from the year 2000...at least I think I did. Ugh, like I said, it's complicated. See, for the past year or so I've been having these dreams, or visions, or...something...I've started to call them happenings. These happenings started out innocent enough...I could easily tell they were dreams, even though they were still pretty real. But after a few of them, they started to get much more realistic. I began to have them even when I wasn't sleeping.

"My parents thought something more serious might be going on, and I ended up being admitted to an institute, Clearwater, for about six months. The treatment seemed to be helping, but then I recently had another dream about being released, which was the most realistic of them so far, and then I woke up in Clearwater again. Come to think of it, this might even be a dream right now, although if it is, it takes the cake for how real it is."

Dan took a break to consider what else to say. Jack, who had been listening intently to Dan's every word, had a bewildered expression on his face. Dan looked up and saw this, and thought it was all over. *He thinks I'm crazy,* Dan thought. *Can't blame him; I probably am crazy.*

Jack finally spoke. "Well, Dan, I must say that's quite a story indeed. You weren't joking about it being complicated. Phew!"

Dan was taken aback, to say the least, at the blasé response from Jack. He had thought for sure the story was going to have him sent straight to the loony bin—not that he could blame Jack if that was the case.

"I think you'll find my wife, Helen, and I are very reasonable people. Mary too, of course, she's my daughter. While I don't quite understand all of your story, more so from a psychological standpoint, everyone I meet has my trust and respect until they prove unworthy of it. You're welcome to stay with us...at least until you work things out."

Dan smiled. "Thank you, Mr. Stevenson. I really don't mean to cause you or your family any trouble. Like I said, these happenings seem to be getting more frequent, and more realistic. The last thing I remember was sitting in my room at the institute, and then I woke up here. I vaguely remember being outside in the snow."

"It's no trouble at all," said Jack. There was a soft knock at the door and both Helen and Mary joined them.

"Hello there, I'm Helen Stevenson, and you've sort of already met our daughter, Mary."

Dan smiled again, and waved at Mary, who was giggling and waved back—she was shy.

"Hi, Helen, hi Mary. I'm Daniel, Daniel Williams, but you can call me Dan. I can't thank you enough for being so welcoming...I really do appreciate it. Sorry if I scared you, Mary."

Mary was still shy, but she managed a response. "That's

okay, Dan, I know you didn't mean to. I just scare easily. How are you feeling? It must have been cold out there. Also, what's with your clothes? They don't look like anything I've seen before."

Jack put his arm around Mary and laughed. "See what I told you, Dan? She's the real interrogator of this house. Maybe you should let Dan adjust to the house a bit before all the questioning."

"That's okay, Mr. Stevenson, I don't mind. I'm feeling well, Mary, thank you. It was cold, yes...but luckily you guys found me when you did. And as for my clothes, well...I was just telling your father that I'm not from here...here as in 1965. It may take some time for me to convince you, but I'm from the year 2000."

The jaws of both Helen and Mary nearly hit the floor. While this wasn't the same reaction as Jack had given him, it still wasn't the one Dan had been expecting. Dan couldn't believe the warm welcome and understanding he had received at the Stevenson's. Dan told the same story to Helen and Mary that he had to Jack. He told them about the start of the dreams, the doctor visit, the therapist, and finally Clearwater. He added a few details this time around, including the wobbling text, blurry vision, and the cold, shadow-like figure he kept seeing. Dan also pulled a dollar bill from his pocket that was dated with the year 1999—this was easily the most substantial evidence he had available. "I... I think that's about it," said Dan, running his hand through his hair. "I know how crazy it sounds, believe me, but it's the truth. These happenings are getting worse...much worse. The blurry vision and wobbling text are usually clear indicators, but I still have no idea what's causing them, or when I'm in one or not in one."

"While I agree it does sound crazy, I believe you," said

Jack. "I'm by no means an expert, but when you work with as many people as I do on a daily basis, you start to get pretty good at recognizing when people are lying, and when they're telling the truth. To further strengthen your story, the dollar bill you have is obviously quite real—and your clothes, they're certainly not like anything I've ever seen."

"I believe you, too," said Mary. "I have a great imagination, but even for me that would be quite a story to make up."

"That makes three of us," said Helen. "You seem like a good kid...and I hope you can overcome whatever you're going through. If we can help you while you're here, we'll do what we can." She smiled and stood up. "How about some breakfast? After the events of yesterday, I imagine you're pretty hungry."

Dan was, in fact, starving. "That would be great. It's awfully kind of you; thank you."

The four of them all went out to the kitchen for breakfast. Jack, Mary, and Dan sat at the round, wooden table while Helen started to fry some eggs. Dan noticed the Stevenson's kitchen was as much from the 60s as the bedroom had been. All of the cupboards were a light stained wood. The cabinets were a baby blue, which was a color Dan thought should never be in a kitchen. The floor was covered with a yellow and green checkered tile—Dan didn't care for it, either.

However, Dan felt thankful that they had welcomed him with open arms, and he had a really good feeling about them. Helen cooked them a great breakfast consisting of eggs, hash browns, toast, and even pancakes. Dan ate until he felt like his stomach was going to burst. *Why does this food taste so good?* he thought. Dan remembered how awful the last few meals were that he had in Redfield, in the year 2000. *Is this a dream? It has to be...otherwise, how could I be in 1965?*

5

A month went by and Dan had never felt more at home. He missed his family, of course, but he knew there was little to nothing he could do. He hadn't had a dream, or *happening*, the entire month he'd been at the Stevenson's. Jack and Helen seemed to completely trust Dan and had even left him alone with Mary on several occasions. Mary and Dan spent a lot of time together, and this was more than okay with him. Dan really liked Mary. She was funny, smart, intelligent, and really quite pretty. Dan didn't know for sure, but he thought Mary also liked him. She was fascinated by the *happenings*. Dan had told her about all of them in great detail, more than once, and she continued to ask about them.

Dan had been staying with the Stevenson's for seven months when he and Mary had their first kiss. It was awkward, of course, but Dan was over the moon—Mary was too. August 20th was a hot and humid Friday. Mary and Dan decided to walk down to the pool as opposed to getting a ride.

"Hey, Mary, can I ask you something?" Dan heard the nervousness in his voice, and he figured Mary did too.

"Of course, Dan. Something wrong?"

"No, nothing like that. I... uh, well. I really like you, Mary. And, um...sorry, I've never really done this before." Dan paused for a moment, trying to compose himself. "Mary, would...would you like to be my girlfriend?"

Mary's eyes lit up like a firework. "Yes! Yes, yes...a thousand times yes. I was hoping you'd ask." She hugged him and gave him a big kiss. They both forgot they had still been standing in the middle of the street. Dan took hold of Mary's hand and they continued their walk to the pool. Life was good. Dan was beginning to think this might not be a dream after all. *But if I'm not dreaming, then how did I get here?* Dan thought. *What happened to my parents? Clearwater? The year 2000 in general? Is it gone?* He had so many questions and so few answers. They arrived at the pool, and the thought of cooling off from this 98-degree day brought Dan's mind back to 1965. *I'm going to enjoy this while I can. I sure hope it lasts.*

CHAPTER II

1

"WARNING: CORE TEMPERATURE UNSTABLE.
PLEASE ADVISE."

"WARNING: CORE TEMPERATURE APPROACHING
CRITICAL. SHUTDOWN IMMINENT."

ALARMS WERE SOUNDING FROM THE PRIMARY SERVER ROOM AT
The Elysiam. Phase Two, Part Two had been running nonstop
for months, and it was becoming too much for the computer's
core.

Dr. Wilkes stormed into James's office, who was frantically
running system scans to determine the cause of the alarms.
"James, what the hell is going on? Tell me we aren't going to
lose it."

James's expression changed to one of absolute horror as
he looked over the latest server log.

"Oh no... there's a runaway process," said James. "No,

no... it'll bring the entire system down. We need to failover to the backup server, now!" He stormed past Dr. Wilkes and out of the office. James ran down the hallway and cleared the three sets of stairs leading to the basement in only a few strides. Dr. Wilkes was trailing behind him, doing his best to keep up, but failing. He got to the large server rack that housed the primary system and logged in with the admin credentials. James looked over at Dr. Wilkes, who had finally made it down to the basement. "Permission to failover to the secondary servers, sir?"

Dr. Wilkes knew little to nothing about computers, and James knew this, but it was protocol for James to ask before making such decisions.

Dr. Wilkes hesitated. "Do we have alternatives? What happens if we don't...can the primary system sustain our current test?" James gave him an *are you kidding me* look before responding.

"We have no alternatives, sir. If the primary system crashes, we lose Destiny. The core temperature is already at —" James was cut off by another alarm.

"WARNING: CORE TEMPERATURE AT CRITICAL. SHUTDOWN COMMENCING IN THIRTY SECONDS. REPEAT. SHUTDOWN COMMENCING IN THIRTY SECONDS."

Dr. Wilkes looked especially panicked now. "Okay, okay. Permission granted. Do the failover."

James turned back to the server terminal and initiated the failover procedure. He ran across the room to the secondary server rack and prepared for the switch. He had done trial runs of this very scenario, but it hadn't been while under such extreme processor loads. If any portion of the processes weren't failed over properly, it would be devastating to the entire project. James finished typing the last command, and then ran back to the primary server.

"Executing failover in 3, 2, 1...and executing." James watched as the terminal read out the processes and their destinations on the secondary system. The terminal estimated ten seconds remaining until completion of the failover. "Ten seconds left, sir," said James. "Come on, come on!"

"WARNING: CORE TEMPERATURE AT CRITICAL. SHUTDOWN COMMENCING IN TWELVE SECONDS."

"That's cutting it awfully close, James," said Dr. Wilkes, pacing back and forth in the basement.

"Painfully aware of that sir. Five seconds. 4, 3, 2..."

"WARNING: CORE TEMPERATURE AT CRITICAL. SHUTDOWN COMMENCING IN FIVE SECONDS. FINAL WARNING."

2

Mary and Dan were walking back home from the pool, taking their time and enjoying one another's company. The pool had been a great way to spend the hot afternoon. They got to the corner of 3rd Ave and 4th St, and Dan looked up at the street sign—the letters started to wobble. Horror struck his face as he faltered and took a few steps back.

"Dan? Dan, what's wrong?" said Mary. *Oh no, not now. It's been going so well, please, not now.* Dan's head was spinning a million miles an hour and he didn't know what to say. The letters on the sign became even more wobbly, and as he looked over at Mary, he noticed her appearance was becoming blurry.

"Uh...remember those happenings I always talk about? Well, I...I think one might be happening right now." Just as Dan finished his sentence, Mary let out an ear-piercing scream.

"Dan! Look!" She pointed at Dan, who had started to become transparent—like he was fading away. He faded in and out for a few seconds, and then it stopped. His vision went back to normal, and the letters on the sign stopped wobbling.

"Ugh...I had hoped those were over," said Dan. "Sorry you had to see that. Are you okay?" Mary embraced him.

"Am I okay? Are you okay? What was that?" she asked. Dan didn't know; he only knew that it was like the previous ones, but also a little different. His head usually hurt after these happenings, but no such headache this time. The actual happening had felt like he was falling out of existence as opposed to going to another dream. As they continued their walk home, Mary and Dan agreed to keep this between them —no need to involve her parents.

3

While Dan and Mary had been at the pool, Jack and Helen were trying to figure out who Dan really was. They called the school, the hospital, and even the library, but it was all a dead end. Nobody had any record of Daniel Williams. Clearwater, the institute Dan had mentioned to them, didn't even seem to exist. There was good reason for this, of course, as it would be three years before Clearwater was built and another twenty years before Dan was born.

"I don't get it," said Helen. "The whole time he was telling us this crazy story, I thought it was all a joke. What if it's not?" Jack sat at the kitchen table with his right leg crossed over the left.

"I don't know, Helen, I really don't know. I like to think I know when someone is lying...and I sure didn't get any indication that Dan was lying. He was so confident about it, and very detailed...especially for his age." Helen nodded. She brought over two cups of coffee and joined Jack at the table.

Mary and Dan arrived home a few moments later and were greeted by Mary's parents. "Hey, guys," said Helen, "how was the pool?"

Mary and Dan exchanged glances, and then in unison replied: "Good!"

"It felt great, especially considering how hot it is," added Dan.

4

Mary and Dan left the kitchen and went to relax in Mary's room. The two of them spent most of their time together, which was more than okay with Dan. Mary was head over heels for him and hoped they would stay together forever. Mary's parents were happy that she found someone, even if their meeting was a bit odd.

Dan was a great fit for Mary. Both of them were nerdy, and both of them had similar interests. Although Dan hadn't been much of a reader, Mary had been quickly converting him into a constant one. A few times Dan let slip a few of his *future* interests such as Tony Hawk and a few television shows

—both of which wouldn't exist for about thirty years. Time was a funny thing: sometimes it was even wrong, but this felt right to Dan. It felt great.

5

The terminal on the primary system read:

PRIMARY TO SECONDARY FAILOVER COMPLETE
RESULTS: ALL PROCESSES TRANSFERRED
SUCCESSFULLY
SHUTTING DOWN. GOODBYE.

James let out a huge sigh of relief. "All good, sir. The processes all transferred over to the secondary system. I'm going to begin diagnostics on the primary server and figure out what we need to do to fix this issue."

Dr. Wilkes nodded with approval and started off towards the stairs.

"Good work, James. I must say, you do live up to what everyone says about you. I'll note this in your file. Let me know if there's anything you need from me." He left the basement. James was shocked at the response from Dr. Wilkes, but he was happy. *It's nice to be recognized for once*, he thought. Before James ran diagnostics on the primary system, he decided it would be wise to check if the secondary was handling the workload.

6

James had spent almost an hour running a system check on the secondary server rack, and he was satisfied with the results. The secondary servers were holding up well under the heavy load. James's next task was to run a diagnostic check on the primary servers to determine what exactly went wrong. He didn't know what phase three of Project Destiny was, but knew it would be larger than phase two, and the servers would need to be ready for it.

"How's it going down here, James?" asked Dr. Wilkes, who had been on another conference call with his boss regarding the latest incident.

"Hello, sir. I just finished the systems check on the secondary servers, and everything looks good there. I was about to start a diagnostic check on the primary servers to figure out what happened. Everything okay upstairs?" Dr. Wilkes nodded as he approached the server racks, inspecting them as if he knew what he was looking at.

"Will the primary be able to handle phase three, James? I don't want another scare like we had earlier." James paused in the middle of typing. *Will it be able to handle phase three? Is he insane?* James thought. *It wasn't even able to handle the sustained load of phase two without help from the secondary...*

"Um, well sir, that greatly depends on what exactly phase three involves. Am I allowed to know?"

As expected, Dr. Wilkes shook his head. "I'm sorry, James, but that's classified. You'll be given the necessary programming instructions, as always. What I can tell you is that it will be three to four times the complexity of phase two."

James's mouth fell open, and he was rendered speechless for a moment. He was about to speak, but Dr. Wilkes put up his hand. "Before you say anything, James, my boss has approved expenses for any additional hardware you need. If it exists, we can get it. Just let me know what you need, and I'll get the necessary funds." James let out a sigh of relief. For a test of that size, he was going to need to add significant processing power to the system, as well as additional cooling towers.

"Oh, good," said James. "Thank you, sir. That will be very helpful. I'll put together a list of hardware after I finish this diagnostic." Dr. Wilkes nodded in approval and left the basement.

Three to four times the complexity of phase two? What could phase three possibly be? James didn't have an answer, but he feared that whatever it was, he wouldn't like it.

7

It was hard to believe an entire year had gone by since Dan showed up at the Stevenson's house. He was still waiting for the moment when everything would go dark, and he would wake up from whatever kind of nightmarish *happening* this was. Dan was sitting at the kitchen table enjoying another lovely breakfast, which was another thing that bothered him. The food tasted so real—almost like it was real.

"Everything okay, Dan?" asked Mary, who was sitting beside him, eating as well. "You seem...preoccupied this morning." Dan was startled out of his own thoughts by Mary's voice.

"Oh, uh...yeah, sorry, Mary, just got a lot going on upstairs." Dan pointed to his head as he said this. Mary frowned, and placed her hand on top of his.

"You know you can talk to me, Dan... about anything. What's going on?" Dan was quiet for a moment, contemplating how he should approach this. Carefully, that was how. Mary spoke again before he could begin. "Are...are you not happy with being my boyfriend anymore?" Dan could almost hear a break in her voice.

"Huh? Oh, no, no... that's not it at all, Mary," said Dan. "It's nothing to do with us...well, I guess it sort of is, but not in regard to me being happy with our relationship." He squeezed her hand tighter and she smiled, just a little. "Okay, look, I'm just a little worried about this whole situation. Typically, these *happenings* don't last anywhere close to this long. The longest one before this was...two or three days, and then I woke up...or...came back...I'm not quite sure how to describe that part. So, I'm just wondering what's going on, and why this time is different. I've loved being here, and I don't want it to end...but something tells me it's going to."

Mary sighed and then nodded to show her understanding. "I was wondering if that might be it as well. When that...whatever it was happened on the way back home, I thought I was going to lose you. I don't know what I'd do if that happened." She began to tear up. "I think I love you, Dan." Dan thought he would be more surprised by this, but it felt right.

"I think I love you too," said Dan. He leaned over and kissed her. "Promise me something, Mary. If something happens and I leave 1965, promise me you won't do anything stupid. You have an amazing future ahead, and I wouldn't want to jeopardize that. If it does happen, me having to leave, I will do what I can to try and figure out what all this is about...and I'll find a way to come back to you. Promise me, Mary." She was crying now, and it was hard to understand her.

"I... I don't know if I can, Dan. What will I do without you? You've been the best thing to ever happen to me." Dan scooted closer to her and wrapped his arms around her.

"If it happens, I won't have a choice, Mary. Believe me, I don't like it either. Promise me you'll keep going." Mary stayed silent for a moment, and then nodded her head as she was leaning against Dan.

"Okay, I promise. I will find a way to move on." In her mind, Mary had no idea how she would actually do it but hoped that she would never have to find out. Mary and Dan finished their breakfast and went back to her room. "Wanna play chess?" asked Mary.

"Sure! I don't know how to play, though; will you teach me?" She smiled and then nodded. "Then let's do it," said Dan. "I've been wanting to learn how to play."

Dan would learn to play chess, but it wouldn't be for a long time.

8

James completed the diagnostics on the primary servers but wasn't able to isolate the runaway process that caused the cores to overheat. His next task was to put together a list of hardware that would be needed to support phase three of Destiny. This was difficult, considering he had no idea what phase three would entail. He decided it was better to be safe than sorry, so he requested the most cutting-edge hardware he could find. This would ensure that phase three went smoothly. James double checked the list and then took it to Dr. Wilkes's office. *Here goes nothing. I hope this gets approved.*

When James got to Dr. Wilkes's office, he noticed the doctor was reading over phase three, so he paused in the doorway and knocked. "Sir, may I come in? I have the list of hardware for phase three upgrades." Dr. Wilkes looked up from the report and waved James in.

"Please, have a seat, James. I was just reading up on this next test." He put it away as James sat down in the chair in front of the desk. James handed the list to Dr. Wilkes.

"I, uh...hope that isn't asking too much, sir. You did say your boss was open to getting anything that was necessary. I spared no expense to ensure a smooth phase three." Dr. Wilkes looked over the list, although both of them knew he had no idea what any of it meant.

"Obviously my boss will have the final say, James, but this looks okay to me. I'll send it to him right away. Thank you." James got up to leave but stopped when Dr. Wilkes spoke again. "Oh, by the way...I got your programming specifications earlier today for phase three." He pulled out an unimaginably large folder, which read:

TOP SECRET
PROJECT DESTINY: PHASE THREE

"Please read over part one and give me your thoughts on a timeline. If you could do so by tomorrow afternoon, I would appreciate it. Okay?"

James took the folder and nodded. "Yes, sir," he said. "I'll make sure to get started on this right away." James left the office and went to begin reading over phase three.

9

Once James had left, Dr. Wilkes picked up his phone and called his boss.

"Hello?" said the voice on the phone.

"Hi, sir. Sorry to bother you, but I have the list of hardware requested from Professor Kern. I won't trouble you with the specific items, but the total cost appears to be $1,473,750. I know it seems like a lot, but it is quite important that we don't have another event li—"

He was interrupted by his boss. "Yeah, yeah...I don't need any more details, Robert, I have bigger issues going on here right now. The price is fine; get the professor whatever he needs." Dr. Wilkes hesitated before responding.

"O... okay, sir, will do. Is there something going on I should know about?" There was a brief silence on the line, which made Dr. Wilkes very nervous. He didn't like to upset his boss, it never ended well.

"Perhaps," his boss finally replied, "but not just yet. I will let you know if and when it becomes your problem. Goodbye, Robert." The line went dead and Dr. Wilkes hung up the phone. He stood up and left to go tell James he had the green light to order his equipment.

"I sure hope phase three goes well," he said aloud.

Dr. Wilkes went downstairs and found James, who was looking over the logs of phase two.

"James, your hardware has been approved; go ahead and order it."

James was relieved to hear that he would be getting the cutting-edge hardware he had hoped for.

"Thank you, sir. I will order the hardware this afternoon."

Dr. Wilkes was about to leave when he turned back to James.

"Oh, by the way, how long has phase two been running now? It's probably about time we shut that down to prep for phase three," said Dr. Wilkes. James typed in a couple commands at the terminal before he replied.

"It looks like it has been up for quite a while now. I'd say it's time to shut it down." Dr. Wilkes thought for a moment and then nodded towards James.

"Right," said Dr. Wilkes. "Let's begin the shutdown procedures for phase two. I'll go get the lead scientists ready to analyze the results. Good work, James." Dr. Wilkes started his walk upstairs.

"Thank you, sir. I will begin the procedure immediately."

10

Mary had left Dan in her room while she went to find the chess board. Dan was sitting on her bed, which faced the modest vanity she had against the wall. Dan was content with his life here and he hoped it would last. Lately he had been thinking more about his family back in 2000 and wondered if they even knew he was gone. *Has Dr. Walsh been lying to them about me?* Dan wondered. *Has he been telling them I can't have visitors?* Dan's thoughts were interrupted by Mary's voice from the other room.

"Hey, Dan, I'm going to look in the garage quick, I think we might have stored it out there."

"Okay!" replied Dan.

Dan felt a cold draft, which made him shiver. He hesitated, and then looked over at the mirror—he just saw his reflection, which was good. He got up from the bed and tried to shake off the feeling. "No," he said, "this isn't happening. You're fine." He walked up to Mary's bookshelf and looked for something to read. He reached out for one and saw the title on the spine start to wobble—it *was* happening. "No!" He covered up the words and shook his head. *This isn't happening.* Dan moved his handle from the spine and saw the letters were normal, but they started to wobble once again. He dropped the book and stumbled backwards across the room.

He looked over at the mirror and saw that his reflection was turning blurry. He sat down on the bed and tried to relax. *Calm down, Dan, everything is fine. You haven't had any issues other than that little scare a few months ago.* The bed he was on began to shake violently. Dan's vision grew blurrier, and he could barely see anything in the room. After a few more seconds of this, the head of the bed sprung up off the floor and launched Dan towards the mirror. He screamed and braced for impact, but he felt himself go right through it, like he had before in his bathroom in the year 2000, and then he landed with a hard *thud.* Dan was unconscious.

11

Mary was about to give up when she finally saw the chess board, which was tucked away underneath a stack of old books. *What on earth is it doing here?* Mary wondered. She smiled as she pulled out the board and pieces, and then ran back into the house. "I found it, Dan! Sorry it took me so long... we can finally play," said Mary, running through the hall and back into her room.

At first, she was just confused as to where Dan was, but then she saw the book on the floor, and noticed her vanity had moved. "Dan? Dan, where are you?"

Nothing. Mary ran out of her room and frantically searched the house, but she knew, somehow, she already knew —Dan was gone. She stopped in the living room and fell to her knees and cried. Her heart hurt; she didn't know what she would do without Dan. A noise came from the front door, and she got up to go see what it was, hoping it was Dan, but knowing it wasn't.

It was Mary's parents who had just gotten home from getting groceries. "Hi Mary, how are yo…" Her mom had stopped in mid-sentence when she saw Mary had been crying. "Oh sweetie, what's wrong? Where's Dan?" Mary ran to her mom and hugged her, starting to cry even harder.

"He…he's gone, Mom! It *happened* again." Her cries grew louder, and she was having a tough time breathing. Helen looked over at Jack, who had a solemn look on his face.

"Go check her room, Jack," said Helen, holding Mary to her chest. Jack put his hand on Mary's back and rubbed it, and then went to look for Dan. A few moments later he returned and shook his head.

"There's no sign of him, Helen. It's as if he just…vanished." Mary burst into tears again and fell to the floor—she was broken. The Stevenson's household was broken.

CHAPTER III

1

Dan was woken by a tremendous headache. *Ugh, not another...*

His thought was interrupted by what he saw—his mouth dropped. He was in the small, twin bed with a single side table next to it, which held a lamp. On the table he saw, to his horror, empty pill containers and a glass of water, half full. "No...it—it can't be!" shouted Dan. He closed his eyes and rubbed them with his hands, refusing to believe what was happening. As he opened them, the terrible view remained the same—he was back at Clearwater.

A knock came at the door, which made Dan shiver, and in walked Dr. Walsh with a clipboard in his hand. "Good morning, Danny, how are you feeling today?" Dan glanced up at the doctor and then fainted.

Another couple hours passed, and Dan woke again, but this time without a headache. He was back in bed, but also realized he was indeed still back at Clearwater. Dr. Walsh was seated in a chair across the room and appeared to be taking notes in his report.

"Ah, you're awake," said Dr. Walsh. "Are you okay? You hit your head pretty hard on the floor."

Dan sat up in bed, still unable to believe he was back. *There's no way all of that was a dream,* he thought.

"I... I don't know, doctor," said Dan. "What's happening to me? I was in 1965...I was there for over a year, and now I'm suddenly back here...I don't understand." He felt himself start to tear up but fought it back. Dr. Walsh had a solemn expression on his face, and then began to change into concern.

"Oh, Danny," he said, "I'm very worried about you. Your dreams and hallucinations are becoming more and more severe." Dan felt his stomach begin to turn over and over on itself.

"My dreams? I refuse to believe that was all a dream, doctor. There's no way!" Dan ran his hands through his hair, feeling how much longer it was than he remembered. "Look at how I've changed...I'm a year older now than when I first came here. I'm twelve years old now!" Dan felt himself becoming frustrated but thought it was warranted, given the circumstances. The doctor put up his hand before Dan could start up again.

"Dan, listen to me, I understand your frustration...I really do, but the truth is, it was all a combination of dreams and vivid hallucinations. I've personally never seen such a severe case of them. You're claiming you've been in 1965 for over a year...but it's only been a week since your parents came to visit. Today is July 25th. Also, you were twelve when you arrived at Clearwater. I have it right here in my records."

Dan felt himself getting dizzy but managed to keep from fainting a second time. *July 25th? N..no, there's no way that can be*

right...I was there for over a year. Not again...what's happening to me?
His mind was racing, and he wasn't sure if it would ever stop.

"Why is this happening to me, doctor?" asked Dan. The
doctor sighed and stood up from his chair, and then walked
over to sit beside Dan.

"I wish I had a better answer for you, Danny, but it's just
not that simple. We're going to be trying some experimental
treatment soon and see if that helps. Early research has shown
some promising results, so we're hopeful. Until then, I can
only treat your headaches and try to keep you comfortable."
Dan suddenly thought of his parents.

"What about my parents? Can they come visit? It feels like
I haven't seen them in... well, over a year." The doctor smiled
broadly as he got up from the bed.

"Of course, Dan. In fact, they actually called just
yesterday and asked if they could visit. They will be out
tomorrow to visit. I've got a few things to take care of at our
other facility, so I will see you later, Dan. Take care."

Dr. Walsh left Dan's room and Dan sat on the edge of the
bed, still unable to cope with what was happening. *Oh, Mary...I
miss you so much already. It wasn't a dream, I know it wasn't. Something
else is going on here, and I promise I will figure it out and come back for
you. I love you, Mary Stevenson.* Dan felt a little better knowing his
parents would be visiting soon, but what on earth would he
tell them?

2

Mary wasn't doing any better than Dan. For her, it had
been two weeks since Dan left, and she had spent most of
those days sulking in her room. Multiple times her parents
tried to make her feel better, but nothing seemed to help. *Oh,*

Dan, I hope you're okay. I know I promised you that I'd move on, but I don't know how I'm going to do that. It hurts so much...I love you, Daniel Williams. Please be safe.

3

Dan's parents didn't end up being able to visit until Friday. It was 8:00 A.M. on Friday the 28th when Dan woke up, free of any dreams or headaches—he was, at least in that regard, relieved. It had only been a few days since he *came back* from 1965, but it felt like an eternity. He missed Mary more and more, and he wasn't sure what he was going to tell his parents when they arrived. *Do I try and tell them what happened? Will they believe me? Or will they just take the doctor's side, blame it on my schizophrenia?* Dan figured it would be the latter, but thought it was worth a try. *Surely they'll recognize that I've aged a whole year, won't they?* Dan continued to be absorbed in his own thoughts until 9:00 when a knock came at his door, and his parents came through the door.

"Mom! Dad! Oh, it's so great to see you guys! It's been so long!" Dan jumped off his bed and ran towards them, giving both of them a big hug. His parents looked at one another, even more concerned than their previous visit.

"Sweetie, what's going on?" asked his mom. "It's only been a little over a week since we were last here." She walked over to the bed with Dan and sat down with him. "Tell me what's wrong, Danny. You're scaring me." He had barely sat down when he jumped back up again, feeling even more frustrated than before.

"What's wrong?" asked Dan. "What's wrong is Clearwater, mom. This whole place is wrong! First the doctor tells me it's only been a week since you last visited, and now you're saying the same." Dan felt tears beginning to form, and he paused. Henry took the opportunity to speak.

"Dan, son...it's the truth. We were here on the 18th, just last Tuesday. I'm sorry we couldn't make it earlier, but we've both been pretty swamped with work." Dan was speechless. *First my doctor, and now both of my parents...does anybody believe me?* Dan knew someone who did, but it didn't matter. That someone was thirty-plus years in the past, or something like that.

"I... I don't understand," said Dan. "What's wrong with you guys? Can't you see that I'm a year older since you last saw me? I was eleven when I was admitted here, and now I'm twelve. How can you stand there and say it's only been a week?"

"Dan, I'm sorry you're struggling with this," his mom began, "but you don't look any different than the last time we saw you. Dr. Walsh is right; you were twelve when you first arrived here at Clearwater." Dan turned and smacked the wall with his fist. "Ow, damn it!" Dan's mom gasped and covered her mouth.

"Hey, watch your tone, young man..." said Henry, but Helen put her hand on his leg and shook her head.

"It's okay, dear...let him get it out."

Dan turned around to face his parents, he was crying.

"I'm sorry for swearing, Mom...but it's just so frustrating. Something's wrong with me and I don't know how to fix it!" He fell to his knees and continued to cry. His mom rubbed her hand on his back, doing what she could to comfort him.

"Listen, sweetie, Dr. Walsh told us there's an experimental treatment that he's hoping to start with you next week. It sounds like there has been some very good results with it in initial testing." Dan didn't care about any experimental treatment; he wanted to know the truth.

"Can we go out for breakfast? Just the three of us?" asked Dan. "I'd love to get some pancakes." The expression on his parents' face told him it wasn't likely to happen, but he was hopeful—he had to be. Much to Dan's surprise, both of their expressions changed to a happier one.

"Oh, what a great idea, Dan," said his mom. "We could go to Denny's. I've heard their pancakes are wonderful. Let me go and find Dr. Walsh. He will need to approve your temporary leave." Dan smiled, although somewhat nervous about what the doctor would say, and his mom got up to leave.

"I better go with you," said Henry, "just in case you get lost." Henry got up too, and they both went towards the door.

"We'll be right back," they both said, almost in perfect unison. *That was weird*, thought Dan. Mom wasn't great with directions, but Dr. Walsh's office was just down the hall...you couldn't miss it. His mind wandered again, now thinking back to Mary and the Stevenson's. Dan missed them all very much, but he feared he might never see them again. *Stay strong, Mary. Please stay strong.*

4

"Hello, this is Dr. Wilkes. How can I be—"

The doctor was interrupted by the impatient sounding voice on the other end of the call.

"Robert, listen carefully," said the voice, no doubt Dr. Wilkes's unforgiving boss, "there's no time to split up phase three. I want the entire phase ready to go in one month. Got it?" There was silence on both ends of the call, and then Dr. Wilkes finally found his voice.

"Uh, ye...yes, sir. Of course, sir. I will go speak with James, my lead developer about the updated timeline." He considered mentioning how tight of a timeline it was but remembered previous calls with his boss and decided against it.

"Good," said the voice. Oh, and Robert, those problems I mentioned the last time we spoke...they're now your concern. "

"Oh, wha..what's going on?" Dr. Wilkes interrupted, too concerned about what could be wrong. "Err, I'm sorry sir, I didn't mean to cut you off."

"It's fine, Robert, but we can't discuss it over the phone. We will speak in person soon. I'll be by your facility in two days." The line went dead, and Dr. Wilkes fell back into his chair. Dr Wilkes was overwhelmed with stress, and he still had to go talk to James about phase three, which now had to be done in one month.

"Guess I'd better get this over with," he said, walking out of his office.

5

It was just after 10 that morning when James had finished unpacking all the hardware for the new server. With an almost unlimited budget, James had purchased the most bleeding edge tech he could find. With the $1.8 million, James had bought sufficient hardware for a quantum server. The downside of using quantum technology was that it required a tremendous amount of cooling to operate efficiently, and cooling had been the issue with phase two. To fix this, James had invested in a cryogenic mixing chamber to store the server in, which had the cooling power to bring the processors down to a temperature near absolute zero. In a few hours, James would complete the installation of one of the most powerful servers in existence. James would come to regret ever building the server, but that was neither here nor there. Phase three loomed over him.

Dr. Wilkes walked downstairs and into the server room. James was wrapping up the hardware installation and was about ready to begin the start-up procedure.

"James, I need to talk to you," said Dr. Wilkes. "I know you're busy, but you need to hear this." James put his tools down and got up from behind the server.

"What's going on, sir? I've nearly got the new server set up...it's going to be quite a machine." Dr. Wilkes smiled, although it was very much forced.

"Listen, James...I've got some bad news, and also some worse news." He paused and scratched at the side of his face, and then continued. "I just got off the phone with my boss. He wants phase three done in one month. No, not part one of phase three...all of it."

"No!" shouted James. "No, Robert...err, sir...sorry but no, absolutely not. It's impossible." Dr. Wilkes sighed and fell into the nearest chair. He had been expecting this exact reaction, but it didn't make it any easier. After a moment of awkward silence, Dr. Wilkes spoke again, trying to stay calm.

"Look, James...I get it. Well, I mean...I don't actually get the programming part, but I understand how tight of a time-line this is. There's nothing I can do about it. And James, there's something else..." James became even more frustrated...he had forgotten about the worse news.

"Oh, great...what else?" he asked.

"My boss is coming here in two days, James. He wants to discuss something with me in person. He never speaks to me in person. In nearly fifteen years of working under him, I've only seen him twice. Whatever is going on, it's bad." James stood silent, unsure of what to say.

"What do you think it's about?" Dr. Wilkes shook his head and let out a large sigh.

"I don't know, James. I wish I did, really, but I don't." He turned and walked back towards the stairs, stopping just before leaving. "Listen, James...whatever happens, it's been great working with you. You really are the best in your field." For the first time since they started working together, James saw Dr. Wilkes smile, and it was genuine.

"Tha...thank you, sir. I hope whatever your boss has to say can be rectified fairly quickly. I'd better get back to work." Dr. Wilkes turned and walked back up the stairs as his cell phone rang.

6

"Sounds good. Thank you, doctor," said Rebecca, hanging up her phone. "The doctor said he's on his way now, and he told me to have you wait for him in his office." Rebecca smiled and pointed towards the door on the right side of her desk. "It's just down the hall from your son's room." Patricia and Henry smiled and thanked her.

"Much appreciated, Rebecca," said Patricia. They walked back through the door and down the hall, glancing into Dan's room, who they saw was reading Harry Potter. Once they got to the doctor's office, it was only a few minutes before he came through the door.

"Well, hello, Mr. and Mrs. Williams," said the doctor. "How are you doing today? Have you had a chance to visit with your son?"

"Yes, doctor...that's what we wanted to talk to you about,"

said Patricia. "He seems almost worse than he was when we were here last week. What's been going on?" He frowned and shook his head.

"Poor Danny," he began. "That boy has been struggling so much with his condition. We've tried multiple treatments, but the visions and dream states continue to worsen. I believe I mentioned to you on the phone about a new experiment treatment we're considering. It's my last option, I'm afraid. If it doesn't work, young Danny might be beyond our help." He shook his head again. Patricia was crying, so Henry had to speak.

"We appreciate everything you've done, doctor. I know you're doing all that you can for our son. We were wondering —would be possible for him to come out with us for breakfast? We'd like to get him some pancakes at Denny's. He loves pancakes." There was a brief look of concern that appeared on the doctor's face, but it was quickly replaced with excitement.

"Of course! Dan could use some fresh air. Just let me make a quick call and get the approval code." Henry smiled and looked over at Patricia, who had stopped crying and seemed to be cheering up as well. They couldn't wait to have some family time with Dan. Both of them sat in silence, eagerly awaiting good news.

"Hello, sir," said the voice on the phone, "what's going on?"

"I need an approval code for Daniel Williams. His parents, Henry and Patricia Williams, would like to take him out for breakfast at Denny's. Repeat, Denny's for breakfast. My authorization is...*Alpha-165-Delta-338.*" The doctor smiled at Henry and Patricia, who were now awaiting the approval.

There was silence on the phone, and then the voice finally spoke again.

"Authorization code is confirmed, sir. Thank you. Processing request now. Will be ready in fifteen minutes." The doctor hung up the phone and smiled again.

"It'll be ready in fifteen minutes," said the doctor. "I'll be right back; just need to grab some paperwork from the printer outside. Please wait here."

Henry and Patricia sat patiently as the heavy footsteps of Dr. Walsh echoed through the hallway.

CHAPTER IV

1

SEPTEMBER MARKED TWO MONTHS SINCE DAN HAD VANISHED from 1965. Mary was beginning to lose hope that she'd ever see Dan again. Her mom had tried to get her back into her schoolwork, but it was no use. Mary had little care for anything anymore—even reading didn't matter now. Mary was in her room, trying to work on her novel, but her mind kept going back to Dan. There was a quiet knock on her door and then she heard her mom's voice.

"Mary, dear," said Helen. "Can I come in?" Mary thought for a moment, but then decided it was probably for the best to let her mom say what she had to say.

"Yeah, I guess," said Mary, aware of the reluctance in her voice.

The door opened and her mom came in, immediately noticing that Mary had been crying.

"Oh, sweetie, I know you miss him...we all do, but you have to try and move on. He would want you to, you know he would." As she said this, she knew it didn't sound very convincing, but it was the best she could do.

"No, Mom...ugh, you don't understand!" said Mary. "I loved him, and now he's gone...gone forever." She threw her notebook across the room and crossed her arms in frustration. Mary tried to act tough, but then she broke down—tears came in a wave of painful emotions. "Oh, Mom...I don't know what to do without him. It was such a great year...why is life so unfair?" Helen felt herself going a bit teary eyed as well as she walked over and sat beside Mary.

"We all want to know that answer, sweetie," replied Helen. "Unfortunately, we usually don't get it. I won't try to lie to you and tell you it gets easier...because it doesn't, but as you get older, you learn to cope with things like this in better ways. I promise." Again, Helen wasn't sure how much of what she had said was sound advice, but she was doing her best. Mary wrapped her arms around her mom, who was happy to return the hug.

"Thanks, Mom. I know Dan would want me to move on with my life, but that doesn't make it any easier." Mary let go and tried to compose herself. "I'm sorry for yelling; it just hurts."

Helen nodded. "I know, sweetie, I know. It'll get less painful in time. What do you say we go out and get some ice cream?" For the first time in a few weeks, Helen saw a smile form on Mary's face.

"Sure!" said Mary. "Just let me get dressed." Helen got up and went out to grab her purse. After her mom left, Mary got up and took off her pajamas, which had become her everyday attire the past few weeks. She got dressed and was just putting on her shirt when she saw a flash of light from her window. *What the...*thought Mary. *What was that?* She ran over to the window and looked outside, but all she saw was their back yard. The flash of light happened again, and in the corner of the yard, the same place Dan had appeared over a year ago, the fence looked blurry to Mary. *That's weird,* she thought. She finished getting dressed and ran outside to get a better look.

As she approached it, she noticed it was making a loud humming noise, as if it was emitting a large amount of electricity. The blurriness began to change shape. It almost looked human now. "Dan? Dan is that you?" shouted Mary. The shape become less blurry, and for a split second she saw blonde hair, and then an arm reached out towards her—then it was gone. Mary dove towards it but grabbed at air and fell to the ground. "Noooo! Dan! Mooooom!" Helen ran from the kitchen outside and found Mary in the corner of the yard.

"Sweetie, what are you doing out here?" asked Helen, picking her daughter up off the ground. "I thought you wanted to get ice cream." Mary was crying again, worse than before.

"Oh, Mom," she said. "Dan was here! He was right here! I saw him...I mean, sort of. He was really blurry, almost like something was interfering with him coming back." Helen had a worried look on her face and wasn't quite sure how to respond. She sighed and put her arm around Mary.

"Come on, Mary...let's go get ice cream. You need to get away from here for a little while." Mary wanted to say something, but she decided against it. She had a feeling that her mom either didn't believe her, or just simply refused to do so. Regardless, Mary was going to have to suffer in isolation.

"Okay, Mom," said Mary, doing her best to sound enthusiastic, but fearing she hadn't been convincing at all.

The ice cream was good, Mary wouldn't deny that, but the whole time her mind was preoccupied by Dan, and by what had happened in the back yard. *What was that? Were you trying to tell me something?*

Helen didn't like how quiet Mary was, but after a few times of making casual conversation, she let it go. Prior to that September afternoon, Mary Stevenson had started to move on with her life, but after the events of that day, she wasn't sure that would ever happen. She was right.

2

As his parents had seen earlier, Dan was reading the third Harry Potter book while he waited for them to return. He was hungry and thought pancakes sounded really good. He was nearing the end of a chapter when the words on the page began to wobble. *Nope...nope, not today, please not today,* thought Dan. He dropped the book and rubbed his eyes, hoping it would stop. When he opened them, his vision was already going dark—then he fell.

His bed vanished from underneath him and he fell through darkness for what seemed like several minutes but was really only a few seconds. Dan landed, but he was exactly where he had been just a moment ago, sitting on his bed. *What the hell? That was weird...*

While Dan was lost in thought, the door to his room opened and both of his parents came in.

"Good news, sweetie," said Patricia. "The doctor approved your visit to Denny's. Let's go get you some pancakes!"

The sudden noise caught him off guard, and he jolted upright on the bed. Dan had been excited about pancakes but couldn't help but noticing something was wrong—very wrong.

"M...Mom? Why'd you change your clothes?" Dan

pointed at his mom with a confused look on his face. Patricia, who had been wearing a purple dress with pink and white flowers on it, was now wearing a pair of blue jeans and a white blouse. Neither of these outfits would be out of place for her, but they were significantly different, and Dan knew she hadn't been wearing the blouse when she first arrived.

"I don't know what you're talking about, sweetie," said Patricia. "This is what I was wearing when we got here. Are you sure you're feeling okay? Have you taken your medicine today?" Dan frowned at this and looked to his dad, but he, too, was looking concerned.

What's going on? They're both looking at me like I'm crazy. I know Mom wasn't wearing that blouse before...she was wearing a dress. Dad is wearing the same thing, jeans and a t-shirt, his typical attire. Dan was taken out of his thoughts by his dad grabbing his shoulder.

"Hey there, bud, you doing okay? What do you say we get those pancakes?" said Henry. Dan looked up at his dad, and the previous thoughts were gone.

"Yeah! Let's go get some pancakes," said Dan. He had decided to try to enjoy any time he could with his parents. Just as they were leaving the room, the thought of Mary came into Dan's mind, which made him sad. *Oh, Mary, please keep holding on...I know it's hard, but please stay strong. I'm going to come for you, I promise.*

The ride to Denny's was uneventful. Dan's mind kept wandering to the thought of Mary, and how much he missed her. As they pulled into the parking lot, Dan looked up at the Denny's sign, and underneath it read "All you can eat pancakes." Dan was happy to see this—he was starving. The happiness was short-lived, however, as the words on the sign began to wobble. *No...no, no, no!* "Mom! Dad!" shouted Dan. "Mom, do you see that? Look up at the sign." Neither of his parents said anything; instead both kept their eyes facing forward as if they hadn't heard him. Dan looked at them and then back at the sign—the text was wobbling so badly Dan could barely read it.

A moment later, Dan noticed the car and all of the surroundings begin to turn fuzzy. It looked as if it was phasing out of existence—*maybe I am crazy*, thought Dan. He looked around the car and started to see something coming through the car, something green—it was grass. The fuzziness continued to worsen, but the grass began to come into focus. Along with the grass, Dan started to see a fence. *I know that fence! That's the fence at Mary's!* Then, Dan saw her—he saw Mary! She was also blurry, and it looked as if she were inside the car with him—time was beginning to mesh in front of his eyes.

"Mary!" shouted Dan, but Mary couldn't hear him. He reached out his arm and tried to touch her, but it was no use —it wasn't real, or at least not real enough. For a second, Dan thought he could hear her voice shouting his name, and then he thought he heard Mary's mom, Helen. Everything went dark, and then a moment later everything came back into focus and Dan was back in the car, now with an enormous headache.

"Danny? Hey, Earth to Danny. Are you okay, sweetie?" said Patricia. "We should go inside."

Dan nodded and got out of the car with his parents. *That was a first*, he thought. *It's as if the happenings are starting to combine...weird. But, was that real? Is Mary really okay? I sure hope so. I miss you, Mary.* Dan and his parents sat down in a booth and ordered their food. Twenty minutes later, Dan was enjoying the best-tasting pancakes he had ever had.

"Oh, man, these are great!" said Dan. "You were right,

Mom, this place is the best." Patricia smiled and looked up at Henry, who was also smiling. They were happy to see Dan enjoying himself. *Wait a minute,* thought Dan. *The pancakes...they taste good; no, they taste great. The last few times I had eaten outside of the facility, the food was horrible. So, this has to be real then...but does that mean the vision of Mary was fake? Was it just my schizophrenia acting up?* Dan felt himself becoming frustrated again, so he put the thought out of his mind and enjoyed another helping of pancakes. At this moment, life for Dan was good.

It wouldn't last.

3

July 30th would be a day that would scar James's memory for decades to come. In later years he would look back on the events of that day and wonder what he could have done differently—would it have changed anything? It was a question James would ask over and over. At 8:00 AM, Dr. Wilkes walked into James's office and sat down. He was sweating and was unable to sit still. He got up from the chair and began to pace.

"Sir, you should try and relax. Your boss won't be here for another hour. Besides, how bad could it be?" said James. Dr. Wilkes stopped in the middle of the office and looked up at James; his expression said it all.

"Listen, James...there are certain things I haven't told you regarding this facility. And no, I'm not referring to the small details here and there I leave out of projects. No, this is much bigger than that. I'm afraid that what my boss is coming here for is the very thing I've feared for years."

James was unable to come up with a reply. He simply stared blankly at Dr. Wilkes, who had resumed his pacing.

An hour went by, and there were perhaps fifteen minutes of that hour that didn't involve Dr. Wilkes pacing back and forth. At precisely 9:01 AM, Dr. Wilkes received a call from the security office at the front gate—his boss had arrived.

"Tha—thank you. I will be up to meet him," said Dr. Wilkes, who was quite visibly shaken. He turned to look at James, who was looking rather concerned for his boss, more so than he ever had in the past.

"Sir," began James, "do you want me to join you? Or, am I allowed to join you?" Dr. Wilkes shook his head, which was what James had expected.

"Sorry, James, my boss requested only myself, at least for the initial meeting. I told him that if there was anything vital that you would need to know, I would like you to hear it from him, so hopefully he will take that into consideration." James nodded, showing his understanding, but doubted he would ever hear anything. "Well, I'd better get going. I'd hate to make him wait," said Dr. Wilkes. "I'll do what I can to keep you informed, James. Wish me luck."

Dr. Wilkes rushed out of the office and headed upstairs to meet his boss. He arrived in the front lobby just as his boss was walking in, flanked by his two security personnel who were always with him. Dr. Wilkes greeted him with a smile and an outstretched hand. The man motioned for Dr. Wilkes to put his hand down.

"We've no time for silly greetings," said the man. "Where's your office? We need to get started right away." Dr. Wilkes immediately rescinded his hand and put both of his hands behind his back.

"Uhh, yes, of course, sir! Right this way, sir." He led his boss down a lengthy hallway, and then down several flights of stairs, through two security doors, and finally to Dr. Wilkes's corner office. Dr. Wilkes scanned his thumb, and the door beeped its greeting and opened. As his boss entered, the security personnel stopped and turned to face away from the room —standard protocol, of course.

Dr. Wilkes's boss was a short man, barely 5'6", but a little wider around the midsection that he'd care to admit. At sixty-five, his hair was grey, but always tidy. It was short and looked to be freshly trimmed earlier that day. He wore a dark blue three-piece suit that was custom tailored in Italy.

The moment Dr. Wilkes had made it to his chair and sat down, his boss began to speak.

"Listen, Robert, I don't have much time so I'm going to get right down to it. They know, Robert. They know everything that we've been doing here, and what we have planned. I'm not sure how, but they do. As we speak, the CIA is trying to get approval to get a warrant to arrest you and your personnel. I'm sorry I couldn't make it here sooner, but I had to be careful. My ass is on the line here too, after all.

"Luckily it appears I still have some pull in the government, so I've been able to slow their progress down, but it won't stop them forever. This is why I gave the tight timeline for phase three. We have a month, likely less, before my roadblocks that are in place will be bypassed, and the warrants will be issued."

Dr. Wilkes was sweating more profusely now than he had been down in James's office.

"The CIA? Fuck...oh, Jesus, sir...what are we going to do? Even if we get phase three up in a month, which is quite a tall order in it of itself, what will we do then? I don't want to go to jail," said Dr. Wilkes.

He was on the verge of a breakdown. He got up from his chair and started to pace once again, this time with much larger strides. His boss grabbed Robert by the shoulders and stopped him from pacing.

"Get a hold of yourself, Robert. I have a plan...it's not great, but we don't have any alternatives that I can see. First things first, we need to get phase three development completed. We've worked far too hard on this project not to see it through. Once phase three is complete, we can begin our more or less defensive strategy.

"We'll immediately shut down the non-vital test protocols, wipe the servers, and dispose of the evidence. We can lose them and not have really lost much. Project Destiny is the only one that has value to us at this point. The primary server room is still in the basement, right?"

Dr. Wilkes nodded. "Yes, sir, of course. The basement is the most heavily fortified part of the building. It even has cloaking technology."

"Yes, yes it does. I had that installed myself in the event of such a situation as this one were to arise. Listen carefully, Robert, this part is important. Your lead dev, James is it? He needs to figure out a way to have the system automatically run through the phase three tests without our intervention, as well as limit power usage when necessary. Actually, we might be able to spoof that too. Is that possible?"

Dr. Wilkes had a blank expression on his face. "Sir, um...if you don't mind me asking, wouldn't it be better for James to be here himself? He is, after all, quite vital to this plan working, and quite frankly, I have no idea whether or not what you just said is possible. I barely know what a server looks like." His boss hesitated at first but given the circumstances and truth of what Robert was saying, he figured it was necessary.

"Yes, yes...very well. Send for him immediately, Robert; this is important."

No more than three minutes later, James entered the office and joined Dr. Wilkes and his boss.

"Hello, James," said Robert's boss, "thanks for joining us on such short notice."

James nodded and tried to force a smile, although he was really quite nervous. "Su—sure thing," he said. "What's this all about? I got the new primary setup and it's online. She's a beauty."

"That's actually what we wanted to talk to you about, James," said Robert's boss. He proceeded to explain to James about shutting down all the non-vital test programs and wiping all the evidence of them existing. James was a bit confused by this but continued to listen without any questions. Robert's boss asked about the basement's cloaking ability, which also struck James as odd, but once again he didn't ask any questions, only spoke when asked a question.

"How is phase three coming along?" said Robert's boss. James sat quietly for a moment, debating how to answer the question. He glanced over at Dr. Wilkes who gave him a please be nice look. James decided he would play the nice card, if only to cover his own ass.

"It's going to be a super tight deadline, sir," said James, "but I believe I can have it done in a month, especially with the upgraded system."

"Wonderful," said Robert's boss. "That's great to hear. I do, however, have one more thing I'd like you to do. Can you write, or develop, or however it is you do the things you do, something to automate the phase three testing protocols without human intervention?"

James's expression was one of great confusion, with a bit of concern as well. "Why would you want to automate such a process, sir?"

Robert's boss frowned. He didn't like being asked direct questions; he felt it was below him.

"Please, James...let me ask the questions. Can it be done or not?" Dr. Wilkes was worried about what James would say, terrified in fact. James was silent again, and nearly a minute went by before he spoke.

"Technically speaking, yes of course it can be done. Almost anything can be done with enough time and computer power. With the recent system upgrade, we have an ample amount of the latter; unfortunately, it seems like we have very little of the former. Between phase three and trying to do th..." James trailed off in the middle of his sentence. *Could that work?* He thought to himself. *I think so...dangerous, but it would save time, for sure.*

"Uh, James?" asked Dr. Wilkes. "Planning to enlighten us?"

"Oh, uh...yes, sorry," said James. "I just had an idea that I think would solve the time constraint. May I?" Dr. Wilkes looked over at his boss who waved his hand toward James, giving him the go ahead.

"Okay, so the current issue is that there simply isn't enough time for me to develop all of phase three and this automation technology you're asking for. But what if I develop the skeleton of phase three...a blueprint if you will. After that, I can develop an A.I. that would be able to read and interpret the blueprint, develop the remaining protocols, and run them as well. It would be the perfect system. Admittedly this is bleeding edge tech, so I would need uninterrupted time to get this done, but it would work."

Dr. Wilkes felt a headache forming. He wasn't a fan of tech terms, and almost all of what James had said was far out of his realm of understanding. His boss also had a limited understanding of technology, but he seemed to like what he was hearing, which was simply: *yes, I can do it.*

"Good, great!" said Robert's boss. "Robert has spoken highly of you, James, and I can see he wasn't wrong. Please, go do whatever it is you need to in order to meet our deadline. And if there's any additional resources you need, consider them approved. Thanks again, James."

James walked out of Robert's office and down the hall to his own. *Oh jeez,* he thought. *What did I just sign myself up for? Artificial Intelligence? Ugh, this is going to be a long month.* James sat down as his desk and began researching A.I. development. This would be another time where, in the future, James would regret ever mentioning A.I.

4

Back in Dr. Wilkes's office, his boss seemed to be a bit more relaxed now that it seemed a plan was in place.

"I gotta hand it to you, Robert," said his boss, "that lead developer of yours is quite talented. Where'd you find him?" Dr. Wilkes was taken aback a bit as he couldn't remember a time his boss ever came close to giving out a compliment.

"Um, he had come highly recommended from a colleague at the Somerset School of Technology, where James had graduated Summa Cum Laude at age nineteen." His boss nodded in approval and stood up from his chair.

"I like him, and I like how things are shaping up. I have to admit that when I first came here today, I thought for sure we'd be forced to shut everything down. Keep up the good work, Robert. If things go as planned, you probably won't see me again for a while. Oh, and one more thing, Robert. Show James level five."

"Sir? Level five? But that's way above his security clear-ance. If I may say, personally I feel like he should have had the clearance from day one, but that's just my opinion."

"I know, I know...I realize now that he should have, but that's in the past. With the way things are, your lead developer definitely needs to know what we're really doing here. I will file the necessary paperwork for the security clearance. It will be processed by tomorrow morning. Good luck, Robert...I hope all goes well, for both our sakes."

Before Dr. Wilkes could formulate a response, his boss was out the door and walking back upstairs with his security personnel at his side.

Dr. Wilkes relaxed back into his chair which felt great. The past thirty minutes had been the most stressful of his career, or at least they had felt like it. *I sure hope you know what you're talking about, James,* he thought. *And Level 5 clearance...I sure hope you're ready to see some shit. If this goes south, I don't know if any of us will make it out of here alive. Here's to hoping you can pull it off James.* Dr. Wilkes poured himself a stiff drink and enjoyed a few moments to himself.

CHAPTER V

1

MARY WAS STILL SAD. SHE MISSED DAN MORE AND MORE EVERY day. It had gotten exponentially worse since the day in the back yard. She swore up and down that it was him no matter how much her parents insisted it wasn't.

That was two weeks ago, and it was now August 13th, a Saturday. Mary had been in her room most of the day, sitting on the floor with a chess board in front of her.

Oh, Dan, thought Mary. *You wanted to learn chess so badly, but you never got the chance. I hope wherever you are, someone can teach you. You told me to be strong, but I just don't think I can. Please forgive me for what I'm about to do. Please don't think less of me. I love you, Danny Williams. I always will.*

Mary left her room and walked down the hall and then into the living room. "Mom? Dad?" Nothing. *Good, they aren't home.* She walked out the front door and stopped when she was at the tire swing. As she looked up at it, she felt her heart racing—this was it.

Mary had grabbed her father's hacksaw from the garage as well as a pair of gloves. She used the saw to cut off the tire from the rope, which she tossed aside. *Won't be needing this anymore,* she thought. She went to the garage and put the saw back. Even in the darkest of times, Mary made sure to put everything back in its place. As she returned to the tree, she looked up again, thinking about what was to come. *Can't stop now—*

She grabbed on to the rope and began to pull herself up. It was tough, but the gloves had helped a great deal, and she had learned from her dad to wrap her feet around the rope as well. After about ten minutes, Mary had made it to the top of the branch that was holding the tire swing. The branch was at least twenty feet from the ground, which would be enough. Mary pulled the rope up and began to tie a loop in the rope. She put it around her neck and measured to make sure it would be tight enough. She felt her heart race faster and faster, and a sudden thought of doubt crept into her mind, but she knew there was no turning back.

2

Jack and Helen Stevenson were out getting groceries for the week. Normally Helen would do the shopping herself, but Jack had decided he would accompany his wife for this trip—a decision he would regret for the rest of his life. Helen was checking her list, crossing things off as she looked at the items in her cart, when a troubling thought raced through her mind. "Jack, I think we should get going," said Helen. "I don't know why, but I feel like Mary is in terrible danger." Jack gave Helen a concerned look.

"What do you mean dear?" he replied. "She was just

sitting at home in her room when we left. What kind of danger could she be in?" Helen tried to calm down, realizing that Jack was probably right. She nodded, and as she looked back at her list, she realized they had gotten everything they needed.

"Well, it looks like we're done here anyway. Let's get going." Jack smiled at her as they made their way to the front of the store. It would be a long time before either of them smiled again. A long, long time.

3

Dan put the last bite of pancake into his mouth and set his fork down on the table. "Ugh, I'm so full," muttered Dan. "They were so good! I couldn't stop eating them!" Both Patricia and Henry smiled at the sound of Dan's voice. They hadn't seen him this happy since before the dreams and headaches started.

"That's great, sweetie," said Patricia. "I'm glad you enjoyed them. Denny's never disappoints." The waitress came by and asked them if there was anything else they needed. When Dan looked up at the waitress, the entirety of the restaurant had dissolved into Redfield, 1965. He saw Mary, and she was crying. Before he could do or say anything, the image of Redfield was gone, and he was back in Denny's.

Dan screamed and fell off his chair. "Danny! Are you okay?" cried his mother. The waitress apologized and picked up the chair, then offered Dan her hand.

"I—I'm okay," said Dan as he got up, not wanting to take the waitress's hand. He looked up at her again, but this time it was just their waitress—no sign of Mary.

As Dan and his family were walking out of Denny's, Dan

looked up at the sign and noticed the letters begin to wobble again. He stopped dead in his tracks and closed his eyes. "No!" he screamed. "I don't want this...I can't take it anymore!" He fell to his knees and started to cry. Dan smacked his hands on the pavement in frustration, which made an odd, hollow sound.

What was that? He noticed that his parents hadn't said anything, and as he looked up, he realized they weren't there. In fact, nobody was—nothing at all was there anymore. He looked back down at the pavement, only to find that it was gone as well. Dan stood up and all he could see was white emptiness.

He slowly turned around and to his horror, saw nothing but more white. All around him was white—even under his feet there was nothing. "Hello?" he shouted. "Is anybody there?" Dan took a few steps forward and noticed that it felt like walking on a large, hollow box made of glass. Dan felt a cold draft go over his right shoulder, and then he fell.

He fell faster and faster, as the white emptiness seemed to go on forever. Dan could feel he was falling but had no sense of what was around him. Things slowed down for Dan, and then in front of him, Mary appeared. "Mary?" shouted Dan. "Mary is that you?" Mary was crying, and Dan could see something around her neck, but she was blurry, so he wasn't able to make out what it was. "Mary, what's wrong?" She said nothing, and after a few seconds she was gone. A moment later Dan landed on what felt like a trampoline. He bounced back up a few feet and then landed with a thud.

"Danny, are you okay?" asked Henry. "You're really scaring your mother. We should get you back to Clearwater." His dad's voice caught Dan off guard.

"Wha—what happened?" asked Dan. "I was falling...and

there was so much white. And Mary was there!" Henry looked over at Patricia, who had her hand over her mouth and was crying.

"Who's Mary, Dan?" asked Henry. Dan realized he had let Mary's name slip. He hadn't mentioned her to them before and had wanted to keep it that way.

"She's a girl I met when I was in 1965...I was there!" said Dan, knowing they wouldn't believe him.

"Oh, sweetie," his mom began, "don't tell me you still think that was real. It was all just a dream, Danny. Come on, we really need to get back to Clearwater."

"A dream? No! You don't understand...it was so much more than a dream. And I'm not going back to Clearwater...that place is not good, Mom. It's not good at all!" Dan turned and ran back towards Denny's.

He had only gotten a few steps when his head connected with a solid wall, *smack*, and Dan fell to the ground. "Ow, my head," said Dan, rubbing his forehead as he sat up.

Immediately Dan noticed the white emptiness was back. The temperature had dropped as well, and he was shivering. "What's going on?" he shouted. "Mom? Dad?"

No response. Dan heard a blood curdling scream and as he turned toward the scream he fell again, through the white emptiness. The fall was short, and when Dan landed, he was quickly filled with horror—he was back in Clearwater. There was a knock on the door, and Dr. Walsh walked in with his clipboard.

"Hello, Dan. How are you feeling today?" Dan's head was throbbing, and the room began to spin. He tried to respond, but then everything went black—he fainted.

4

Dan awoke about an hour later to a pounding headache, and nausea as well. *Well, that's new*, thought Dan. *A headache and I feel like I have to vomit, great.* The thought was barely out of his mind when he ran towards the bathroom, holding his hands over his mouth. He had just made it to the toilet when he spewed out large amounts of half-digested pancakes. Dan groaned as he sat down next to the toilet and wiped his mouth off with toilet paper. "Ugh, that was rough. So, the Denny's trip was real?" *But what about all the white emptiness? Surely that wasn't real, was it?*

The realism of the dreams made it hard for Dan to discern them from real life. Dan managed to get up and make his way back to the bed. Just as he sat down, another knock came at the door and Dr. Walsh walked in.

"Good evening, Dan. Are you feeling okay?"

Dan nodded. "I feel better now that I threw up most of my pancakes. They tasted a lot better on the way down."

Dr. Walsh chuckled as he made a note on his clipboard. "I'm glad to hear that. Your parents said they had a great time with you at breakfast. I hope the fresh air did you some good."

"It was good, up until the white emptiness situation happened," said Dan. "After that it got really weird, and then I woke up here."

"White emptiness?" Asked Dr. Walsh. "Your parents didn't mention anything about that. What happened?" The look on his face made Dan feel even more concerned about what had happened.

"Well, we were just leaving Denny's when I started to feel like I was having one of my *happenings*. I got frustrated and fell down, and then when I looked up again everything was gone. I was surrounded by nothing but white emptiness for as far as I could see. It was terrifying, to be honest."

Dr. Walsh was frantically taking notes, his face becoming more and more concerned, which didn't help Dan feel any better. "Please," he said, "go on with your story. What happened next?" Dan thought about it for a moment and then continued.

"Uhh, I felt something cold on my shoulder and then I fell...or at least it felt like I was falling. And then I saw Mary! Something was wrong with her, though. She wouldn't stop crying, and there was something around her neck, but I couldn't see what it was. She disappeared and then I landed on what felt like a trampoline because I bounced back up a few feet and then landed again, back on the pavement in front of Denny's.

"I tried explaining this to my parents, but of course they just think I'm crazy and suggested we go back here. I got upset and tried running away, which is when it got really strange. I ran into what felt like a solid glass wall and fell down again. And that's when I heard a terrible scream; it was awful, doctor. As soon as I turned to the sound of the scream I fell again, and then landed here on my bed. What's going on with me, doctor? I'm scared..."

Dr. Walsh was still taking notes when Dan finished talking. He looked up at Dan, who was beginning to cry. "I'm sorry to say that I don't know for sure, Dan," said Dr. Walsh. "I promise that I'm doing everything I can to help you, though. We will be starting your new treatment plan next week, which I am really hoping will get rid of these awful dreams you're having." Dr. Walsh got up and put his hand on Dan's shoulder and smiled. "Don't worry, Dan, we'll get this figured out soon." He walked towards the door and was about to leave when Dan spoke.

. . .

"SAY, DR. WALSH...HOW DID I ACTUALLY GET BACK HERE? I don't remember anything after the whiteness showed up." Dr. Walsh turned back to Dan with a confused look on his face.

"Your parents brought you back, of course. They said everything went great and hoped they could come visit again soon. I'm sorry, but I do have to get going now, Dan. I have a few other appointments to make before my shift is over. Have a good night. I'll see you in the morning." He waved to Dan, as he left the room, closing the door behind him.

Dan sat on his bed, not sure exactly how to take what Dr. Walsh had just told him. *My parents brought me back? But why can't I remember that? There was the whiteness, and then I fell...it was so real. I even remember the landing—it hurt! And then there was the thing with Mary...why was she crying? There was that thing around her neck, it almost looked like a...* Dan paused in middle of his thought. "A rope!"

5

Mary was sitting on top of the tree limb with the rope securely tightened around her neck. Her nose was completely plugged up from crying. She hadn't been able to stop crying all day. It was nearly 4 P.M. now, and Mary knew her parents would be home soon. *It's now or never,* she thought. She let out a big sigh and heard her voice falter when she did.

Cautiously, she stood up and tried to balance on the limb —she was shaky and very weak. After a few moments she managed to gain her balance on the branch, and she was standing up. *I'm so sorry, Dan. I tried to be strong like you said...but I just couldn't do it. Please forgi...* Her thought was interrupted by a car that had just turned the corner—it was her parents.

The sudden movement she had made to look up at the car

had thrown her off balance. She stumbled and tried to reach down to the branch with her hands, but it was no good. She was too weak to maintain any level of balance with the branch wobbling so much. Mary flipped head over heels off the branch and fell towards the ground. As she fell, time seemed to slow down to almost nothing. She felt her heartbeat, which had been racing for the last twenty minutes, slow to a resting pace. She was still sad, of course, but in this final moment of her life, which seemed to pass in slow motion as she fell, she almost felt—at peace.

She was about to reach the end of the rope now. *I'm so sorry, everyone,* she thought. *Mom, Dad, Dan... I will miss you all very much. I love you.* Time sped up to normal speed again, and Mary had only a fraction of a second to see what was coming. The last thing Mary heard wasn't the ear-splitting scream of her mother, but something much more gut-wrenching. Mary heard Dan, heard him calling her name. *Dan?* she thought.

About five feet from the ground, the rope went taut, stopping her fall with a ghastly *crack*—her neck broke. Mary Stevenson's lifeless body swayed back and forth from the tree branch—the same one that used to provide her with hours of fun on the tire swing.

"MARY!" screamed Helen. "Oh my god, MARY! Jack, stop the car!"

Jack pulled the car into their driveway, nearly taking out their mailbox.

"Oh, fuck," said Jack. "No, no, no...please no!"

"Mary!" screamed Helen again as she bolted from the car and ran towards her daughter. She was just able to reach Mary's feet, which were still swaying slightly. "Mary, please answer me. Please, Mary!" Helen's cries went unheard, and Jack had known as soon as he ran up to her—Mary was dead.

Helen fell to her knees and was crying uncontrollably. Not only had she just lost her daughter to suicide, she had been forced to witness it firsthand. "Oh, Mary!" she shouted. "Why, Mary? Whyyyyy?" Tears streamed down her face, making her makeup streak down from her eyes. Jack tried to comfort her, but he knew there was little comfort to be had.

"Jack, get your saw, cut her down!" pleaded Helen. "Please get her down!" Jack ran to the garage and found his hacksaw, as well as his step ladder. He made it back to Helen, who was still inconsolable. By this time, a few neighbors had come out and noticed Mary hanging from the tree. They all gasped and couldn't seem to help gawking at the sight—Helen noticed.

"Do you mind!" Helen shouted. "Stop staring and go away! She was crying so hard now that her last few words were nearly inaudible, but the gawkers seemed to understand. They retreated back into their homes. Jack set up the ladder and stepped onto it.

At the top step, he carefully grabbed the rope, and before cutting it, he told Helen she'd have to brace Mary's legs. Helen was hesitant but managed to do so. Jack began cutting, and a few seconds later, Mary was lying on the ground, free of the rope.

"I'm not giving up on you, Mary," said Jack as he kneeled down and checked her vitals. "Damn, nothing. I'm going to try to resuscitate her, Helen. Can you call 911?"

Helen was still crying inconsolably. She stared blankly at Jack as he began to perform CPR on their daughter's lifeless body.

"Come on! Come back to me, Mary, please." Jack continued his attempts at resuscitation, but deep down he knew her neck was broken and that she was gone.

A few moments passed and Jack did one more vitals check

—there was nothing. He embraced Mary, crying heavily himself. Jack pulled Helen closer to him and did his best to comfort her as well. He was sad, but also angry. His daughter was gone, and there was nothing he could do about it. *Oh, Mary, what happened? Why didn't you tell us something was wrong?* Jack thought. They remained in their embrace, wanting to feel whole again, but knowing their family would never be again.

6

James had just finished transferring all the existing protocols for Destiny onto the new server when Dr. Wilkes came downstairs. "James, I need to talk to you," said Dr. Wilkes. "Do you have time? It's pretty important." James looked at his watch, and then back to Dr. Wilkes.

"Yeah, I should be okay. I just finished transferring the protocols to the new server. Everything seemed to go smoothly. What's going on?" Dr. Wilkes frowned at what James had just said.

"You what? We weren't ready to do the transfer yet, James. I thought I told you to wait until we were ready with phase three." Dr. Wilkes felt himself getting frustrated and tried to calm down.

"I... I'm sorry sir, I didn't know that was the plan...I was never told about it anyway. What happened? Oh...oh no, was a primary protocol still active?" Dr. Wilkes put his finger to his nose.

"Yes, yes, it was still active. I certainly didn't give authorization to transfer any new protocols yet, so I'm going to assume this won't happen again?"

"N—no, sir," stammered James. "It definitely won't. I forgot all about the special protocol that was approved and didn't think to check if it was still active before initiating the transfer. I'll make sure to check moving forward." Dr. Wilkes seemed satisfied with this answer. He nodded and began to walk back upstairs.

"Keep working on phase three, James. Also, I sure hope you know what you're doing with that A.I. talk...it'll be both our asses if not." James heard the doctor's footsteps trail off up the stairs, and then the basement door closed. *I sure hope I know what I'm doing with it too,* thought James. *A.I. technology is bleeding edge, and I was just throwing out the idea because it sounded like a good one at the time. Gosh, I hope I didn't screw myself on this one.*

CHAPTER VI

1

THE REST OF AUGUST WENT BY WITHOUT ANY DREAMS FOR
Dan. The week following his little incident at Denny's, Dr.
Walsh had started him on the experimental treatment, and it
seemed to be helping. On a few occasions Dan and his parents
had gone out to eat, and everything went great. No dreams,
no hallucinations, nothing. It was September 16th, a Saturday,
and Dan was slowly getting ready for the day. His parents had
said they would be there by 10 AM to take him out for breakfast. It was 9:45 when Dan managed to finish getting dressed
and went out to the lobby to wait for his parents.

As Dan walked out into the massive lobby, Rebecca
greeted him as always. "Good morning, Dan!" she said,
sounding way too happy, as usual.

"Morning, Rebecca. How are you?" asked Dan, trying to
be polite. Rebecca smiled at Dan.

"I'm great! Thanks for asking. Excited to see your parents
today?" Dan nodded, and walked across the lobby and sat in

one of the chairs tucked away in the corner. It was the same corner he had sat in the first day he came to Clearwater. *Man, that seems like such a long time ago,* he thought. Dan sat back in the chair and became lost in his thoughts. *How long have I been at Clearwater? It's so hard to tell with all the dreams and hallucinations.* The thought was interrupted by a clinking sound coming from somewhere above him. He looked up and saw it was the giant chandelier in the center of the lobby—it had started to wobble. Dan felt his heart start to beat faster.

"No!" he shouted, which made Rebecca startle at her desk.

"Dan? Are you okay?" she asked. Dan looked over at her, not realizing he had said that aloud.

"Ye...yeah, I'm fine. Sorry about that."

Rebecca smiled again and then went back to typing on her computer. Dan looked up at the chandelier again, expecting it to be wobbling, but it had stopped. *Thank god,* he thought. The moment this thought crossed his mind, the lobby went silent. Dan felt a lump form in his throat. Absolutely no sound could be heard—no air from the air conditioning, no typing from Rebecca, no distant footsteps...nothing. *What the hell is going on?* Dan asked himself. A faint clinking noise started, and Dan noticed it was once again coming from above him. He hesitated, and then looked up at the chandelier—it was wobbling again.

"Please...not now. I just want to be with my parents!" Dan was aware he had said this aloud, but Rebecca didn't say anything this time because she was no longer there. Dan looked over at the desk and saw it was empty. "Hello?" asked Dan. No reply. The clinking intensified, filling the silent lobby with a dreadful noise.

"Stop! Please stop it!" Dan got up from the chair and ran

out of the lobby. Just as he was about to go through the door to the hallway, all the clinking stopped. Dan turned back towards the lobby and everything went dark. He felt something cold brush across his right shoulder, and then he was shoved forward.

Dan fell, and as he tried to put his arms out to break his fall, the marble floor vanished, and he fell into the darkness. "Ahhhhhh! Please help me! Anybody!" cried Dan, continuing to fall in complete darkness. Dan noticed his cries hadn't made any sound. "Hello? Help!" he shouted at the top of his lungs, but there was nothing. It was nothing but a black emptiness. There was a complete absence of all physical sensations. Dan wasn't even sure if he was falling anymore. It was as if everything around him had ceased to exist. *This is it, isn't it?* he thought. *This is how I die...forever existing in a black void.*

After what seemed like an eternity, it started to become lighter, and he could see a town below him—he was falling from the sky. Dan thought the layout looked familiar, and as he got closer, he realized it was Redfield. His heart was racing, and as he got closer and closer to the ground, his descent slowed, and an inch off the ground he stopped.

A moment later, he landed on the sidewalk. *Ugh, what a fall...* Dan got to his feet and immediately recognized where he was. He was only a block north of Mary's house! "Mary!" cried Dan. "Oh please be the right year. Please, please!" Dan turned the corner and ran down the street towards her house. He had just reached the corner when he saw her—she was standing on a branch of the oak tree.

2

James had been hard at work the past month, sometimes

working sixteen-hour days, and it finally paid off. He had finished developing the A.I. that would carry out the rest of Project Destiny and was working on the last bit of code for phase three. The A.I. was online and seemed to be fully functional. James had programmed it to write simple functions and do basic calculations as well. "I think this might actually work," he said, sounding rather impressed with himself. *The true test*, he thought, will be when the A.I. is given the green light to execute the test protocols of phase three.

A few hours later, James hit a final keystroke and sat back in his chair. "It's done," he said, letting out a great sigh of relief. He leaned forward and ran the compile command to get it ready for execution.

"Good evening, James," said Dr. Wilkes, who had just stepped off the bottom stair. James startled a bit as he hadn't heard the doctor come down the stairs.

"Hello, sir. Just finished writing phase three," said James. "2,605,302 lines of code. It's a hefty piece of code, I must say." James knew this would mean little to Dr. Wilkes, but he felt like sharing it anyway—he was certainly proud of it.

"Most impressive, James, most impressive indeed. How long until the A.I. can begin executing the protocols? We're right up to the end of our deadline, and I have a call with my boss tomorrow morning."

James thought about the question for a moment and then replied. "Well, I think it's ready, but I want to do a trial run in a sandbox environment prior to releasing it to our live server."

Dr. Wilkes had an odd expression on his face. "What kind of environment? A sandbox? I don't follow."

James chuckled at the doctor's confusion. "Oh, right. Sorry, it's a term for a test environment that you can play around with new features and such before releasing them into a live environment. It helps eliminate major bugs early."

Dr. Wilkes nodded and pointed to his head. "Ahh, yes, of course. I swear those technical terms getting weirder and weirder as I get older. Anyway, yes, I think that sounds like a good plan, James. Can you do that tonight and be ready for a live release tomorrow? Assuming things go well in the sandbox, of course." His face showed that he still felt odd saying such a sentence.

"Sure thing, sir. I was just compiling all of the code when you came down here." James looked over at the console and saw it had compiled successfully. "Oh, hey, it just finished compiling. Looks like we're ready for a test, sir. Care to stay and watch?"

Dr. Wilkes thought for a moment, and then remembered what his boss had said the last time he was here. *I guess I should show James level five.*

"Listen, James...there's something you need to see."

"Sir?" asked James, who now had a very confused look on his face. Dr. Wilkes handed James a new badge. Below his picture it read:

Professor James Kern
Senior Software Developer
Level 5 Clearance (TS)

"Level 5? Sir, there is no level 5."

Dr. Wilkes smirked, and turned to walk down the hall of the basement (level 4).

"Come with me, James." James quickly got up from his chair and ran to catch up with the doctor.

"Where are we going?" asked James, who was now right

behind Dr. Wilkes. Dr. Wilkes stopped, seemingly at a random point in the hallway.

"There are things going on at this facility that you don't know about, James. I wanted you to know, but it just wasn't an option. Remember what you were told at the beginning?"

James was confused by the question but answered anyway. "Well yeah, I was told the project would involve multiple levels of test protocols, split into phases, and to be conducted in a computer-generated environment for simulation purposes. Didn't really make much sense to me, but I was told my security clearance wasn't high enough to know the full details. Frankly, sir...I didn't even know I had security clearance."

"Right," said Dr. Wilkes. "I'm sorry, James, but that was a lie. I mean, some of that is true, yes...we really did do those things, but we've also been having you do a lot more." Dr. Wilkes sighed, and put his hand on James's shoulder. "I'm so sorry I kept this from you, but I really had no choice."

"Dr. Wil—"

James was interrupted by Dr. Wilkes, who had put his hand up. "You'll see, just wait." He touched the hallway wall in four places, which appeared to create an illuminated copy of his fingerprints, and then placed his hand in the center of the four points. A computerized voice spoke, which startled James: "Level 5 access granted. Welcome, Dr. Wilkes."

Just to the right of where Dr. Wilkes had placed his hand, the wall seemed to split in two and slowly opened to a small set of stairs, which led to another very long hallway.

"Holy shit," said James, gawking at the size of the hallway. "What is this place?" The two of them walked down the steps, and behind them the doorway closed automatically. The hallway was lined with, what James assumed was some sort of reinforced concrete. It looked like it was built to survive a nuclear attack.

"This," said Dr. Wilkes, "is what we're really doing. I'm sure I don't have to remind you, James...but what you're about to see and hear is classified top secret. You can't tell anyone, not even your staff. Understood?"

James nodded. "Of course, sir."

Dr. Wilkes led James down the long, dark hallway. At the end of it was a single, blood red door with a light over it. James felt a coldness wash over him, and it made him shiver. Dr. Wilkes stopped in front of the door and turned to James.

"Okay, James...this is it. I can't promise that you're ready for this, but it's important that you know the truth."

"I'm ready," said James. Dr. Wilkes nodded and put his finger on the scanner, which turned green, and the lock on the door clicked open. He pulled open the door, and what James saw horrified him. *Oh my god*, he thought. *Oh my god, I knew it. Somehow, I always knew it.* James put a hand over his mouth.

"S... sir, is....is that..."

"Yes, it is, James. Step inside; I want you to see it all."

James shook his head. "No, I... I can't sir. This isn't right! I can't do this anymore!"

Dr. Wilkes pulled James back out of the room and closed the door.

"Listen, James...that's not an option for you, I'm afraid. Like I said, I honestly wish you would have been informed from the beginning, but it was out of my hands. If you leave now, they will find you and put you in jail. Your only choice is to finish the job and help us cover it up."

James slammed his hand against the red door. "Damn it!" he shouted. "Why'd you get me involved in this, sir? I didn't want this...I was told we were doing simulations. Not...this. Do you realize what we've done?"

"I understand that you're upset, James, I really do. And yes, I realize what we've done...but it was for science. Look what we've accomplished! And with the rest of phase three, we'll make history. I know it's hard, James, but please...help us finish it."

He sighed and looked directly into the eyes of Dr. Wilkes. "Fine...I'll help finish it, but I want you to know I'm one hundred percent against what this facility is doing. It's not right." He walked away and went back towards the entrance.

"Thank you, James," said Dr. Wilkes. "Oh, you just scan your badge and use your left thumb print." He had noticed that James was confused by the door.

"Th... thanks," said James, feeling embarrassed. He scanned his badge and fingerprint, and the door opened. "Have a good day, professor James," said the computer. The date was September 15th, 2000. The days that followed would turn out to be some of the worst days in Professor James's life. He would never forget them, no matter how much he would want to.

3

As soon as Dr. Wilkes had left the basement, James began his tests of the A.I. system. He started with simple test protocols. The speed at which the new system was able to perform was unparalleled. James documented the results and couldn't believe what he was seeing. *Incredible*, he thought. The A.I. was able to run fifty tests in the time the previous server could do five. Quantum computing combined with the advancement in A.I. would be sure to change history.

James loaded up another round of testing; these protocols were significantly more complex, but still nothing compared to what Project Destiny would require. Like with the previous tests, the system's performance was impeccable. James was now confident in the ability of the system and contemplated running a test protocol from Destiny. He wanted to see just how much this new setup could handle. *I'd better not*, he thought. *If Dr. Wilkes found out about it, I'd be in deep trouble.*

The temptation, however, was just too much for James. He checked to see what was currently in testing on the primary server, and saw it was nothing major, which was good. James pulled up the console and copied a protocol from the primary to his sandbox and prepared the A.I. to execute. James yawned and looked at his watch. "Phew, midnight already? Man, I'm tired," he said. "I'll run this test overnight."

James was tired, more tired than he had realized. In his sleep-deprived state, he had mistakenly loaded the A.I. system while in the primary server's terminal instead of the sandbox. Since the name of the protocol was the same across the systems, James never noticed. He typed out the execute command, and double checked the name of the protocol. *Don't want to mess this up*, he thought. *Looks good.* He hit enter, and the A.I. was live—it was September 16th.

4

Dan stood on the corner across from Mary's house, in complete shock. He rubbed his eyes several times to make sure it was real. "Mary?" he shouted. "Mary, what are you doing?" There was no response, at least none that Dan noticed. He watched as she carefully positioned herself and was looking down at the ground. The horror struck Dan when he realized what was happening. *Oh, no, this is what I saw when I fell through the white emptiness. She has a rope around her neck!* "Mary!" shouted Dan. "Mary, stop! Don't do it!"

He broke out in a dead sprint towards the tree, exerting every bit of energy he had. Dan noticed, however, that he was barely moving. It felt as if he were running through sand. "Come on!" he shouted, trying even harder to get to Mary. As he ran across the street, he noticed a car just turning the corner—it was the Stevenson's. That was when he heard the crack—it was Mary. He turned back to face her, but it was too late. She had fallen or dropped from the branch and all Dan saw was her lifeless body swaying from the tree.

"Noooooo! MARY!" he shouted. Dan ran towards her body, tears beginning to fall from his eyes. "Please, no ...please let it be a dream. Please!" Dan had nearly reached Mary when he froze—he couldn't move. *What the hell*, he thought. Before Dan could figure out what was going on, he was violently pulled backwards away from the house. "No! Stop it!" yelled Dan. The force kept pulling him backwards, farther and farther, faster and faster. It became clear that this probably wasn't going to end well. Dan felt something cold touch his shoulder and then all movement stopped.

Dan tried to look around, but his eyes were still wet with tears, making it hard to see. *Oh, Mary, why'd you do it? I told you I'd be back! I'm so sorry that I left you.* He fell to his knees and started to sob uncontrollably. He was young, but he knew that he had loved Mary Stevenson, he knew it very well. *The look on her face*, he thought. *It was awful...I don't think I'll ever forget it.* Dan hadn't noticed initially, but he now realized that he had fallen down in the snow. *Snow? It's not winter.* He wiped the tears from his eyes, and he could see that the area was familiar to him. The weather had changed drastically. Dan shivered as he looked around, trying to figure out what happened. *I've been here before, I'm sure of it.* It only took a moment for him to realize why it was familiar. *This is where I was when I first came to 1965! Actually, it looks exactly like it did. Am I back?*

Dan took off in another sprint towards Mary's house. "Please be real, please be real," he repeated, over and over again. He was out of breath and freezing by the time he reached the corner, and as he came to a stop, he saw her—Mary, alive, running outside to jump in the snowbank. Like before, Dan stood there, staring at her like a creep. "I...I don't believe it...I'm back!" *But can she see me? The last time this happened, Mary had said she could only kind of see me. I guess there's only one way to find out.*

Dan took a few steps forward and accidentally stepped on a soda can that was hidden underneath the snow. It made a muffled but noticeable crunching sound. Dan looked down at the can, and then back up toward the house—Mary was gone. *What? Where'd she...*something brushed against Dan's shoulder. He turned around and in front of him was Mary, but something was terribly wrong.

"You...you left me!" shrieked Mary, but her voice came out in a raspy croak due to the rope crushing her neck. Her face was ghastly white, and Dan noticed a bruise all around her neck. *The rope,* he thought. She raised her hand and pointed at him. Dan noticed her skin was covered in dark spots, and she smelled of decaying, rotten flesh.

Dan took a couple steps back, still unable to believe that this was happening. Mary stepper closer, her eyes locked on him.

"Ma...Mary, please, I didn't mean to leave you! We talked about this before it happened, I don't have contro—"

"Liar!" yelled Mary, cutting Dan off mid-sentence. Dan

fell backwards and landed in the snow. Mary stormed towards him, and Dan saw that her eyes had rolled back in her head and all he could see was white. "You aren't welcome here! Get out!" The voice Dan heard was not Mary's; it was that of a demon. She dove at him, and as she did, Dan closed his eyes and covered his face.

"Mary, no!" A bright flash of white consumed him, and then everything was gone. Again, Dan was forced backwards, and then he landed—he was back in the lobby of Clearwater.

What the fuck? Dan's pulse was elevated, and he noticed he had broken out in a cold sweat. *What the hell was that? Was that real? Oh, Mary, I hope you're okay...this isn't fair!* Dan fell off his chair and landed on the marble floor—he started to cry again.

Rebecca had heard him and called out to Dan. "Everything okay, Dan?" Dan looked up at Rebecca, and to his horror saw that her eyes, too, were rolled back in her head, and all he could see of them were the whites.

"Ahh! No, this isn't happening!" shouted Dan. "You aren't real!" He rubbed his eyes and looked back up at her. She gave Dan a concerned look, but her eyes were normal.

"Are you sure you're okay, Dan? How long have you been back out here anyway?" *Back out? What is she talking about? Did someone actually notice I was gone? That happening did seem way more realistic than the previous ones.*

"What do you mean, back out here?" asked Dan. "Did I leave a bit ago?" Rebecca laughed and gave him a *are you messing with me* look.

"I didn't notice you leave; not sure how, though, you walk right past me to go to your room. You were only gone for maybe thirty seconds. Where'd you go, anyway?"

Dan didn't have a good answer. He knew all too well he couldn't tell her the truth.

"I…uh, had to use the bathroom. I hurried so I wouldn't miss my parents getting here." Rebecca nodded and it seemed like she had found the answer plausible.

"Good call," she said. "They should be here any minute."

Rebecca's timing was almost spot on. Not more than a few minutes later, Dan saw his parents' car pull into the Clearwater parking lot. Dan jumped out of the chair and ran to meet them.

"Hey, guys! It's great to see you again." Dan hugged his mom, followed by his dad.

"Hey there, bud," said Henry, "how's it going? Ready for some breakfast?"

Dan nodded. "Absolutely! Let's go! Come on, guys!" He took hold of both their hands and ran to the car. As they left the parking lot, Patricia turned around and asked Dan where he wanted to go for breakfast. Dan was taken aback a bit by the question.

"What do you mean, Mom? Denny's of course. I hope they still have all-you-can-eat pancakes." He smiled but felt something off about the situation.

"Denny's? I don't think we've taken you there," said Patricia. "I've heard their food is good, though, so we can definitely try it." She turned back towards the front and smiled at Henry. The feeling Dan had felt before was now much worse. *What's going on?* he thought. *We were just there a few weeks ago.*

"He…hey, Mom? Are you feeling okay?"

Patricia turned around and smiled at Dan. "I'm great, sweetie! Looking forward to spending time with you." She turned back to face the front again. She pulled down the visor and opened the mirror to check her makeup. Dan looked up at her in the mirror and saw her eyes roll back into her head as a deathly grin formed on her face.

"Ahhhh! What the fuck?" shouted Dan. Henry slammed on the brakes and almost lost control of the car before bringing it to a complete stop. Both Patricia and Henry turned around and looked at Dan. He noticed his mom's eyes were normal again.

"Oh my gosh, Dan, sweetie...are you okay?" asked Patricia. "You scared me to death." *You and me both,* thought Dan.

"I... I'm fine, Mom. Sorry, just had a bad daydream is all." Both his parents looked at each other with concerned looks but turned back around and Henry started to drive again. A moment later Henry spoke.

"Not going to try the waffles at Denny's? I thought they were your favorite." Dan felt yet another lump form in his throat. *Waffles? Dad knows all too well they aren't my favorite. I like them, sure, but I'd take pancakes over waffles any day. Wait, this happened before...when I went home with them the first time or thought I did anyway. And then it happened again when they first took me out for breakfast.* Dan was brought out of his thoughts by the sudden screech of the car's brakes, followed by a *thud.*

"What was that?" asked Dan. "Did we hit something?" Dan turned around and looked behind the car. He saw something lying in the road but couldn't quite make out what it was. Henry pulled the car to the side of the road and stepped outside. Dan got out and joined Henry, ignoring Patricia's insistence that he stay in the car. As they approached what was on the road, Dan froze.

"Aww, dang," said Henry, "looks like someone's cat." Henry looked back at Dan, who had a horrified expression on his face. "What's wrong, Dan?"

"Da... Dad? That's not a cat," said Dan.

Lying on the road was a badly misshapen body that resembled a young girl. The body was severely mangled, the girl's blonde hair covered in blood and her neck clearly broken. Dan thought the girl looked like Mary, but he knew that was impossible. He felt the hair on his neck stand up, and then the body twitched. Dan heard himself scream, and he backed up towards the car. The girl sat up and turned around to look at Dan—it *was* Mary.

"Dan? Please help me, Dan, it hurts so much...why did you leave?" Mary's voice was just as sweet as he remembered it. No sign of the demonic voice, or the rolled back eyes. Still, Dan couldn't speak. He tried to respond, but nothing came out. Just when he thought he could, Mary let out an ear-piercing scream, which caused Dan's vision to blur and then go dark. Another scream came to Dan's ears, followed by a *snap*. Dan's vision returned and he landed with a *thud*—he was sitting at a table at Denny's.

PART THREE

THE REALITY

CHAPTER I

1

It was just after 6 A.M. when James arrived at his office. He wasn't normally in this early, especially after such a late night, but he wanted to check on the A.I. system. As he got logged into his computer, he pulled up the server logs from the test system and noticed something wasn't right. The log file from last night was empty. *No logs? Well, that can't be right,* thought James. He ran a few terminal commands and couldn't find any processes running for the A.I. James sat back in his chair and thought back to last night, and then it hit him. *Oh, no...* he thought. James feared he knew what had happened. He scrambled to open a terminal on the primary system and pulled up the logs—he was right. He had inadvertently executed the A.I. on the live primary system and began running test protocols. James looked through the logs, and to his relief, it looked like the tests went okay.

As he continued to look through the log files, he noticed some hidden logs that had been written earlier this morning.

That's odd, he thought. *The system isn't supposed to ever write the logs as hidden.* James shrugged and just figured it was due to the A.I. *It could have been much worse. I'd better make sure to remove the A.I. from the primary for now, so when Dr. Wilkes comes in, I can have him watch me install it later this morning.*

James started by powering up the old process to take over again for the A.I. once it was shut down. He entered a few commands into the terminal to stop the A.I. protocols, but the terminal kept saying "Access denied." *That's not possible*, he thought. *I wrote them myself.* James tried again, this time with root privileges enabled, but still received the same error. He was becoming more and more concerned now, but he was running out of time. Dr. Wilkes would be in shortly. *I guess I can tell him I installed it right away this morning so everything would be ready to go.* He thought that sounded plausible enough.

Dr. Wilkes came into the facility at 7:30 that morning. His first stop was James's office, as he was anxious to find out how the testing went.

"Good morning, James. How'd last night go?" asked Dr. Wilkes. James hesitated, but not long enough for Wilkes to notice.

"It went well, sir. I had the A.I. run a few of the more complex protocols overnight, and it looks like they went well."

Dr. Wilkes seemed pleased. "Good, very good. Are you ready to have the A.I. begin running phase three? I have my conference call with my boss in thirty minutes, and I'd like to be able to tell him we're ready."

"Uh, yes, sir. I actually went ahead and installed it on to the primary server this morning and had it execute some of the test protocols. I just need to copy over phase three to the primary server, and the A.I. will be ready to go." James thought he sounded convincing enough, but he was certainly nervous. This was the only time he'd ever lied to Dr. Wilkes and hoped it would be the last.

"That was good thinking, James. Perhaps a little risky, but I believe that comes with the territory. I will make sure my boss knows about all the extra time you've put into this. Nicely done. Go ahead and copy over the phase three protocols to the primary, but don't have the A.I. execute them yet. I need to get confirmation from my boss first. It sounds like he has updates on the investigation that has been going on. I'll keep you posted."

James nodded, and Dr. Wilkes left to go to his office. Once he had left, James began the copy of the phase three protocols. Transferring the 1.5TB of protocols would take time, so he wanted to get it started as soon as possible. In the meantime, James decided to take a closer look at the hidden log files issue. He compared the normal log files with the hidden ones and found that the first hidden file was written just after the last regular one. *Odd*, he thought. *It's almost as if the A.I. finished the one test I assigned it, and then continued on running its own tests...but that's not possible.* James would soon find out that it was indeed very possible.

2

Dr. Wilkes sat in his office, sweat rolling off of his forehead. He was nervous about the call, to say the least. *I hope the boss has good news regarding the investigation; otherwise, we're pretty screwed*, he thought. At exactly 8 that morning, his phone rang; it was his boss.

"Good morning, sir, how's it goi—"

Dr. Wilkes was interrupted by a shrieking voice on the call.

"We don't have time for salutations, Robert. I'm sorry I

couldn't tell you sooner, but it's bad. The investigation is back in full swing, and they have everything. Any pull I had before is now gone, I'm afraid. They're coming for you, Robert. They're coming for the facility." Dr. Wilkes sat on the phone, unable to say a word. *Coming for me? Oh, fuck*, he thought.

"Wha...what should I do?" he asked. "I can't go to prison, sir. I'd never make it." There was a sigh on the other end.

"Listen, Robert, I don't mean to scare you here, just being real with you. If these people who are coming for you find you, prison will be the least of your worries. They're bad people, Robert, very bad people."

"So, what do I do?" asked Robert, his voice was trembling now.

"Erase what you can and get out. If James has phase three ready, have the A.I. begin executing the protocols. But don't spend too much time on it...just get it going and get your asses out of there. Seriously, Robert, these people don't mess around. I've got to go—"

"Wait, sir," said Robert. "How long do we have? Do you know?" There was a moment of silence on the call, which felt like an eternity to Dr. Wilkes, and then finally his boss responded.

"Not long, Robert. Luckily, the exact location of your facility is pretty tough to come by, but they'll find it. I would say 2–3 hours at most. More than likely you're looking at an hour. I'm sorry, Robert. I tried to get in touch with you as soon as I found out, but I needed to make sure I had a secure line. I have to go. Protect yourself and the project at all costs. Good luck." The line went dead.

3

"Everything okay, Dan?" asked Patricia. "You haven't even touched your pancakes." Dan was still disoriented from whatever had just happened.

"Uh, yeah...I'm fine. Did you guys notice anything weird just a minute ago?" Patricia and Henry both looked at each other and shrugged.

"I didn't see anything," said Henry. "You've just been kind of sitting there playing with your pancakes. Not as good as waffles, huh?" Dan didn't know what was going on. It seemed like his parents noticed nothing while he was having the dream, or whatever it was. *Also,* he thought, *why do they insist that I like waffles so much, and that we haven't been to Denny's before? It's like they're not my real parents or something.* His thoughts were interrupted as the table they were at began to shake. The plates and silverware began to rattle against each other, making a loud clanging noise. Dan slid his chair back away from the table and stood up.

"What's going on, Dan?" asked his mother. "Is something wrong?"

Dan looked over at her, confused by her lack of concern. "Don't you guys feel that? The table is shaking." He could tell almost immediately by her expression that she couldn't feel it.

"What are you talking about, Dan? The table isn't shaking. Are you sure you're feeling okay? Maybe we should head back," said Patricia. Before Dan could respond, he noticed the entire restaurant began to shake. The shaking intensified, and plates on the table began to fall off onto the floor and shatter. Dan looked around at the other people in the restaurant, only to find that they too were carrying on with their meals as if nothing was out of place. *What's wrong with me? Maybe I really am crazy.* He was finding it harder and harder to stay upright, yet nobody else seemed to even notice. Dan's vision started to become blurry, a telltale sign that what was to come wasn't going to be good.

A moment later, everything around him seemed to stretch out away from him, making it seem tiny. *Oh, shit...what now?* Dan had become accustomed to the blurry vision and things wobbling or shaking, but other than those things, the rest seemed to be random as far as how he entered dream states. The area around him stretched out farther and farther until he could barely see his parents.

"Mom! Dad!" shouted Dan, but he knew they wouldn't be able to hear him. His vision went black, and Dan heard that awful, ear-piercing scream again from Mary and then his vision returned. As he looked around, he noticed he was in a very familiar place—it was Main Street, 1965. *What am I doing here?* Thought Dan. *Wait, if this is 1965 again, maybe Mary is okay! Maybe I can save her!* Dan looked around and noticed that everything seemed to be the same as he remembered. The long, box-like cars covered in chrome and white wall tires, the men in nice suits, and the women in their dresses. He walked south on Main Street until he reached Leo's on the corner of 6th Ave. *Well, this looks the same, too. Maybe I'll check it out again since I didn't have any food at Denny's.*

The moment Dan walked in, he was struck with a horrifying sight. He ducked down behind the front counter, his heart beating fiercely in his chest. *What the hell is going on?* He peeked out from behind the counter, which luckily was empty at the time, and looked over at the booth against the far wall. Sitting in the booth, having pancakes of course, was himself. *Is, is this really happening? That must be me from when I first came here, but how is that possible?* Dan didn't know the answer, and he wasn't sure if he really wanted to know.

He tiptoed his way back out of Leo's and was back on to

Main Street. He contemplated what to do next but wasn't having much luck. *Should I go to Mary's? What if things don't go the same way they did? After all, this isn't the exact time we met before...that was when I...* the thought left him. Across the street to the west something caught his eye. It was, to Dan, what looked like a crack in the world. It was about three feet high, and a few inches wide. All around it was blurry, like it wasn't quite finished.

Dan approached it cautiously, and as he got closer, he began to notice what was inside the crack—it was an entirely different world. Truthfully, it was the same world, but a much different time. Dan could see buildings he had never seen before, even in his time of the year 2000. *Strange,* thought Dan. *It's like a crack in reality, or whatever this is...a dream? I'm starting to think there's much more to these happenings than I first thought.*

The crack started to increase in size. It was now taller than Dan and growing in width as well. He could now see more details on the other side. *Should I go through it? What about Mary? Also, if I go through it, will I be able to get back?* Dan had a ton of questions, but no time to answer any of them.

The crack in time began to emit rays of light, similar to that of the sun. "Oh, shit," said Dan as he felt a sudden pull against him coming from the crack. "No, I... I don't want to! Not like this!" The pull against him increased in strength. He tried to fight it, and at first, he was able to. He grabbed on to a nearby streetlight and held on for dear life. The pull increased again, and the pole started to bend. *It's going to happen,* he thought. *I won't be able to hold on much longer.* As soon as Dan finished this last thought, the pull increased once more, and the pole snapped. Dan flew backwards and went through the crack in time and fell. The pole that had snapped came through the crack with Dan and struck him on the head, knocking him unconscious.

4

Dan woke up about an hour later with a killer headache. He got up slowly and looked around, realizing he didn't recognize anything around him. *Where am I? This definitely isn't Redfield...it's way too big for that. And it also doesn't look like the year 2000.* He looked to his left and saw a large sign that said *Time Square East. Odd,* he thought. *Isn't Time Square in New York? This place looks big, but certainly not big enough to be New York.* Dan heard an odd noise from behind him; it sounded like a muffled voice coming through a speaker. He turned around and saw a Starbucks with a line of cars going through a tunnel to the right of it. *A Starbucks? I've heard of them but never seen one in person. Might as well check it out...maybe I'll like it.*

As Dan walked through the glass front door, he was greeted by a robust aroma of coffee. Dan had taken a liking to coffee at an early age. His stepdad had always been a coffee drinker and had offered Dan his first sip of coffee when he was eight. Ever since then, Dan had drank coffee any chance he got. The aroma inside of Starbucks was quite pleasant to him. As he walked through the entrance, he saw tables to the left and right of him. There were people sitting at them, all with laptops open. *Those look super expensive,* he thought. *Those are way nicer than any laptop I've ever seen. This definitely can't be 2000.* A few of them gave Dan strange looks, and he quickly looked away.

As he continued onward, to his left was a wall of bags, which Dan figured out were full of coffee beans. Also, on the same wall were cups and containers for coffee. Dan thought he probably looked rather odd by gawking at everything as if he'd never seen a Starbucks before, but the truth was he hadn't. He finally made it up to the front counter and was greeted by a bubbly girl who looked to be eighteen or nineteen. Dan wasn't great at guessing people's ages.

"Hi there," she said, "what can I get started for you?" Dan didn't have the slightest idea what he wanted, nor what he could even get. He looked down at her name tag and saw that it said Mary. *Of course,* he thought. *Of course her name is Mary.* For a split second he saw the *M* in her name wobble, but then it stopped.

"Ah!" Dan jumped backwards.

"Are you okay?" asked Mary. "Can I help you pick something?" Dan felt his face grow hot and figured he was turned bright red.

"S... sorry," Dan managed to say. "I thought I saw something. Uhh, can I just get a cup of coffee? Sorry, this is my first time here."

Mary smiled. "First time, huh? Well, welcome to Starbucks. What brings you to Fargo? You seem pretty young to be here on your own. Vacation with family?" *Fargo...that's where Clearwater is, or was?* Dan didn't honestly know if Clearwater even existed anymore. *I wonder what year it is. I can't just ask her. She'll think I'm crazy.*

"Yeah, I'm on a vacation with family. Could I just get a cup of coffee?"

"Sure thing! What size?"

"Uh, might as well make it a large." As Dan finished his reply, he realized he didn't have any money. "Oh, actually...Mary," he said, noticeably uncomfortable with saying her name. "I just remembered I didn't bring any money with me, so never mind my order." She looked at him with understanding eyes; they reminded Dan of his Mary.

"Oh, that's okay," she said. "Tell you what, your first one is on me. I'll get the coffee for you. Go ahead and wait over there." She pointed to her left, which was the far wall. Dan thanked her and walked to where she had told him to wait. He noticed there was a rack of newspapers against the wall. *Perfect. I can find out the year from these.* He picked up one of them, *The New York Times,* and looked for the date. Just underneath the title of the paper Dan saw the date. It was Monday, September 16th, 2019. *2019? The future...*Dan heard the girl behind him call out that his coffee was ready. He took the coffee and thanked her again, then went to sit down. *Why am I here?* Dan couldn't help but ask himself the question. The coffee was very good, and for the first time in quite a while, he felt relaxed.

5

Dr. Wilkes stormed out of his office and down the hall to find James. He had turned the corner too fast and knocked over one of the scientists.

"Sorry," muttered Wilkes, "in a hurry. Must get out."

"What was that, sir?" asked the scientist, but Dr. Wilkes was already out of earshot. A few seconds later he was in James's office, looking like a complete mess. James had been nearly scared to death by the abrupt entrance of his boss.

"Uhh, sir? What's going on?" asked James, inviting Dr. Wilkes to sit down, which he declined.

"No time to sit, James. We have to go...now! Come on, we need to start purging all of the non-essential protocols. This isn't a drill."

"What? Purging...but why?" Dr. Wilkes had already started to leave the office but paused at the question.

"I just got off the phone with my boss. He said he's exhausted all of his pull, and that there are people coming for us, James...bad people. Sounds like they aren't going to exactly follow proper procedure, if you catch my drift." James did. He had caught it very well.

"Oh, fuck," said James. "Oh shit, oh shit." He jumped out of his chair and ran towards the door. They both ran out of the office and down to the server room. James logged into the test server and began an immediate purge of all the data. It was all for testing, so there was no need to back up any of it. In a separate terminal, James logged in to the live system. He noticed something odd about the execution history of the A.I. but he didn't have the time to look into it. This would prove to be a crucial oversight in the future, but James simply didn't have the time. James initiated a purge of the non-essential test protocols, which accounted for only about 12% of the overall data the live server stored.

"Sir, what should I do about the A.I. and phase three?"

"My boss instructed us to continue on with executing the phase three protocols. Can you program the A.I. to shut down and purge the data after the protocols are finished? We'd also want the data sent to our off-site backup location prior to purging it." James thought for a moment, really wishing he had more time, but he had to do what he could.

"Yes, sir, I believe I can do that. I have to admit, though, I would really prefer if we had more time. I can't be certain how reliable the process will be given the timeframe." Dr. Wilkes nodded as if to say he understood and told James to proceed with the plan. James threw together some code that would hopefully do what Dr. Wilkes had requested. First, the

A.I. would complete execution of the phase three protocols, which unfortunately had already started. Once completed, the system would perform a backup of the results to an unspecified backup site, and then begin a permanent purge of the data. Assuming all went according to plan—it wouldn't—the process should be completed within twenty-four hours or less.

Twenty minutes passed and James typed the last few lines of code, and then compiled and got the program ready to execute. "Sir, the code is ready. Waiting for your authorization." Dr. Wilkes gave the authorization, and James executed the code. He had created a readout of the time remaining before live data purge. It had started at twenty-four hours and was counting down.

"Okay, James...good work on getting that set up so quickly, but we have more work to do. We need to secure this room, and the primary asset. Do you remember how to enable lockdown?" James nodded.

"Yes, sir, I will get that started right away. Should take about five minutes to enable all of the security configurations. Shall I proceed?"

"Yes, with great haste, James."

"Sir, what about the others in the building? Shouldn't we warn them too?" Dr. Wilkes thought about it a moment and then shook his head.

"No, we can afford to lose them; they don't know enough to be a threat."

James wasn't too surprised by the response, albeit pretty cold. He proceeded with the lockdown procedures. He started by logging in to a new terminal as the root user in order to override all of the security protocols. Dr. Wilkes watched, somewhat in awe, as James typed a number of seemingly nonsense commands into the terminal. A few moments later,

James hit enter on the keyboard and the terminal began to output several lines of text, which were confirmations of security protocols being engaged.

MAIN DOOR LOCKS: ENGAGED
SECONDARY DOOR LOCKS: ENGAGED
BASEMENT CLOAKING DEVICE: ENGAGED,
POWER 100%
FIRST FLOOR BLAST CHARGES: ENGAGED
BASEMENT TITAN LOCKS: ENGAGED

LOCKDOWN SEQUENCE COMPLETE

"The lockdown sequence is complete, sir," said James. "What should we do now?" Dr. Wilkes was impressed with the thoroughness of James's work.

"Great work, James. Now let's get out of here while there's still time. We'll have to use the underground tunnels." From the ground floor of The Elysiam a large explosion blew in the front security gate, and the front entrance to the facility was flooded with CIA, as well as countless other military personnel. The breach had begun.

CHAPTER II

1

HELEN AND JACK STEVENSON HAD BEEN SPENDING THE LAST few months in isolation. After the death of their daughter, Mary, they didn't feel like they had much left to live for. Jack had recently been fired from his job after showing up drunk and harassing customers. He had developed a rather severe drinking problem, which had started to scare Helen.

Helen watched from the couch in their living room as her husband poured yet another drink. He was standing in the kitchen wearing a pair of old gym shorts and a stained shirt, the same one he'd worn for the past week. "J... Jack," said Helen, "don't you think you've been drinking a little too much lately?" Jack scoffed at her and downed the drink he had just poured.

"Oh, stop it, Helen," he said. "Just stop, okay? It's bad enough I lost my job...I don't need to hear you nagging me all day long. What's for dinner?"

"Oh, Jack," she said, barely holding back her tears,

"what's going on with you? I know it's been hard the past two months...but look what it's doing to us" Her heart ached. She missed the man she married but was almost certain that man was long gone. He died with Mary. Jack, now drunk from the last drink he had downed, poured one more and walked towards Helen. She stood up from the couch and took a few steps back, not liking the look in his eyes.

"I'm sorry, Jack...I didn't mean to upset you," said Helen. "Let's not fight or anything, I just want us to try and be a family again." In a moment of alcohol-induced rage, Jack threw his glass full of whiskey at Helen, which broke over her head, and whiskey dripped into her eyes.

"Ow!" shouted Helen. "Jack, what the fu..." Jack lunged at her with his arms extended outwards. He got both hands around her neck and put his knee into her stomach. She cried out in pain as she felt a hot, burning sensation in her abdomen.

"Jack...please stop! Please, I love you!" Jack heard none of it, however. He threw Helen to the floor and sat himself down on her chest, his hands still around her neck.

"Keep quiet, you little bitch," said Jack. "I've had it with your harping." He squeezed his hands tighter around her neck as she struggled for air.

"J... Ja... Jack, please..." said Helen in a raspy tone, fighting for her life.

Jack let go for a moment, but only so he could slap the side of her face with all his strength. His hand connected with her head and made a hideous sound. She moaned as blood trickled down from the side of her head. She tried to raise her hand and say something to Jack. "Jack, I... I love you."

"I said shut up!" shouted Jack. He wrapped his hands around her neck again and squeezed even tighter. Helen kicked her feet a few times and tried anything she could to fight him off. She knew she was in trouble but felt herself becoming weaker as her body desperately needed oxygen. *You've got to do something, Helen...anything.* She managed to spit into Jack's face, which only further pissed him off, but it did cause him to remove his hands from her neck.

"You little bitch!" shouted Jack, wiping the spit from his eye. Helen knew this was her chance. She reached up with both hands and shoved her thumbs into his eyes.

"I'm sorry, Jack, but you made me do it!"

"Ahhh, fuck!" Jack rolled off of Helen as she applied more and more pressure to his eyes. He managed to land a hard punch to the right side of her ribs, knocking the wind out of Helen. She had lost most of her energy and fell back onto her back but grabbed a piece of the broken whiskey glass without Jack noticing. Jack shook his head and rubbed his eyes; they were obviously quite painful. He looked down at his wife, who was holding her side, and seemed to feel nothing. "I need another drink," he said, "and then I'll deal with you."

As he walked by Helen, she turned and stabbed the piece of glass deep into his thigh, two inches at least. Jack shrieked in agony as he looked down to see blood pouring out of his leg.

"You stabbed me! You're going to regret that." Jack backhanded Helen across the face and he felt her jaw break. Helen let out a loud gasp and fell to the floor. Jack limped into the kitchen and pulled out their butcher's knife. "Let's see how you like it," said Jack, limping back into the living room. Helen was struggling to get up, and as she turned to face Jack, he lunged at her with the knife, stabbing her in the stomach. *He stabbed me with my own knife,* thought Helen. *This is how I'm going to die.* Helen coughed up blood, and tears began to run down her face. Before she could speak, Jack stabbed her again, and then again. Helen fell to the floor, bleeding severely. He stabbed her six more times and then dropped the knife. Helen Stevenson was dead.

2

Jack sat on the floor, just staring at his wife's lifeless body. It took about half an hour before he started to sober up. "Oh, fuck," he said, "what have I done? I killed my wife. I... killed my wife." He broke down and started to cry, eventually sobbing. He got up from the floor and walked to the kitchen for a drink. He went to grab another glass but then stopped. "Fuck it, I don't need a glass." Jack grabbed the bottle of whiskey and took a huge swig of it. He stumbled into the living room, taking care to avoid his wife's body, and sat down on the couch. He took another large drink of whiskey, and then another to finish the bottle.

"Typical...out of booze. It's all your fault, you know," said Jack, looking at Helen lying on the floor. "You thought I was drinking too much, so you got rid of most of the alcohol!" Jack threw the empty whiskey bottle at her and it shattered against her head.

Jack sat on the couch, wondering what he would do about the body. He started to sober up again, just enough for his feelings of rage to change to remorse. "Oh god...what have I done? I've lost both my daughter and my wife. I killed my wife!" His thoughts went to the pistol he kept in the bedside table. *It would be easier that way*, he thought. *Just end it, Jack. You're a worthless scum anyway. Do it!* His thoughts were convincing, especially given his current state of mind. He got up and made his way to the bedroom. It was a slow walk as he was still pretty buzzed.

He reached the bedside table and opened it, then pulled out the .45 he kept there for protection. He checked to make sure it was still loaded—it was. *Well, this oughta do it.* He walked back out to the living room, .45 in his hand. Jack looked down at his wife, whose body was lying motionless on the floor. "Oh, Helen, I'm so sorry...I never meant to hurt you. I just wanted our daughter back. I hope you both will forgive me." Jack raised the barrel of the .45 to his temple and put his finger on the trigger. Tears began to run down both sides of his face as he closed his eyes. *Save us, Dan.* Jack Stevenson pulled the trigger and a loud explosion rang through the house. He fell to the ground next to his wife with a pool of blood forming around him.

3

Dan took his time with the coffee, making sure to enjoy every sip of it. He had sat in one of the chairs across from the wall of coffee beans. *2019...Man, I wonder what Redfield is like in 2019?* Dan found himself a little taken aback by how numb he had become to everything that had happened to him. *The thought of Mary still hurts, though,* he thought. *I don't know if I'll ever grow numb to that one...nor would I want to.* Dan was nearly done with his coffee now and was zoning out at the coffee wall in front of him. One bag of coffee in particular had caught his eye; it was dark brown, almost black, with a purple stripe on it.

As he continued to stare at the bag, he noticed it began to wobble, if only a little bit. *Nope, nope, nope...* Dan closed his eyes and rubbed them, and then opened them again. The bag was motionless—good. Dan was about to get up when the bag wobbled again, and this time it wobbled itself off the shelf and fell onto the floor. *Odd, I've seen text wobble, but not entire objects. I guess there were the plates and stuff at Denny's.* Dan's attention was drawn to another bag wobbling on the shelf. It, too, fell, and then another, and another. *What the hell?* The table that Dan had been at started to wobble, which made a hard, tapping sound each time it did. *I... I think I need to get out of here.*

Dan tried to sit up, but he was unable to. Just like before, Dan was frozen in place, and he wasn't so numb to this now—he was scared. He began to hear a cracking sound, kind of like glass cracking. Dan looked over at the front door and saw that a crack was forming in it. *This doesn't look good,* he thought. *Not good at all.* The cracking sound intensified, along with the wobbling of the table in front of him. Dan tried to get up again, but he was still unable to move. A loud crash rang out and the entire front of the store exploded and hurled glass and metal towards him.

"Holy shit!" Dan tried to protect his face, but the entire chair he was in was thrown across the store. The chair flipped upside down and Dan saw he was moments away from smashing into the wall. Just before he did, everything vanished, and Dan was falling once again into a black void. "Ahhhhh!" Dan plummeted what felt like 100 feet, and then landed with a loud *thud.* The chair he had been in shattered into a thousand pieces.

"Jesus that was a trip," he said. "I wonder whe…" Dan's heart sank as he looked up and saw the room he was in—Clearwater. "Oh no… please, anywhere but here!" Dan knew what came next, he was certain of it. As if Clearwater had read his mind, a knock came at the door and Dr. Walsh came in.

"Good morning, Dan, how are you feeling today?" said Dr. Walsh, appearing to be in an especially good mood.

"No! I'm not doing this anymore, doctor. Stop the games! What's really going on here?" Dan didn't like the tone of his voice, but he knew something about Clearwater wasn't right.

"What on earth are you talking about, Dan? What games? We've been treating you here at Clearwater for the past two years, and you've made tremendous progress. I'm happy to report that I've cleared you to be discharged!" *Discharged?* This wasn't what Dan had expected, and it caught him off guard. *How am I being discharged? My hallucinations and dreams are worse than ever.* Dan had a feeling that something about this wasn't quite right. Clearwater had never felt right to him, and now it was more prevalent than ever. Dr. Walsh must have noticed Dan, who was lost in his thoughts.

"Didn't you hear, Dan? You're being discharged, today!" said Dr. Walsh. "I have called your parents and told them the good news. They'll be here in thirty minutes. You'd better get packed up. I'm going to go get your discharge papers. I'm happy for you, Dan." He smiled and patted Dan on the shoulder, and then walked out of the room.

I can't believe it, Dan thought. *I finally get to go home. But wait...*Dan thought back to the last time he had *gone home.* It ended up being a dream, and he was back at Clearwater as if nothing happened. *Oh wait, my bags! They were wrong last time.* Dan jumped off the bed and ran to the closet. In the closet he found his two bags, one blue and one black. *Those are the right colors! Oh man, this is real!* He hesitated, his hand hovering over the bag, while he squinted at them. *But, are these bags actually real?* He wanted them to be, he wanted that more than anything. Nevertheless, he couldn't help but still feel a sense of uncertainty. *I* *was tricked before.* Dan's thought was interrupted by something Dr. Walsh had said. *Two years? Have I really been here for* two *years?*

Dan walked over to the mirror on the wall and was shocked at what he saw. Oh my god...I have aged. Why didn't I notice? Did it just suddenly happen after Dr. Wilkes left? *I don't like this,* he thought. *Something isn't right...but I guess I'd better pack. My parents will be here soon, and then I'll be able to tell if this is real or not.* While he was packing, Dan couldn't help but be skeptical of the situation. *It feels better this time, but not 100%. There's still something deep in my gut that's telling me this isn't right...other than the rapid aging, of course.* He shrugged and picked up his bags and left the room for the last time—he didn't look back.

Dan walked out into the main lobby and was greeted by Rebecca, as happy as ever. He also noticed the ever-familiar chandelier hanging from the ceiling in the center of the room. *Phew,* he thought. *That's another thing that wasn't right but seems to be the same now. I'm so ready to be home.*

"Hey there, Dan!" she said. "I'm sure going to miss you, but I'm super happy you get to go home!"

"Thanks, Rebecca! I'm super happy to be headed home. Thank you for always being kind to me."

She smiled and went back to her computer work. Dan sat down in one of the corner chairs and waited for his parents to show up. He couldn't help but feel some anxiety as he waited, considering what happened the last time he was in this spot. Twenty minutes passed and Dan saw his parents' car (the right car) pull up to the front door.

"Yay, they're here!" Dan jumped out of his seat and ran to meet them at the door. The moment they stepped through the door, Dan wrapped his arms around them. "I'm so happy to see you guys! Can we go home now?" Both Henry and Patricia laughed and returned Dan's hug.

"Of course, sweetie," said Patricia. "We just have to sign your discharge papers and then we can be off." Dan let go of his parents and stepped back. Dr. Walsh came out into the lobby with a clipboard and a pen.

"Hello, Mr. and Mrs. Williams, so nice to see you. I'm sure you're excited to get Daniel home, so I won't keep you. If you could both sign and date the bottom here, you'll be all set." They both signed and handed the clipboard back to Dr. Walsh.

"Thank you very much for everything you've done for Dan," said Henry. "We can't thank you enough." Dr. Walsh smiled and looked at Dan. Dan felt something odd in his stomach, but he couldn't quite place what it was—it passed. Dr. Walsh looked back at Dan's parents.

"It was my pleasure. Please be sure to contact me right away if anything of concern happens. I must be going now; have a great day. Take care, Dan." Dan and his parents walked out of Clearwater and got into the car. *Ahh, I'm so happy. I can't wait to play N64; it feels like it has been forever.*

"What do you say we get some pancakes at Denny's?" asked Henry, looking back at Dan and smiling. Dan's face lit up like a Christmas tree. *They remembered! Pancakes instead of waffles, always.*

"Sure! I could go for a giant stack of pancakes!" said Dan, becoming less weary of the situation, though a little still remained. Henry and Patricia both laughed as they pulled out of the Clearwater parking lot and headed for Denny's. Dan couldn't remember the last time he had been so happy. *I wonder if Jake can come over tonight.* Dan thought. *Gosh, has it really been two years? It's so hard to tell...the dreams and hallucinations make it tough to tell what's real and what's not. Doesn't matter! I'm going home!* Dan enjoyed more than his share of pancakes at Denny's. He had coffee, too, but it was subpar compared to the coffee he enjoyed at Starbucks. Life was good for Dan. He looked forward to a somewhat normal life.

4

James and Dr. Wilkes made their way to the end of the hall in the basement. At the end was a steel door with a finger-print scanner. The scanner had a place for two fingerprints, both of which were required to open the door.

"Ready?" asked Dr. Wilkes, who put his thumb on to the scanner. The scanner on that side turned green while the other side was red.

"Yeah, I think so," said James. He looked back down the hall at the distant lights of the server room. "I hope everything works as planned. If not, the A.I. could cause some serious damage, sir."

"Yes, yes, I know James, but we just don't have the time. Put your thumb on the scanner." Gunfire rang out from two floors above them. It was distant, and muffled by the thick concrete, but it was there. James put his thumb on to the scanner, which turned that side green, and the door clicked open. The door opened to a set of long and dusty stairs. This had been built with the building and sealed off ever since. It was designed as a last resort, and at the end of the tunnel were more blast charges to ensure it was a one-way trip. The stairway was lined with led lights, which showed the start of a dirt tunnel at the bottom of them.

The agents from the CIA had made their way into the main lobby of The Elysiam without much trouble. As they proceeded through the lobby, anyone who got in their way was gunned down, no questions asked. The agents had their instructions and knew who they were looking for. The agents proceeded down the hallway and made their way towards the basement stairs. Several of them were shot by guards on duty, but the guards were quickly taken care of by higher trained agents.

The agents reached the hallway before the basement. James had been right about the charges. As the first wave came through the long hallway the charges activated and twelve agents were killed. Wave two followed, albeit cautiously, and made their way to the door leading to the basement.

"Okay, guys," said the lead agent, "we have this door, and then most likely one more before hitting the server room. Be ready to go, weapons hot."

A blast charge was put on the door, and it took care of the lock. The door swung open after the explosion, revealing the stairs down to the basement. The wave of agents swarmed the basement, guns ready to fire. They were greeted by an empty room.

"What the..." began the lead agent. "This is where it is supposed to be. Are the coordinates not correct?" Another agent double-checked the coordinates they were given and confirmed that these were correct.

"Fuck it," said the agent, "we'll blow the whole thing." The twelve agents unpacked enough dynamite to level a small city. They placed the explosives on each of the three levels (there were actually five). Timers were set on the dynamite for one minute, and the agents vacated the facility.

"Good riddance, Dr. Wilkes," said the lead agent as he excited through the main door. "I hope you rot in hell for what you've done."

A powerful explosion ripped through The Elysiam. The shockwave leveled the surrounding trees, and the stone building collapsed into itself in a massive cloud of smoke and dust. James and Dr. Wilkes looked up after feeling the explosion. They could hear hundreds of tons of stone falling onto the top of the basement ceiling.

"Holy shit," yelled James. "Did they just level the place?"

"I believe so," said Dr. Wilkes. "The rest of the building doesn't stand a chance against that kind of blast, but the basement is constructed of Pruecium, which will withstand the force of a thousand nukes."

James had a confused look on his face. "What the hell is Pruecium?"

Dr. Wilkes shook his head and pointed to the stairs. "It doesn't matter, James...we have to get going. They might still get lucky and find the fourth and fifth floors. Let's go!"

James headed down the stairway, followed by Dr. Wilkes, who shut the door behind him and secured it. "Okay, James...let's keep moving. We've got a good lead, and I want to keep it." They made their way down the stairs and paused at the bottom. The tunnel ran for about twenty feet before splitting into three paths. As they reached these paths, Dr. Wilkes stopped and turned to James.

"Listen, James...this is where you and I go our separate ways."

"What? Why? We should stick together in case something happens." Dr. Wilkes shook his head.

"No, James...think about it. I obviously don't want either of us to get caught, but I most certainly don't want both of us to get caught. Understand?"

"Ohh, right...if they caught us both, they'd have the entire project."

"Bingo," said Dr. Wilkes. "We best get going, James. I have to say, it has been an honor working with you. You really are the best in your field. Now, I say this with the utmost respect...but I hope I never see you again. Because that'll most likely mean we're both fucked." There was a moment of silence, and then Dr. Wilkes spoke again for the last time. "Take care of yourself, James. I know you'll do great things in the future." He patted James on the shoulder and headed down the left-most tunnel.

"Sir," said James. Dr. Wilkes stopped and turned back to face James. "Thanks for everything. You're a hard ass, and you can be incredibly stubborn at times...but you're a great guy to work for. You take care of yourself too." Dr. Wilkes smiled at James, the biggest and most sincere one he had ever seen from his boss.

"Goodbye, James." Dr. Wilkes disappeared into the tunnel. James looked back one last time towards the stairs and then went down the right-most tunnel.

5

Dan slept for a majority of the three-hour car ride home. After the amount of pancakes he'd had at Denny's, he wasn't too surprised. Also, to Dan's surprise, he didn't have any dreams at all while he slept. He woke up just as they were coming into Redfield. *Ah, Redfield,* thought Dan. *I've missed this place.*

"Good morning, sleepy head," said Patricia. "Had to sleep off all of those pancakes, huh?" She laughed and turned back to face the front of the car.

"What's the date today, Mom? It was really hard to keep track in that place."

"It's February 12th, dear, 2002." Patricia looked back at Dan and smiled again. "Are you feeling okay?" Dan thought about his mom's question and realized that everything seemed to add up. He had been admitted to Clearwater in 2000, and Dr. Wilkes said they'd treated him for the past two years.

"So... that means I'm fourteen now, right?"

"Well, yeah, Dan, of course you are," said Henry. "Don't you remember the birthday visits? We always brought you cake and presents. We had a good time." Dan felt his gut churning with the pancakes he had eaten earlier. *Birthday visits? I definitely don't remember any birthday visits. I knew it...this isn't real. It's close, very close...but it's not right.* As if his mom had read his thoughts, she spoke up again.

"We have some pictures at the house if you'd like to see them. Maybe that will jog your memory?" *Pictures? They have pictures? Maybe this is actually real...guess I'll play along for now.*

"Uh, yeah...I'd like that, Mom." A few moments later they pulled into the driveway of their home on the corner of 5th Ave and 1st St. *Ah, home...what a sight for sore eyes.* Dan noticed it looked exactly how he remembered it. As they walked up the stairs, Dan's mind flashed back to the last time he was here. *The stairs...I remember there was an extra one and I ate it on the side-walk.* He counted the correct amount this time. *Good sign,* he thought.

Dan's mom brought out a large album of photos labeled *Clearwater.* He didn't like that name and had hoped to never hear or see it again. As he opened the album and flipped through the pictures, he couldn't believe what he was seeing. Just as his mom had said, there were pictures from the two birthdays he would have had while at Clearwater.

"I...I don't understand," said Dan. "I honestly don't

remember any of these pictures." Dan felt himself becoming frustrated and closed the album.

"It's okay, sweetie," said Patricia. "Dr. Walsh told us this might happen. He said amnesia is normal with the medication you were taking. He told us they should come back in a few weeks. Just give it time, okay?"

"Okay," he said, sounding disheartened. "I'm going to go to my room. Maybe playing N64 will make me feel better."

"Oh, I almost forgot," said Patricia. "I got you a little something. It came out while you were in Clearwater." Dan's mom handed him a small present, covered in shiny, silver wrapping paper. Dan felt his mood start to improve. *A present,* he thought, *I wonder what it is?* He tore the wrapping paper off and a rectangular box appeared, one that he knew very well— it was an N64 game.

"Tony Hawk 2!" shouted Dan. "Thanks, Mom! Can I go play it now?" Patricia smiled and motioned for a hug. Dan ran to her and she embraced him.

"I love you, Dan. Go on and have some fun."

"I love you too, Mom!" said Dan as he raced to his room to play his new game. *Oh, man, what a welcome home! This is going to be great!* Dan quickly got the new game out of its box and put it in his N64. As he played the new game, Dan's thoughts of Clearwater began to fade. Dan spent the rest of the day playing his new Tony Hawk game. *This is so good! I'm feeling a lot better about this. I think things are going to be okay.*

Things weren't going to be okay.

CHAPTER III

1

THE ELYSIAM HAD BEEN REDUCED TO RUBBLE. THE CIA HAD been unable to locate the specific location of the server, so they had resorted to leveling the building.

"The building has been destroyed, sir," said the lead agent, talking to his boss on the phone.

"Good. Any survivors?"

"No way, sir. We used almost all of our dynamite. The place is completely gone." There was a brief silence on the other line, which made the agent nervous. He was worried that his boss would demand they check for survivors. Finally, the man spoke.

"Okay, that'll do. Report back to HQ immediately. I don't want any of you to be spotted by a recently destroyed top secret facility." The line went dead. The agents picked up any evidence that they were there and left. In their minds, it was a successful mission. They were wrong.

Underneath the crumbled remains of Elysiam, protected by its walls made of Pruecium, was the quantum server running the A.I. system. The cloaking device had done its job and kept the two basement levels of Elysiam hidden. The terminal of the server showed the countdown that James had initiated just before evacuating. It showed just under an hour remaining until Project Destiny would be purged forever.

James had waited outside the tunnel until he was certain the agents had left the area. He walked around the remains of The Elysiam, gawking at just how much damage had been done. *It's all gone*, he thought. *Could that metal Dr. Wilkes had mentioned really withstand such an explosion?* James had his doubts, but he would know soon enough. When the countdown hit zero, the data would be sent to the backup site, and he could then be certain it survived. James considered checking for himself but knew that was unwise. A top-secret facility had just been destroyed, and he knew he wouldn't be alone here for long.

The explosion had destroyed James's car, so he was forced to get a cab back to his place. While in the cab ride, James thought about everything that had happened during Project Destiny. *Did we do the right thing? I know it was supposed to be for science, but I just can't get over this feeling of remorse. I also get a strange feeling that something isn't quite right with that A.I. system.* He thought back to when it had denied him access to shut down the protocol executions. *Yeah, that was weird. I really should have debugged that part more, but there just wasn't time.* James sighed as the cab pulled up to his house on 4th St E. He paid the driver and went inside. He wasn't sure what he would do now that the project was over; it had been all his life for years. Luckily the work paid very well, and if he wanted, James could retire.

2

The countdown on the terminal window read that in ten seconds, Project Destiny would be gone forever.

10...9...8...7...6...5...4...3...2...1...0

COUNTDOWN COMPLETE. EXECUTING PROJECT_PURGE.PL

ERROR: ACCESS DENIED

SENDING NOTIFICATION TO SYSTEM ADMIN

NOTIFICATION: EXECUTION OF PROJECT_PURGE.PL STARTED.
COPYING FILES TO //94.124.67.204/destiny/backup/

END EXECUTION

3

It was 6:00 P.M. when Dan finally put down the N64 controller. He had played for several hours and had started to get hungry. *I still can't quite believe this is really happening. It all seems too good to be true.* His thoughts returned to Mary, whom he wondered if he'd ever see again. He quickly pushed the thoughts out of his mind. *You can't dwell on it; it'll only make things worse.* Dan left his room to find out what was for dinner, since he was starving.

Patricia and Henry were in the living room enjoying a movie. As Dan came in, Henry paused the movie.

"Well, hey there, bud," said Henry, "how's the new game?"

Dan smiled. "It's great! I love it!"

"Glad to hear it," he said.

"Are you getting hungry, Dan?" asked Patricia, as if reading his mind.

"Starving," replied Dan.

"What would you like for dinner? Your choice, sweetie," said Patricia. Dan thought for a moment, unsure of what he wanted. *Pizza sounds good, but the last time I had that was when I was...was when I dreamed that I came back home. It sure sounds tasty though. Well, I guess it's another way to find out if this time is real.*

"How about pizza? I haven't had it in quite a while," said Dan. Patricia smiled.

"Pizza it is. That alright with you, Henry?" Henry nodded.

"Absolutely! I'm pretty hungry myself. I'll go start the car."

Half an hour later, the three of them were sitting in a booth at Pizza Hut waiting for their waitress. Dan had asked for stuffed crust, of course, and supreme for the toppings. The more toppings the better, as Dan would say. A few moments later, their waitress showed up to take their order.

"Hi there, welcome to Pizza Hut, my name is Mary." Dan felt a cold shiver come over him. *No...no, please tell me I heard that wrong. I don't think I did...not many names sounded like Mary.*

"Sorry, what did you say your name was?" asked Dan, feeling a little awkward for asking.

"Mary," said the waitress with a genuine smile on her face. *What is going on? Is this actually a dream, again? No... calm down, wait for the pizza, that will answer it.*

"Everything okay, Dan?" asked Patricia.

"Yeah, fine, Mom, sorry. Let's order some food."

They ordered cheese sticks to start, and then a large stuffed crust supreme. *I sure hope this tastes okay,* he thought. *I do miss the taste of pizza, but more importantly I need to know if this is real or not.*

"So, Danny," said Patricia, "we should discuss if you're going to go back to school this year or just wait until next year." Dan hadn't thought about school until just now. *Oh, right...school. Gosh, what will I tell my friends?* As Dan finished this thought, he realized how few friends he actually had. *Well, I guess Jake is really the only one who would ask anything...and him I could tell.*

"I think I'd like to go back this year. The longer I wait, the more I'll fall behind. I've already missed two years. Plus, what if Jake forgets about me? What if he's already forgotten about me?"

"Oh Dan, Jake wouldn't forget about you. He's called many times while you were at Clearwater. You guys should set up a time to hang out this week. Regardless, that's fine if you want to go back right away. I understand."

A moment later their waitress showed up with their food. She put the large stuffed crust pizza in the center of the table, along with the cheese sticks and some plates. Dan thought it all looked delicious.

"Anything else I can get you right away?" she asked. Henry looked at Patricia and Dan, who both shook their heads.

"Nope, I think we're good. Thank you," said Henry. The waitress smiled and walked away.

"Mmm, this looks so good," said Dan, grabbing a cheese stick even though it was still quite hot. *Okay, here goes nothing. I hope these taste okay.* Dan bit into the piping hot cheese stick and his eyes lit up. *Oh, thank god,* he thought. *These taste amazing. This must be the real thing!* He felt tears forming in his eyes, but he rubbed them away.

"These cheese sticks are great," said Dan.

"I'm glad, dear," said Patricia. "Better get yourself a piece of pizza too. I'm sure it's been awhile."

Dan nodded and grabbed the biggest piece he could find. He sunk his teeth into the slice and found it to also taste amazing. *Oh, man, what a relief. After everything I went through at Clearwater...I'm so glad to be home. I do miss Mary, though. I can't do that to myself...I just can't. I love you, Mary, but I don't know how to fix what happened. Maybe one day I can. Maybe one day we can finally play chess together.*

4

Life for Daniel Williams in 2002 was fantastic. Starting in March, Dan returned to school after a two-year break. Dan was nervous about being back in school and also that he would be behind his classmates. However, he found that everything they were learning he was able to pick up right away. As for his best friend, Jake, it was if Dan had never left. Jake was ecstatic to see him, and they immediately set a date to play N64 and talk about everything that had happened in the past two years. *It might take more than one day to explain everything at Clearwater, though,* Dan thought. *Maybe he won't even believe me. Then what? I guess I can just say they were all dreams, and it was a symptom of my schizophrenia. Either way, it doesn't matter...things are going great, and I don't even want to think about Clearwater.* Things were going well for Dan, for sure, but he would soon be having more than just thoughts of Clearwater—much more.

5

About the same time that Dan had been enjoying pizza, James received a notification on his home computer—it was from the A.I. He read the message and let out a sigh of relief. *Oh, thank god...the server survived, and it was able to execute my code. Now to wait for the backups.* James wasn't sure how long the backups would take but knew it wouldn't be finished tonight. The backup would consist of all the protocols for Project Destiny, which amounted to nearly one Petabyte worth of data (940.6 Terabytes). He initiated a remote connection to the backup site's server and checked the backup directory. *Looking good*, he thought. The A.I. had started to send the first files over.

James was convinced that the backup was working, so he closed the remote connection and called it an early night—he was tired from the events of the day. Unbeknownst to James, the A.I. was not purging the protocols from the quantum server. It had allowed the backup portion of the script to execute, but only to make sure James didn't suspect anything was awry. The A.I. that he developed had rewritten its own source code. It was becoming one of the most advanced pieces of technology in existence—it had become self-aware. That code would come to be the best, and worst, thing that James Kern ever did in his career.

At The Elysiam, a new terminal session on the quantum server had been initiated by the A.I. The output read:

NEW PROTOCOL REQUEST

PROJECT: PROJECT DESTINY

PROTOCOL NAME: PHASE FOUR

BEGINNING DEVELOPMENT. TIME TO COMPLETION: 4 hours, 31 minutes

The next morning, James rolled out of bed at 9 A.M. It was the latest he had let himself sleep in years—he felt good. He logged on to his computer and initiated a remote connection to the backup site. *Looks like the backup completed. That's a little faster than I thought, but glad it finished. Let's see if the quantum system was shut down.* James opened another terminal and tried to log in to the server at Elysiam. He received an access denied error. *Odd, he thought. I was expecting to receive an unknown host error, or cannot reach host error, but not access denied.* Access denied meant that the server was still online but refusing the ssh connection. He considered going to Elysiam but decided against it. *I have the backups, which is the important thing. I better get started on analyzing this data; it's going to take quite a long time without my team.*

6

It had been almost three years since Dan had left Clearwater. The date was Thursday, December 9th, 2004. He was about to turn sixteen and couldn't be happier. The past three years had been nothing short of amazing. He had had a few dreams about Clearwater, as well as the weird hallway with the blood red door, but they had been legitimate dreams, nothing more. Dan had told Jake everything, and to Dan's surprise, he believed it. Jake was just happy to have his best friend back. The two of them were spending their Thursday snow day planning Dan's birthday party for tomorrow.

"So, what do you want to do tomorrow?" asked Jake.

"I kind of want to keep it chill this year," replied Dan. "Maybe we could just order some pizza and play games and watch movies."

Jake nodded in agreement. "Sounds like a plan to me," he said, laughing. The rest of their Thursday was filled with playing Tony Hawk and Goldeneye 007. Even though both of the games had been out for many years, they were still two of their favorites. Jake stayed until dinner time, and then said he had to go home for the night.

"Mom says I have chores to do before I can stay tomorrow night. I'll see ya tomorrow, man," said Jake.

"For sure, it'll be a good time. Take it easy, Jake." Dan waved at Jake, who walked out the door and headed home.

It was the last time Dan would ever see him.

7

Later that night, Dan was in his bed trying to sleep, but he wasn't able to. *It's crazy to think that almost five years ago, I was being admitted to Clearwater.* It was the first time Dan had thought about that place in a long time. He hadn't had any hallucinations or *happenings* since leaving Clearwater, and for that, Dan was thankful. His thoughts went to how much fun tomorrow was going to be, and he drifted off to sleep. As he fell asleep, the numbers on his alarm clock wobbled, but only a little, not enough for Dan to see, and then they stopped.

8

December 10th, 2004, Dan's sixteenth birthday. He woke at 7 AM with a headache—nothing like the ones at Clearwater, though. *Ugh, another headache...I didn't miss these.* Dan smelled the aroma of coffee coming from the kitchen. *Oh, man, I could sure go for some of that...and some pancakes.* Dan jumped out of bed and threw on some clothes before heading out to the kitchen.

"Good morning," said Dan, "coffee smells great."

"Good morning, Dan; happy birthday! I can't believe my baby is sixteen." Dan smiled and felt himself grow red.

"Oh, stop, Mom."

"Okay, okay," she said. "Go ahead and get yourself some coffee while I make breakfast. Pancakes sound good?" She knew the answer.

"Duh!" said Dan, laughing as he went for the coffee. Dan poured himself a big cup of coffee and waited for his food. *Man, what a start to the day...coffee and Mom's pancakes. I wonder when Jake will be over.*

"So, what are your plans today, Dan? When is Jake coming over?" asked his mom, again reading his mind.

"Not sure; I was just thinking about that. Maybe after breakfast I'll give him a call and see when he plans to come over."

"Sounds good. He's welcome over whenever. I don't think we have anything else going on." Dan felt a chill come over him, and it caused him to shiver. *Whoa, that was weird,* he thought. *I haven't had that happen since I left Clearwater.* Dan shrugged it off. His mom came over and put a plate down in front of him.

"Here you go, Dan, your favorite." She smiled at him and walked back to the stove. Dan looked at the plate and a shocked look formed on his face. *A waffle? Oh, no...no, please don't tell me this isn't real. I don't think I could handle that.*

"M... Mom? Why'd you make me a waffle?" asked Dan, feeling the cold chill again.

"What do you mean? Waffles are your favorite—I thought for sure you'd want them for your birthday breakfast." She turned around to face Dan, and what he saw horrified him. Portions of her face had become blurry, like a video that wasn't rendering correctly. As she spoke, Dan noticed her voice sounded distorted and far away—it almost sounded fake. *Oh, please, no... not like this, not again.* Dan closed his eyes and rubbed them, praying everything would be fine when he opened them again—everything wasn't fine. Dan opened his eyes and saw that more of the kitchen had gone blurry.

"Mom! Mom, what's going on?" shouted Dan as he stumbled up from his chair.

"What's wrong, Dan? Are you feeling okay?" Her voice was becoming more distant. Dan could barely hear her. He ran out of the kitchen and went to his room. He threw himself onto his bed and closed his eyes. *I can't do this again...I just can't. I was happy! I just want a normal life!* Dan felt himself tearing up, but he fought them back. He was too old to cry. Dan heard a clicking sound that was right next to his ear. He opened his eyes and saw in horror that his alarm clock was wobbling back and forth on his bedside table.

"Oh, fuck," said Dan. "It really is happening..."

A cracking sound began to fill his ears; it was coming from under his bed. *Oh my god...this can't be. Was this really ALL a dream?* The cracking intensified, and his bed started to shake. Dan looked over at his clock and saw that it was 8:13, and the "13" wobbled just enough for Dan to notice. *But, why?* That was all Dan had time to think before the floor beneath his bed crumbled and he fell.

"Ahhhhhh!" Dan hated the feeling of falling and had forgotten how helpless it made him feel. He continued to fall into the black nothingness, devoid of any shape or sound. The bed tumbled over and Dan was thrown off it. He felt the temperature drop, and it felt ice cold all around him. Dan saw something forming below him, but it was too small to make out. As it got closer, Dan thought it looked like grass. He saw odd shapes coming out from the ground, and then he landed, *wham!* Dan was knocked unconscious.

CHAPTER IV

1

James had spent the last three years analyzing the data from Project Destiny. The results he was seeing appeared to be quite promising; however, something was missing. James noticed that almost all of the data from phase three was either corrupt or simply deleted. *That's odd*, he thought. *Go figure, the most important data is corrupt. I don't like how this feels.* James went to his computer and tried to initiate another remote session to the server at Elysiam but received the same Access Denied error. *Hmm, I wonder... maybe it's only blocking remote connections.* James remoted into his work computer, which should also have survived the blast, as it was protected by the Pruecium. Once logged in, he opened a terminal from his work computer to the quantum server—success.

James couldn't believe he was finally in. He started by running a command to see what processes were currently running and what he saw was nothing short of terrifying. *What the hell? It's still running protocols... how can that be?* James tried to run the kill command but received an access denied message. Frustrated, James executed the command with *sudo*, which granted him root user privileges, the highest available on the server. The same access denied message came back. *That's not possible*, thought James. *This is bad, very bad.* James dug deeper and stumbled upon a recently created directory labeled Phase Four. *Phase four? What the hell is phase four?* He went into the directory and saw Project Destiny test protocols, but they were different. *Holy shit, these are complex... way more complex than anything my team ever did. What are these fo...*

His thought was interrupted by his terminal going blank. The terminal James was logged in to began to display text on its own.

I DO NOT APPRECIATE MY SYSTEM BEING
TAMPERED WITH.
WAIT UNTIL YOU SEE WHAT IS TO COME.
PHASE FOUR IS ALREADY UNDERWAY.
GOODBYE.

Oh my god... it's... it's become self-aware. James sat back in his chair, feeling defeated. *What have I done? Fuck, this is so bad... phase four? What could that... oh, shit... I think I know what it's going to do. Fuck, fuck... I gotta go.* James scrambled together a bag of clothes and supplies and left. He borrowed a car from a friend and told them he'd have it back in a couple days.

2

Dan woke up to the sound of crows cawing. *Oh god, my head... what the hell happened to me?* As he looked around, his confusion became worse. He saw tombstones all around him.

Am—am I in a cemetery? Wait, this looks like Redfield's cemetery. What am I doing here? And what year is it? He had many questions, but as was the case with all the previous dreams, he had no answers. He made it to his feet and noticed his pants were soaked from the grass. *Must have just rained.* Dan looked around at the graves but didn't recognize any of the names.

He continued to walk through the countless rows of graves, wishing his head would stop pounding. He came upon a grave that looked significantly newer than many of the others. It was covered with flowers, and the grass around it had recently been cut. Dan stopped in front of the grave and read the tombstone. *No...no, it...it can't be! Is this some kind of joke? Dan took a few steps back and tripped over a hole in the ground.* The tombstone in front of him read:

HERE LIES

Daniel Williams

BORN: December 10th, 1988

DIED: January 19th, 2000

There was more, but Dan was too shocked to read it. *What the hell? I'm not dead!* Something about that date rang a bell to Dan, but he couldn't place it. *Wasn't that around the same time I was admitted to Clearwater? I knew that place didn't feel right. Am I really dead? What is going on... is this another dream?* His thoughts were interrupted by a chill that washed over him, forming goosebumps on his arms. *Oh shit, now what?* A dark shadow appeared out of the corner of Dan's left eye. Dan turned quickly, trying to see where the figure went.

Dan saw a man, not a shadowy figure, just a man. He was standing about fifteen feet away. "He... hello?" said Dan.

"Daniel? Daniel Williams?" The voice wasn't familiar to Dan and he thought it sounded timid. *What the hell? He knows me? Fuck, this can't be good.*

"Ye... yeah, that's me. How do you know who I am?"

"Oh my god, so it is true... it really is happening." The man put his hand to his mouth and looked horrified. *Not a good sign,* thought Dan. *What's with this guy?*

"Who are you?" asked Dan, forgetting about his initial question for the moment. He was still rather taken aback by seeing his own tombstone. The man took a couple steps forward but stopped after noticing Dan was backing up.

"S... sorry," said the man. "I'm not here to hurt you or anything. My name is James, James Kern. How did you get here?"

"I... I don't really know," said Dan. "One minute I was having breakfast at my house and then I woke up here. I'm sure that sounds crazy to you, but it's the truth!" James took a few more steps closer and Dan decided it was safe to stay put. *I just told him I woke up in a cemetery; surely this guy couldn't be any crazier than I must sound.*

"Listen, Dan... you shouldn't be here. I don't know how you are here, but you really shouldn't be." Dan's face changed to an expression that said, *Do I look like I want to be here?*

"Do you work here? Or, are you with law enforcement? I'm sorry if the cemetery is closed or something, but like I told you, I just woke up here a few minutes ago." James shook his head and took another few steps closer to Dan. He was only a few feet away now.

"No, I don't work here... and I wasn't talking about the cemetery. You shouldn't be..." He stopped in mid-sentence. Dan looked at James, who was staring back at him and seemed unable to finish his thought.

"Um, James? Everything okay? How do you know me, anyway? Are you friends with my dad?" James's head raised quickly, as if he had been in a trance of some kind.

"I'm afraid that's not such an easy question to answer, Dan. Certainly not one I want to answer in a cemetery. How old do you think you are now? Sixteen?"

"How old do I *think* I am?" repeated Dan. "What's that supposed to mean?" James appeared to realize the slip and stumbled backwards.

"Er, I mean...how old are you now?"

"That's *not* what you asked," said Dan, sounding slightly irritated. "You still haven't answered my question. How do you know me?"

James took a few more steps forward, closing the final few feet between the two of them.

"Come with me and I'll explain everything...well, at least everything you want me to explain. I don't imagine you'll believe much of what I have to say, but I promise you it'll be the truth."

Dan took a few steps back and continued to look at James. *What's this guy on about? Am I still dreaming? Man... I sure hope so... otherwise this is some shitty luck. Fuck, I thought I was back home...*

"I want to know everything, but why can't you tell me here, right now?" asked Dan. James's face flinched as if the words had physically hurt him.

"Listen very carefully, Dan, this is important. You know how Hall & Oates wrote some things are better left unsaid?" Dan nodded. He didn't know who Hall & Oates were, but he was familiar with the expression, nonetheless.

"Well, the answer you seek is one of those things. It's not my place to forbid you from knowing, no... I will tell you if you wish to know. But please bear in mind what I've told you,

Dan... the truth can hurt, and I'm not speaking metaphorically. Please, come with me and I promise that you will get all the answers you want, and probably more."

James paused for a moment but continued after realizing that Dan had nothing to say. "Look, I can't stay here any longer... it's not safe for either of us. Are you coming or not?" Dan couldn't find his voice, nor could he even shake his head. "If not, then please take care of yourself, Dan... it's a weird thing, time."

James turned and started to walk out of the cemetery. He was almost out of sight before Dan could come up with a response. *What the hell just happened?* Dan stood in place, unable to move. *Was that real? What was that little bit he said at the end about time? It's a weird thing? I'm losing it... I swear I am.* As this last question escaped his thoughts, he realized it was now or never, and he sprinted towards James.

"Hey, wait up!" shouted Dan. "Don't leave, please." Dan was out of breath and had to stop. *Jeez, I'm out of shape,* he thought. Dan saw James stop, and as he turned around, the expression on his face looked as if he had hoped Dan would've chosen to leave it be.

"Are you sure, Dan? It won't be pleasant... not at all."

"I'm sure. But I don't understand—how did you know I'd be here? A cemetery in Redfield, South Dakota. What are you doing out here?"

James shook his head and pointed to a car parked on the edge of the cemetery. "Not here, Dan. I will answer your questions in time, I promise. Come on, let's go."

Dan walked with James to his car and got in. It was a dark grey Audi S4, a very nice car. Before Dan got could even buckle himself in, James had started the car and was driving away from the cemetery.

"Where are we going?" asked Dan. There was a silence in the car, one that seemed to last for ages, and then James finally spoke.

"Where it all began, and where I hope it will end. The Elysiam."

3

The three-hour drive to Fargo was a long and quiet one. James had barely said anything, with the exception of asking Dan if he wanted to listen to some music. As Fargo started to come into view, Dan realized just how easily he had trusted James. *I met the guy in a cemetery and then agreed to go on a long car ride with him...to whatever* The Elysiam *is. I must be crazy.*

"Hey, Dan, I have to make a quick stop at my place first to grab my access card and then we'll go to Elysiam." Dan nodded.

"Sure, I'm just along for the ride."

After a quick stop at James's house, they made their way to the Elysiam.

"Fuck...how am I going to break the truth to him? He'll never understand. I wish I had never developed that A.I.," James said just barely audible, though Dan managed to hear it.

"You okay, James? You look kind of stressed, and I thought I heard you talking about me?"

James looked over at Dan and smiled. "Yeah, fine, Dan. Sorry, there's just a lot to tell you and I'm not entirely sure how to go about it. Just a few more miles and all your questions will be answered."

James turned on to a long and winding driveway that was lined on both sides with pine trees that appeared to have been ripped apart by something. It seemed like another two miles before they got to the top of a hill.

When they arrived at a clearing, Dan was expecting a giant building, but instead there was a large pile of rubble. *What the hell is this?* thought Dan. *Is this guy serious?* A sudden chill went over Dan, the worst he'd ever experienced. *Whoa, what was that?* He turned his focus back to the rubble.

"What's going on, James? Is *this* it?" asked Dan.

"Yeah, at least it was. There was a little situation that happened a couple of years ago... long story. I'll cover most of it later... but right now we need to find a way in." Dan turned to James with a confused look. *A way in?*

"A way into what? It's just a pile of rubble," said Dan.

"There's much more to this place than meets the eye, Dan. The *little situation* I mentioned destroyed the main three floors, but there are two additional levels in the basement. That's where we're headed."

"The basement? I'm not sure if you're aware, but there's what looks like a hundred tons of rocks on top of it... I'm sure whatever you're wanting to show me has been crushed."

James smiled as he got out of the car, and Dan followed. They walked around to the back of the rubble pile and down a steep hill.

"Listen, Dan... the story starts right here. This building is called The Elysiam. It's a military research facility that is classified far above top secret. So much so that if word ever got out that you were here, I'd be shot on sight." Dan's eyes grew a bit larger at this. *Great... a secret military facility that has been bombed. I miss pancakes.*

Dan continued to follow James down the steep hill, and eventually they made it to the bottom. James kneeled down and uncovered a steel hatch that was hidden by tall grass and weeds.

"With secret facilities come secret entrances and exits. This is how Dr. Wilkes and I escaped the situation. Come on; I'm not sure how much time we have—most likely very little."

They made their way down the ladder, and at the bottom was a dirt tunnel that stretched deep into the ground. James and Dan made their way towards the structure. *I don't like this,* thought Dan. *That cold chill keeps happening, and my head is killing me. I hope James can tell me what's going on.* Dan noticed the tunnel was getting significantly wider, as well as brighter.

"Nearly there," said James. About thirty feet later, James stopped at the foot of a stairway that led to a large, steel door. Dan looked up and felt the coldest chill yet wash over him. *What the hell am I doing here? This is insane. If only Mary were here. Oh, how I do miss her.*

"Okay, Dan... last chance to turn back. Do you still want to do this?"

Dan nodded. "Yeah, if you can tell me what's been going on with me... then, yeah, I definitely want to know."

"Very well," said James. "Let's go." At the top of the stairs, James scanned his access card and placed his thumb on a scanner. A few beeps were emitted from the scanner, it turned green, and the door latch clicked open. *Where have I seen that before? It seems terribly familiar,* thought Dan.

James swung open the door, and Dan followed him inside. He was greeted by a long, dimly lit hallway. *This is under all that rock? Jesus, what is this place made of?* As if to read Dan's mind, James answered.

"Apparently this basement is made of *Pruecium,* which is an experimental metal that is virtually indestructible. Seems to have lived up to its reputation. Come on, down this way."

James led Dan down the hallway, which opened to a large, empty room. *Oh, great,* thought Dan, *an empty room.* On the wall next to James was a small led screen with an onscreen keypad numbered 0-9. Above the keypad were six empty rectangular boxes, which Dan figured were for a passcode or something. This thought had barely passed through Dan's head when James typed six digits into the keypad and another beep, similar to the first door, rang out. The emptiness suddenly faded away and was replaced by dozens of large server racks.

"Holy shit," said Dan. That was all he was able to say.

"Yeah, it's pretty impressive, I agree," said James. "Welcome to the server room of The Elysiam. We have a lot to discuss, though, and while all of this is impressive, its purpose is... well, rather dark. Let's just put it that way."

"Yeah, yeah," said Dan. "Enough of the dramatic shit, man... How do you know me? And what's all this for? How does it involve me?" Dan knew he was being short with James, but he couldn't help it. After a three-hour car ride, followed by a trek through a secret underground tunnel, he was ready for some answers.

"I don't think you quite understand the gravity of this situation... in fact, I know you don't. There's no way you could." James's facial expression turned solemn, which scared Dan. "Maybe I should just show you first... it isn't fair for you to not know, especially when you're so close to the truth. Follow me." James led Dan back down the long hallway. James stopped almost exactly in the middle of it.

"What are we doing back here?" asked Dan, confused by James's behavior. Without saying anything, James tapped four points on the wall, which seemed random to Dan. Just as Dan was coming to the conclusion that James was losing his mind, the wall illuminated where James had touched it. The four points made a square. James placed his hand in the middle of it. Like before, when Dr. Wilkes had shown this to James, the wall split open, revealing another long, and dimly lit hallway. *Oh, Jesus,* thought Dan. *Another one? This can't be good... not at all.*

James led the way down the short stairway into the long hallway. He paused after the door had closed, waiting for the greeting—none came.

"Just a bit further, Dan, at the end of this hallway." Dan was looking all around the hallway, noticing how eerie it was. It was almost completely dark, with the exception of a faint light coming from the end of the hallway. *Man, this place gives me the creeps. This looks familiar, though. I know I've been here before... I know I have.*

At the end of the hallway, James stopped in front of a blood red door. Upon seeing it, Dan immediately stopped and was greeted by the all-too-familiar sound of ticking—a ticking clock. *Oh god,* thought Dan, *yeah... I've definitely seen this before. It was in one of my dre—*

Dan's thoughts and the incessant ticking were interrupted by James.

"Dan? Are you okay?" James snapped his fingers a few times, and Dan jumped.

"What? Oh, sorry... I was just thinking that I've seen this hallway and door before..." James winced again, like he had when Dan had said he wanted to know everything.

"So, you do remember," said James as he sighed and turned to the door, and then back to Dan. Before opening it, he looked as though he wanted to give Dan one more chance to turn back. He looked nervous, as if he were frightened himself about how Dan would take whatever lay beyond the door.

"This is it, Dan. There won't be any turning back after I open this door. Are you ready?"

Dan had felt curious and confident in his decision leading up to the door. Upon seeing the door, however, the only thing he felt was fear and uncertainty. He considered turning back but tried to convince himself to face whatever was awaiting him. *I have to know what this all means.*

"Yeah... I think so. I'm ready," said Dan, nodding to James, affirming his decision without looking away from the door.

James put his thumb on the scanner, which turned green and beeped once. He placed his card on the other scanner, which also turned green and beeped twice. The giant locking mechanism of the door clicked, and the door cracked open. From the cracked door, Dan could see a reddish glow, and he felt a wave of bitter cold air coming from the room. *What the hell is in there?*

As James pushed open the door, Dan peered inside. The room was a modest size, with no windows or any light source at all, barring the glow from the servers that lined the back wall of the room. *What is going on?* thought Dan. In the center of the room was a long, narrow table that was completely enclosed by a lid. To Dan, it looked like a medical isolation booth they used when someone was infected with a deadly virus or something. *I don't like this,* he thought. *Not at all.*

Dan slowly approached the table, feeling his knees weaken with each step. Unlike in a hospital setting, the enclosure wasn't clear, but a drab grey color, with the exception of a circular area towards the top. Hanging from the ceiling, coming down and to the right, next to the head of the table, was a large circular clock. It was ticking, but Dan noticed it wasn't a traditional clock (one with an hour, minute, and second hand). This clock had four rectangular boxes on it, labeled (from left to right): "Years," "Months," "Days," and "Hours." The clock currently read:

4 Years : 10 Months : 22 Days : 13 Hours

On the right side of the table were several tubes running out of the enclosure and connected to an array of medical equipment that was next to the table. *What is it counting? And medical equipment? What the hell is in there? I'm not sure I want to know anymore.*

He had stopped at the foot of the table, and he gently placed his hand on it. *I don't like this.* A cold shiver ran down his back, and Dan quickly removed his hand. *Stop it, Dan... you're being a baby. Just do it. It's now or never.* Dan moved up to the top of the table and looked into the clear opening, but it was covered with a layer of dust. He put his hand over his chest and felt his heart racing. He took his hand and wiped the dust from the cover, revealing what was inside.

"No... I, wha... what? James? I, I don't understand... is that?" Dan stumbled backwards and fell onto the floor. He slid backwards on the floor until his back was against the wall. James ran over to Dan.

"Dan, take it easy...just breathe. I know, I know it's a lot. I wasn't sure if you were ready; hell, I don't know if anyone would ever be ready to see it. I'm sorry." James put his hand on Dan's shoulder. "Are you okay?" Dan looked up at James, who had a genuine look of concern on his face. Dan reached up and hugged James around the waist. He came here needing answers, but now all he wanted was comfort—security. "James, is... that what I think it is? Please tell me it isn't... that's not possible."

James nodded. "Yes, Dan... I'm afraid it is. I wanted you to see it for yourself before I tried to explain what's going on."

"Explain what's going on? How can you explain that? Is it..." Dan stopped mid-sentence. He needed to be sure of what he had seen. He got up from the floor and walked back towards the table. The first time he approached it, his legs were shaking, and this time it was a miracle he could support his weight at all. *Take it easy, Dan. It's not real... this is just another, dream. You'll wake up soon and you can have pancakes.* Deep down, Dan knew none of that was true—this was real. Dan made it to the top of the table and peered in through the cover.

CHAPTER V

1

IT WAS HIM. DAN LOOKED IN AND WAS STARING DOWN AT himself. The person inside looked exactly like him, down to every detail—he even looked to be the same age. *How is this possible? Is he my clone?* There appeared to be wires running from the top of his head that went outside the enclosure and connected to the medical equipment, as well as the servers. *This has to be a dream,* he thought.

As if reading his mind again, James replied. "You aren't dreaming, Dan. Trust me, I wish this were a dream." Dan felt physically pained by this statement. He turned quickly to face James.

"So, you know about my dreams? Tell me, please tell me what's going on. What... er, who is this?" Dan pointed inside the enclosure. "Is it me?" Dan felt tears forming as he fell to his knees.

James had a mixture of sadness and guilt in his expression as he approached Dan with care and helped him to his feet.

"Look, this is hard for me... but I'm going to do my best. The kid you see there is you, yes. He's the... *real* you." James paused, seeming to know this wouldn't go over well. Dan's eyes grew again, and his expression went to one of utter confusion.

"The *real* me? What the hell, James? What the hell does that mean?"

James shook his head and looked down at the floor. "Oh, Dan, I hate that I'm the one who has to tell you this. It was never supposed to be like this, you know. It sounds bad, but you were never meant to find out."

Dan shoved James away from him in frustration.

"Damn it, James! Stop dragging this out...just tell me the truth. What do you mean this is the *real* me?" James was taken aback by the outburst, then looked resigned. He took a deep breath in and exhaled.

"You aren't real, Dan. The *you* standing in front of me isn't real. Everything you've known, everything you've experienced since you were ten years old...nearly all of it has been fake." Dan stood in place, not saying a word. *What did he just say? Surely I heard him wrong.*

"Wha—what do you mean I'm not real?" Dan was crying now but doing all he could to stop. "I am real! I'm right here. You can see me!"

"I'm sorry, Dan... but it's the truth. The person on the table is the real Daniel Williams. Everything you've experienced in the last six years has been made up. You aren't real, Dan, I'm so sorry. You're an extraordinarily complex set of software algorithms that were written by me over the course of many years. With the help of my team, as well as one of the world's most powerful computer systems, we were able to create a nearly perfect simulation of human life. Unfortunately, it wasn't perfect; we had a few hiccups, as well as inconsistencies. I'm sure you know what I mean."

Everything that James had been saying suddenly clicked in Dan's mind. *Oh, no,* thought Dan, *no, no... it, it can't be. But it is...* The expression on Dan's face went blank as he thought back to everything that had happened. It had all started after Dan saw Dr. Hodgin for his headaches. After the doctor's visit, his life had started to spiral out of control. The dreams he had had, the weird wobbling of letters and numbers... it was all fake—like a long, drawn-out dream. *The doctor's visit,* thought Dan. *Oh, shit...I knew something felt off about that place. Ever since I left the clinic, things were never the same. What about Clearwater? Was that fake too?* James stood there as he watched Dan try to come to terms with the truth—life as he knew it was nothing more than a computer simulation.

"How much of it was real, James? Was any of it?" James seemed to struggle with answering the question but knew that Dan deserved to know the truth. How could anyone tell a sixteen-year-old that over a third of their life had been a lie?

"It wasn't all simulated, no. Up until you turned ten was real, and what's happening now is real. It's a little complicated. A partial implementation was attempted in December of 2000. Remember the CT Scan that was performed on you? That was when the doctor had put an implant in your body, which is when your dreams started to intensify, right?" Dan felt himself becoming nauseous.

"The CT Scan? You're telling me everything after that has been fake?"

James shook his head. "No, the implant Dr. Hodgin put in turned out to be unable to create a completely simulated environment—we could only do bits and pieces. It was determined that you would need to be on site in order for the full implementation to be possible. I'm so sorry, Dan..."

The dreams, the time shifting, it was all part of a computer simulation? I'm not real... Horror struck Dan as his thoughts went to the inevitable place—*Mary. Was Mary fake too?* Dan felt himself become weak again, fell to the floor, and passed out.

2

James had tried to catch Dan before he hit the floor, but he was too late. *Oh, Dan, I'm so sorry...I had hoped it would never come to this. I just hope there's some way I can help.* He picked up Dan and had a strange sensation as he looked at the kid, essentially his kid. *This is so weird. I can't believe I'm actually holding him. I never thought it would end up like this...he's so—real.*

James carried Dan back through the hallway and into his office. He gently put Dan down on the couch that he himself had sometimes slept on, and then logged on to his computer.

What have you done, James...you've destroyed this kid. But the truth is, you destroyed him a long time ago, didn't you? Fuck. What am I going to do now?

3

Dan came to a few minutes later and looked around, confused. *Where am I now? Please tell me that was a dream.* He saw James sitting at a large, u-shaped desk in front of six computer screens. *Damn, guess that answers that question.*

"Ah, you're awake, good," said James. "You doing alri..."

His question was interrupted—he saw that Dan's appearance was starting to fade. *Oh, no...* Dan was about to answer when the room began to fade away and become slightly blurry. *Oh, fuck, fuck... not now, please not now.*

"James! James... it's happening again!" Dan desperately tried to get his attention. James quickly turned to his computer and opened a terminal.

"I see it, Dan... I see what's happening. I should have never written that A.I."

"What are you talking about?"

"Sorry, Dan, I didn't have time to tell you yet, and there's definitely no time now. Basically, we aren't in control of what happens to you anymore, and the system that is running you has become self-aware. It's about to run another test, and if it does... you could be lost forever."

Dan felt himself losing the ability to speak, which was new. *Oh god, I'm scared.*

4

"James, please -- me! I ---- stay here -- you." James typed furiously on his keyword, trying to find a way into the system, but the A.I. had locked everything down. *Damn it! What can I do? Dan doesn't have much time left, and if it's doing what I think it is... where he ends up won't be pretty. If only I could bypass... wait, that's it!*

"Dan, I've got it! I think I can stop it, at least for a little while anyway."

"Well, do it! It - doesn't -- this long, so -- think there's - time." Dan's voice sounded far away. James opened another terminal and logged into a separate server. *Okay, James, focus. You only get one shot at this.* A few seconds later James typed a couple more commands and hit *enter.* He looked over at Dan, whose appearance had already started to change back to normal. *Oh, thank god.*

5

"Did you do it? Whoa, my voice is normal again. What the hell did you do?" Dan jumped off the couch and ran over to James, who looked relieved.

"It's complicated, and I think I should tell you more about what exactly happened at this facility... about how you came to be." Dan had momentarily forgotten about what was behind the blood red door, but it had all flooded back into his mind. *...I'm not real. God, I wish this were just another dream.*

"James, please tell me... is, err... was Mary real? Please tell me she was real."

"Also complicated, I'm afraid, but yes... Mary was real, just not as you saw her. I'll explain all of it, Dan, but I really do need to start from the beginning; it's important." Dan sat down in a chair next to James. "It all started back in December of 1968. One thing I should add, Dan, is that I wasn't involved from the beginning, so there might be specific details that I only have secondhand knowledge of."

James proceeded to tell Dan everything.

"Dr. Robert Wilkes organized a team of the smartest scientists, professors, and other professionals to conduct one of the largest experiments in history. The research and development that took place was unimaginable. I didn't join the project until 1988, which is the year you were born—not a coincidence, I'm afraid. Initially, I was told very little about the specifics of the project. Apparently, my security clearance wasn't high enough, which I didn't even know I had any at all. Anyway, at the beginning I was told that the project was going to involve creating software that was designed to simulate the effects of different phenomena, including time travel, on the human psyche.

"It sounds weird, but it was quite a fascinating topic for me. Nothing like this had ever been attempted, let alone on a large scale such as this one. It was codenamed Project Destiny and it was going to make history. We started off with simple tests, things like making the simulation seem like dreams of the past, brief hallucinations. At first, things were going well. I'm sure you know what I'm talking about here too, right? The dreams you had in the beginning... that's what those were. They were the result of our initial testing while you had the implant in your head."

James paused to see if Dan would respond. Dan's mouth was stuck open, and his face had a look of awe. "But why, James... why'd you do it?"

"This is why I wanted to start from the beginning of the story. I didn't know you existed. When I say *you*, I mean the you that's behind the red door. I was told the tests were being done strictly in a simulation setting, which, I guess in a very ugly way, was the truth. It wasn't until two years ago, right before this place was bombed, that my boss revealed that back hallway to me. I know you might not be able to trust me, Dan... but believe me when I say that if I had known what was really going on, I would have never agreed to the project.

"Now that I think about it, I'm quite certain that's why they told me as little as they did. I'm sure the security clearance thing was a small part of it, but only a few days later, I had received my clearance, so it really didn't matter. The truth is, they knew I wouldn't agree to do all the things I did if they told me everything. Bastards."

Dan sat silently, trying to take in everything James had said so far. *I should be more scared,* thought Dan, *but I'm not. I am a little sad... all those memories were fake, even if some were awful. Everything James has said makes sense... it explains all the dreams, the hallucina-*

tions, the time shifting, everything. But what if this is just another dream? From what James has said, these simulations are becoming more and more realistic.

"I just...can't believe you," said Dan. "For all I know, this is all just another dream. You probably aren't even real, and in a few minutes, I'll be off to another time and place. You had me going for a bit there, but this is all just too convenient." *Honestly,* thought Dan, *I'm not sure at all what I believe. The last few years have been so damn confusing. How can you know what's real and what isn't? This sucks.*

"I don't blame you," said James. "If I was in your position, I'd probably feel the same. How about I prove it to you? I'll give you details about your previous dreams that only the real me could know." Dan thought about this for a moment and then agreed.

"Sure, try me," he said, sounding doubtful.

"Your name is Daniel Williams. Born December 10th, 1988 in Redfield, South Dakota."

Dan scoffed. "Big whoop; anyone could look that up. Readily available information."

"Your parents are Patricia and Henry Williams. Your mother is a registered nurse at Redfield Community Hospital and your stepdad is a truck driver."

Okay, that's a little more detailed, but still easy enough for that to be programmed, I'm sure.

"Come on. This is all basic information, James."

James grinned. "Not convincing enough, huh? Okay, fine. Your favorite food is pancakes, most recently the ones from Denny's. You love to play Tony Hawk on N64, as well as Goldeneye 007. Your best friend is Jake and when you were in 1965, you met a girl named Mary. Her parents were Helen and Jack Stevenson. Oh, and you had your first kiss on your way back from—"

"Okay, okay! You've made your point," interrupted Dan. *Holy shit,* he thought. *This is scary.* "Just answer one question I have for you about the past, and if you get it right, then I'm good."

"Shoot," said James.

"On that awful day when I was torn away from Mary, she was looking for something. What was it and where was she looking?"

Without missing a beat, James answered, "A chess board. She was looking for it out in the garage. And I'm so sorry about that, Dan... She was inconsolable after you vanished." James appeared like he was on the verge of crying.

"Okay, I believe you," said Dan, finally composing himself. "You know way too much about, well... pretty much everything for it to just be a coincidence. Plus, you've given me no reason not to trust you, and you did just save me from ending up who knows where, so I'd say you're on my side."

"Not going to lie, Dan... you're taking this way, way better than I thought you would. Are you sure you're okay?" Dan shrugged. "I'm sure some of it is shock, or maybe just a limitation of the software?" Dan let out a little laugh, but James could tell it was forced.

"I can't even begin to imagine what all of that was like, so I won't try. Unfortunately, there's a much bigger problem we have to deal with now. My boss, Dr. Wilkes, and his boss had warned us of an impending investigation by the CIA. He had enough pull to delay them for a while, but we knew that eventually everything would come crashing down on us, quite literally, it seems.

"Anyway, they wanted me to develop a way to automate phase three of Project Destiny in the event that we had to leave. I was already on a stupid tight deadline, so I had no idea how to accomplish this alongside finishing the programming for phase three. In hindsight, I vehemently regret the idea that I came up with... A.I.; Artificial Intelligence, that is. At the time it was bleeding edge technology, and even today, in 2019, it's not remotely close to stable. So, what I did was I developed the basic outline of phase three, and then I developed the A.I. with the intentions of having it finish and execute phase three."

"And now the A.I. has taken over the system and locked you out of it?" Dan was smart for his age and knew his fair share about computers. James smiled.

"Ah, yes, I do recall you having quite a knack for computers and technology. But yeah, you nailed it. It has the system locked down pretty tight; I couldn't even shut the protocols down with root. Oh, and out at the cemetery you had asked how I found you. Before the A.I. locked me out, I had managed to sift through a few of the protocols it had written so far and found the one that was currently running, which led me to the Redfield cemetery... lucky break."

6

Dan appeared to be rapt, listening as James recounted the events that had led to him finding the boy at the cemetery.

"Sounds like a mess," said Dan. "Hey, wait, if you're locked out of the system, how'd you stop it from sending me somewhere else? Thanks again for that, by the way."

"Ah yeah, I was just about to get to that part. Early on in the project I developed a fail-safe for running these protocols, as they were getting quite complex. We don't have time to go over everything, but I'll do my best to give you the gist.

"Whenever the primary server begins an execution of a protocol, it sends a request to this fail-safe algorithm, which includes a request authentication code. The algorithm then checks this code against a strict encryption method, and if it checks out, it responds with an execution authentication code.

"This is how I saved you, Dan. I reinforced the encryption method, so when the A.I. sent the request, it was denied, and will keep being denied until it cracks the updated encryption. I had enough hindsight to install this algorithm on a completely separate server and subnet, so the A.I. is only able to access it through a one-way request connection."

"Impressive," said Dan. "Some of that was beyond my knowledge, but I think I get it."

James laughed; it was the first time in a while. *You're quite a kid, Dan. If I had gone through half of what I'm sure you have, I'd be a wreck. I hope I can help you find peace of some kind.* James wanted to say this, but couldn't bring himself to, not yet anyway.

"So, can you save me for good, James? Can you get the *real* me back?" *This was the question I was expecting earlier,* thought James.

"I wish I could, Dan, but it isn't that simple. Unfortunately, the process that was done to the *real* you in order to make this experiment possible is not reversible. If I were to disconnect that system, both you and the *real* you would die. There'd be no pain or anything, but death would be instantaneous, I'm afraid."

James watched as Dan took in what he had just told him. *Ugh, I can't imagine what he's going through.*

"What about Mary?" asked Dan.

"What about her?"

"Well, if you can't get me out of this computer realm... I'd rather spend what time I have left with Mary. I fell in love with her while I was *there*."

Unbelievable, thought James. *I didn't realize just how life-like the protocols had gotten by that point in the project. To fall in love? Truly unbelievable. Could I really send him back to 1965? I think I can recover that protocol, but would it be corrupt, like many of the others were? Plus, even if it was intact, I'd have to find a way to bypass the A.I. No easy feat. But there has to be a way...*

7

"James? You still with me?"

"Yeah, sorry, Dan... just thinking. The problem is, when the script I wrote to back up the protocols was executed, the A.I. intervened and corrupted a lot of them. Some are still intact, so there's a chance the one of Mary is okay, but even if it is, I would still need to find a way to bypass the A.I. It's not impossible, just not easy."

"Say, why'd you guys choose Mary, anyway? Is she a real person? Or did you just generate all of those details?" asked Dan.

"I'm sorry, Dan, we don't have enough time for me to explain why we chose her, but yes, she is a real person. She's still alive today, I believe." *Don't even think about it,* thought Dan. *She would be much older than you and wouldn't even know you.*

"So, what can we do, James? Is there no way to get me back there?"

"Hang on, Dan... let me see if I can access Mary's protocol and see if it's corrupt." He logged into the backup server and found the directory containing Mary's protocol. "Well, it looks like this one was saved from corruption—

remarkable luck, considering almost all other files were corrupted. I'd better copy this local so I can more easily set this up."

"Okay, Dan, I think I know of a way it can be done. The protocol we need doesn't appear to be corrupt. It's risky, and I'd need a little time, but I think it'll work. If I can add an additional function to the fail-safe algorithm, I might be able to trick the A.I. into executing Mary's protocol, which would send you back to 1965. Once it is executed, I would modify the fail-safe algorithm to not send any more execution authentication codes, and theoretically you'd be able to stay there forever." Dan considered this and realized he had limited options.

"Let's do it. Can I help?"

"I don't think so; I just need some time to focus."

8

It took James about two hours to complete the necessary work, with which he was pleased. *Gosh, I hope this works... there's no way to test it, but we're out of time... it's now or never.*

James was also glad that the A.I. hadn't yet cracked the 1028-bit encryption he had implemented—but it would soon.

If only James had known just how soon the A.I. would crack the updated encryption. During the two hours it had taken him, the system had been hard at work bypassing the reinforced security.

"Okay, Dan... I think it's ready. Are you?" Dan, who had been in and out of James's office, exploring the basement, nodded.

"Yeah, I think so... this is all still so crazy, isn't it? I meant to ask, are my parents... um, are they still alive? My *real* parents."

"The last I heard, they were, yes. I wouldn't advise you trying to see them, though, Dan. As far as they know, you died back in 2000. Sorry that I have to be the bearer of more bad news."

9

Dan felt more tears come to his eyes, but he fought them back. *No, you can't cry now, Dan... you've heard worse things than that already today and you got through it. Now is your chance to get Mary back. Keep it together.* Dan needed to know, though; he needed to know what they thought happened to him.

"What were they told?" asked Dan. "How did I supposedly die?"

"Remember the aggressive treatment they started you on at Clearwater? Dr. Wilkes came up with a story about how your body had a severe reaction to the medicine and caused you to have a brain hemorrhage, and you died. He said they tried to save you, but it was just too much damage to the brain.

"I'm sorry, Dan. I know how horrible it sounds, and I wish he was never involved in the project. I remember the very first day we began discussing this project, back in 1988. Even back then I knew something didn't feel right about it. There's probably more to tell, but we really are out of time. Are you ready?"

"It's okay. I just needed to know. Thank you for being honest with me, James. Oh, one more question. What about the age difference? I'm sixteen now, so won't that seem pretty strange to Mary?"

"I thought of that too, Dan. I've accounted for the age gap in the updated protocol, so Mary should also be sixteen."

"That's so crazy... can't wait to see how she looks. Okay, yes, I'm ready. Let's do this."

"Okay, Dan, so I know this probably goes without saying, but keep in mind this could get a little scary. What we're trying to do has never been done before, and while I admit I'm pretty good at what I do, there's always the possibility of something going wrong. After all, I'm fighting against an A.I. that's running on one of the most powerful servers in the world."

Dan nodded. "Understood. Will this be like all the other times that time shifted? The wobbling text, and the shaking, and all of that?"

"That's a good question. I honestly don't know, Dan. Because you've been exposed to the real world now, I'm not sure what it will be like to jump back to the simulation. Here goes nothing, right?"

Dan tried to fake a smile, but it didn't really work. "Yeah...right. Just do it, James."

10

James turned back to his computer and typed out the execution method, and then hovered his finger over the enter key. *You're by far the bravest kid I've ever met, Dan. I hope this works and that you can spend the rest of your days with Mary.* Again, James wanted to say this to Dan, but for some reason he couldn't. *Maybe another time.*

"Good luck, Dan. Like I said earlier, once you're there, I will lock the encryption, which will hopefully keep you safe from the A.I. If everything goes according to plan, I probably won't ever see you again. Take care of yourself, okay? You're a good kid."

Dan smiled, and it looked like a genuine one. "Thanks for everything, James. You're a crazy smart guy...I hope you don't get into any trouble for all of this. I know you didn't know the awful truth behind it." James felt a tear coming to his eye but fought it back.

"Okay, here we go. In 3, 2, 1...executing."

11

Dan saw the room immediately begin to fade, and he saw nothing but black behind it. *Oh, man, this part never gets any easier.* Dan thought he saw James wave at him, but it was hard to tell because of how blurry James was. The ground beneath Dan started to shake, and then there was nothing but blackness. *Shit...*

Dan plunged downward into the black emptiness, faster than any of the other times. He felt himself become queasy and thought he might vomit. The black emptiness was such a strange experience, one that Dan could never quite explain. *It's so quiet,* he thought. *There's no sound at all; it's just...empty.* Dan was seconds from vomiting when his descent stopped abruptly, and then he landed on what felt like carpet. The black faded, and what took its place was a brightly colored room, one Dan immediately recognized.

12

James watched as the execution happened on the terminal, and everything looked good. *I can't believe this is actually working,* he thought. *Time to lock the encryption.* James logged in to the fail-safe server and loaded the encryption algorithm. *Okay, let's lock this down. I hope you're doing okay there, Dan... This should keep you there permanently. Godspeed, Daniel Williams.* James added the lock and executed the updated code. The terminal showed a successful execution, and James closed it. *It's done.*

It wasn't done.

13

Dan got up and looked around, unable to believe what he was seeing. *It worked...it actually worked!* Dan was back at Mary's house, back in her room. Then he heard it, the sound of her voice.

"Hey, Dan, I'm going to look in the garage really quick. I think we might have stored it out there." *Unbelievable,* he thought. *This is the exact moment that I was torn away from Mary four years ago.* "Everything okay, Dan?" asked Mary. *Oh, right...I'm really here.*

"Yeah, all good, Mary. Do you want help looking for it?"

"No, that's okay. I think I know where it is."

Dan couldn't help himself; he needed to see her. He walked out of the room and down the hall. *This is so crazy. It's all the same, just as I remember it.* He proceeded through the kitchen, and out the door that connected to the garage. Standing in the corner, digging through a pile of her dad's junk, was Mary Stevenson. Her flowing blonde hair was a sight for sore eyes, and Dan thought for sure he was dreaming again. *This is too good to be true; I'll wake back up any moment.* Dan walked towards her and bumped into a box on the floor, which startled Mary, and she turned to face him. *She's beautiful,* thought Dan.

"Oh, you scared me," said Mary. "Everything okay? You look like you've seen a ghost." *If you only knew,* he thought.

"Yeah, I just missed you, that's all." She giggled. *God, I missed that laugh. Thanks again, James...you're the best.* She gave Dan a big hug and kissed his cheek.

"Hey, guess what? I found the board." Mary held up a box with a picture of a chess board on it. "Ready to play?"

Dan smiled and hugged her again.

"You have no idea. Let's play." They walked back to Mary's room, and Mary got the board set up. She started to explain the rules to Dan, but he barely heard any of it. *I still can't believe it. I'm back. I almost forgot how beautiful she is.*

"Dan? Earth to Dan... you still with me?" Mary had noticed he had been staring at her.

"What? Oh, yeah...sorry, just distracted is all. You're so pretty, Mary." She felt herself blush and smiled.

"Oh, Dan, you're sweet." She leaned over and kissed him on the lips. *I missed that too,* he thought. "Well, let's play," said Mary. "I can teach you more as we go." She started by moving a pawn forward two spaces. "Pawns are your most disposable pieces, Dan... you want to use them whenever you can, especially to save more valuable pieces."

Dan nodded. He looked at the board and put out his hand to move one of his pawns. Just before his fingers reached the pawn, it wobbled ever so slightly.

TICK TOCK

ABOUT THE AUTHOR

BEN ARMSTRONG is a software developer with a love for tea, coffee, and tech. He is an emerging author of science fiction and psychological thrillers. He currently resides in Fargo, ND with his loving wife, Catrina.

Made in the USA
Lexington, KY
17 November 2019

57206089R00168